THE NURSING HOME

JAMES J. MURPHY III

I&J Publishing
P.O. Box 833
Shrub Oak, NY 10588

THE NURSING HOME

All rights reserved. Without limiting the rights under copyright reserved above, no part of this publication may be reproduced, stored in or introduced into a retrieval system, or transmitted in any form or by any means (electronic, mechanical, photocopying, recording, or otherwise) without the prior written permission of both the copyright owner and the publisher of this book.

The Nursing Home is a work of fiction. The names, characters, places, incidents, and dialogue are products of the writer's imagination or have been used fictitiously and are not to be construed as real. Any resemblance to persons, living or dead, actual events, locales, or organizations is entirely coincidental.

I&J Publishing
P.O. Box 833
Shrub Oak, NY 10588

Copyright © James J. Murphy III 2009, 2010

0-9842731-0-7
978-0-9842731-0-2

Library of Congress Control Number: 2009910922

Publisher's Cataloging-in-Publication
(Provided by Quality Books, Inc.)

Murphy, James J., [date]-
　　The nursing home / James J. Murphy, III.
　　p. cm.
　　SUMMARY: When patients and employees begin dying at Rigg's Nursing Home, the police, resident Morris Grover, and a group of newly hired young staff want to know why. What they discover is more shocking than they had imagined.
　　LCCN 2009910922
　　ISBN-13: 978-0-9842731-0-2
　　ISBN-10: 0-9842731-0-7
1.. Nursing home patients--Juvenile fiction.
　　2. Teenagers--Juvenile fiction. 3. Nursing homes--Employees--Juvenile fiction. 4. Murder--Investigation--Juvenile fiction. 5. Detective and mystery stories.
　　6. Ghost stories. [1. Nursing home patients--Fiction.
　　2. Teenagers--Fiction. 3. Nursing homes--Fiction.
　　4. Murder--Fiction. 5. Mystery and detective stories.
　　6. Ghosts--Fiction.]　I. Title.

PZ7.M95338Nur 2009　　　　[Fic]
　　　　　　　　　　　　QBI09-600203

Printed in USA

Credits

Editor: Lisa G. Murphy

Cover Art: Jill Bauman

Cover & Interior Design: ATG Productions, LLC,
Christy Moeller-Masel

Interior Typesetting: ATG Productions, LLC, Cory Olson

www.atgproductions.com · Surprise, Arizona

— Dedication

The Nursing Home is dedicated to the grandmothers of both my wife and I: Josie B. and Jean B. They had both been in nursing homes when this story was thought of.

Chapter I

"Jude, I never thought this day would come."

"I know, Sam. But we both know that your father is not getting any better. He doesn't take his medicine, he ignores his doctor's orders, and most importantly, he won't even listen to us. Maybe this is for the best." Jude tried to make her husband feel better about the situation.

"I just wish that there could be some other way."

"Get up, Todd! It's Sunday!" Jude screamed to her son from the living room.

"I know it's Sunday! Let me sleep!"

"Get up now! We're leaving in fifteen minutes!"

With absolutely no enthusiasm, Todd slipped out of bed. "Come on... Why do I have to go? Grandpa ain't my problem."

"No, Todd, he's everybody's problem lately," Sam interrupted. "Now move your ass! I'd like to get home in time to watch the Marlins game."

THE NURSING HOME

"Why don't you just set the tape, Dad?" Todd replied with sarcasm as he marched down the stairs, knowing that his father was not up to date. Todd was lucky enough to know what a VHS tape was; his generation was growing up with DVDs and had the luxury of TiVo and DVR.

"Don't be a smart ass," Sam told his son, knowing in the back of his head that he was behind on the times.

"Great... I wanted to sleep late today. I hope we get home early, Dad. There's a concert I want to go to."

"What concert might that be, Todd?"

"Arise Befall! They are the best local band in Alachua. Maybe even the best in Florida!"

"You know something, Todd? When I was younger, I had to give up things that I enjoyed because my father made me do work around the house."

"Oh, like your baseball game?"

"I'm going back to when *I* was a teenager. Do you know how many times I've missed rock groups that came around?" A smile came to Sam's face as he remembered his high school years.

"Remember those songs you used to always annoy me with?" Jude giggled.

"Which ones? There were so many." Sam began snapping his fingers to a Tommy Tutone beat. Todd was hoping the subject would change so his father would stop acting like a fool.

"Todd, we all have to make sacrifices sometimes," Jude said, trying to calm everyone down. "Let's just do what we can. We will try to make it back here early."

— JAMES J. MURPHY III —

"Hey, Dad! Are you ready?" Sam called out.

"I'm not going!" Morris complained from his bedroom.

"You brought this upon yourself, Dad. Maybe if you listened to me or the doctors for once in your life, you wouldn't be in this predicament. You can't even remember to take your medicine every morning. You are a stubborn, old son-of-a-bitch who doesn't give a fuck about anybody except yourself."

"You don't know what I've gone through in life, Sam!"

"Oh, not this story again. Poor little Morris: abused as a child, tormented in school... Oh, boo hoo! Cry me a storm!" mocked Sam. "Well, guess what, Dad? You weren't the best father, either, so stop your bitching. Now let's get the fuck out of here. Today's game is against the St. Louis Cardinals and Sunday traffic is the worst. It's bumper to bumper."

Deep down, Morris knew his son was right. He knew he was as helpless as a three-legged dog, but had too much pride to admit it.

"Dad, I know you hate me right now, but believe it or not, this is for your own good."

"Sam, what's the name of this place again? Rick's?"

"For the hundredth time, it's Rigg's Nursing Home," Sam reminded his father.

"Rigg's!? Are you fucking kidding me? Sounds like a tire place."

"We already packed everything. If there is anything else you need, you'd better grab it now."

"Let me grab my new word search book," Morris said as he tried to come up with ideas of what could keep him busy in his spare time. He figured he would have a lot of it.

—— THE NURSING HOME ——

"It has over a hundred pages of searching for me to work on. That should last me a few weeks."

"How about you take some of Todd's, as well? He won't miss 'em."

"Alright. At least it will give me something to do." It finally started to sink in that he would have to find new ways to occupy his time. He had gotten used to having family around to entertain him.

Morris wondered how it got so bad. Looking back, he realized that he had bad knees for half of his life. He started landscaping in the 1940s and continued until the 1960s. At first, it was only a gig. He did it for extra money; off the books, no taxes. This is my meal ticket, he had thought. Things had been going right down Morris's alley. He had thought of all of the things that he could buy Gertie and how he could improve the house.

Then one afternoon, June 11, 1962, Morris had been landscaping on the roof of a building. He'd been layering bricks and ran out of cement. Being in a certain position for so many hours had caused him to lose his stepping when he was getting up to get more cement. After losing his balance on the ten-foot roof that summer, Morris fell off and injured his leg. After his leg had healed, he worked for another two years. Doctors advised him not to, but Morris's attitude about 'being a man' got in the way. He thought, 'I bring home the bacon,' plus, he had to provide an income to support his family. Morris had thought, 'I'm forty-one. I can't be doing this shit anymore; it's killing me.' He finally quit, although he was pissed off at himself about it. For the next fifteen years, Morris had worked at a bank until he retired in 1979.

Gertie had always been there for Morris through thick and thin, even when her husband was wrong. She had his two sons. With Gertie, Morris believed he could do anything and always tried to. Their relationship started to go a little sour after Morris broke his leg. He was prescribed painkillers, but refused to take anything, especially something a doctor would give. Gertie had wished that Morris would accept help once in a while. Their relationship got even worse five years later, after what happened to Ben. Gertie had seen the way Morris acted towards Ben. If they hadn't been father and son, they would have been best friends. They shared everything that a father and son would share. Then one day, the unthinkable happened. Ben was killed in a car crash. A drunk driver ran a red light and hit him on the driver's side at an intersection. Ben died instantly. Morris was devastated. His family tried to make him feel like he still had people who loved him, but it didn't snap him out of that fog. That was not his only problem. Morris hadn't been getting any younger; his knees were getting worse and worse. Gertie had always been there for her husband and, at that point, was there for him more than ever because he was practically confined to a wheelchair. She loved her husband, but had wished that he'd listened to the doctor's orders to prevent him from being in that kind of situation.

People had always thought Morris would pass away before Gertie, as he himself thought, but life played a mean trick on him. Gertie, healthy as a horse, died in her sleep, out of nowhere.

THE NURSING HOME

This day was inevitable, Morris thought to himself as he picked up the word search, getting ready to leave for the nursing home. He knew it would come sooner or later, but was hoping that it wouldn't be sooner. Morris started getting teary eyed and felt a lump in his throat as he realized that it might be his last time in his room. Or the house, as a matter of fact.

Chapter 2

October 7, 2007 was a cool autumn Sunday and leaves were falling off the trees. Some of the houses on the block already had their Halloween decorations up and carved pumpkins on display. More leaves than usual had fallen off the trees for an October in Hawthorne, Florida. Neighborhood families were raking them up while their children were playing in the piles, and the Grover family was taking Morris to the nursing home. Sam backed out of the narrow driveway in his beat-up 1993 gray sedan that had approximately 203,880 miles on it, not to mention rust spots, and away they went. They'd been in the car for ten minutes and there was no sign of traffic yet. Sam was thinking about how great that was. Then, just as he was about to merge onto the highway, everything seemed to come to a complete stop.

"What could be the damn hold up, Jude? It can't be road work - It's Sunday!"

"I don't know, Sam."

— THE NURSING HOME —

"Fuck! We're stuck in traffic!" Sam yelled. "We were making perfect timing and now I'm going to miss today's game." It was obvious that Sam was beginning to stress out as he started twiddling the hairs of his dark brown mustache, which was beginning to grow some whites.

"Told ya you shoulda set the tape, Dad," reminded Todd.

"Shut up, Todd! I don't need this right now. I just knew we should have taken you to Rigg's yesterday, Dad. Marlins and St. Louis Cardinals; game of the year! Don't even mention the word 'tape,' Todd."

"Okay, okay."

"You only care about your precious baseball game, Sam, and you don't give a damn about me," said Morris.

"We all care about you, Morris," interrupted Jude.

"Then why am I going to Rick's Nursing Home?" asked Morris for the hundredth time.

"I give up, I give up," said Sam.

"Sam, we both know that you are doing this to seek revenge," Morris told him.

"What do you mean, Dad?"

"We haven't been close for years and we both know this, Sam. All those times you'd call and talk to your mother, I'd hear her ask if you want to talk to me and you'd always say 'Maybe next time.' Why didn't you want to talk to me? I tried being a good father to you."

"Tried, my ass, Dad. You gave up on me when I was six or seven."

"That's not true, Sam."

"Yes, it is. Ever since Ben died."

"Don't you dare mention Ben's name!" Morris demanded.

"You are still defending his name – He's dead! Get over it! Move on!"

"I tried, Sam. I really did. I wish we could go back in time, but we can't. I loved you and your mother very much and she knew then and she knows now that I still do." After Morris said that, everyone was silent for five minutes, with the exception of Morris's huffing. Todd browsed through a magazine, pretending that nothing happened. He wished he had headphones with him, so he wouldn't have to hear them bitch. There was so much tension in the car, not even a knife could cut through it.

"I know that you love us, Dad," Sam finally said. "I don't like the idea of this either, but you are very forgetful and this is effecting our lives as much as your own. I've worked another six-day week at the brokerage firm. You know I work in the stock market department, so when people lose on stock, they come to me when they want out. Do you know how many people bitch at me every day? Whether it's my boss or someone on the phone, someone's always on my case. I'm tired and I'm stressed out and I need to unwind. All I wanted to do was watch the game, maybe munch on a bag of chips, and enjoy a nice, cold beer. Is this too much to ask?" explained Sam as he removed his seat belt from his small stocky body just to stretch.

"I don't mean to be a pain in the ass," replied Morris. "Asking you for help is the last thing I ever wanted to do. Do you think I like being a cripple, Sam? I don't even

—— THE NURSING HOME ——

feel like a man anymore." Tears filled Morris's deep dark brown eyes. He shook his head in shame.

Finally, the traffic began to move. The Grovers got off Exit 4 of the Tigress Highway, heading towards Tera Lane. What was supposed to be a forty minute drive up to Hampton took an hour and a half as they finally approached the twists and bends that lead to the entrance of Rigg's Nursing Home. The parking lot was packed with families and friends visiting patients. Wind blew the leaves off the trees and onto the fields surrounding the property. Cabbage Palms had been planted around the brick building. Etched in stone was '1841,' the year in which the development was established.

Morris stared up in awe as he took in amazement the size of the nursing home. "This is Rigg's?! It's the size of a mansion. I'm gonna get lost in this place."

"That's the idea," Sam kidded.

"Don't worry, Morris. You'll find your way around soon enough," reassured Jude.

"I just want to go home." Morris sighed.

"Dad, I'm afraid this is your new home," Sam reminded his father.

Todd snickered. How harsh, he thought to himself.

When Sam parked the car, Todd went to the trunk to get Morris's wheelchair and he and Jude helped him into it. It took a little while to get Morris settled, as usual. As they headed for the door of the nursing home, two middle-aged nurses sitting on the bench studied their new potential patient as they continued smoking their cigarettes on their lunch break.

Within one minute of walking in, the Grovers were

— 18 —

greeted by a woman with light red shoulder-length hair and what Morris considered to be a fake smile. Who the hell does this woman think she is walking around like she owns this place? We had a word for women like this years ago, Morris thought to himself. Too bad he couldn't remember it. The woman introduced herself as Cyndi Gillian, the head of the nursing home. The Grover family shook her hand and let her know that they were given a prior tour of the nursing home just a few weeks ago by her assistant, Martha. Cyndi told them that she was informed of their visit and was given notice of Morris's arrival. She smiled at Morris, expressing genuine interest. All Morris did was growl.

Cyndi gave the Grover family another tour, introducing Morris to the staff and some guests. He only grumbled what sounded like a 'Hello' to each person he met. Morris complained to Sam about how the whole building smelled like crap. He then made a sarcastic comment to Sam, saying, "Hell, why don't you bring Todd and his friends here? They won't need to smoke pot; they could get high on the smell of shit that's in this place."

"Your father is quite a character, Mr. Grover. He will fit in real fine here; real fine. Trust me, your father is in good hands. There is no need to worry," Cyndi told him with confidence.

"I know you'll take care of him real well," said Sam.

"Make sure he eats his greens!" Todd joked.

"Quiet, Todd!" Jude shot a look at her son. "Morris, we'll come see you in two weeks. Please try to make some friends. The people here seem very nice. The staff appear to be very professional," she reassured him. Morris sighed.

THE NURSING HOME

Jude is the gullible type. She can't see through any act, Morris thought.

"Yeah, Dad. You'll make friends," said Sam.

As Cyndi turned to greet another visitor, Morris took what might be his final chance to vent before his family would be leaving. "Why do I need friends when I have such a wonderful family that abandons me in a strange place to leave me for dead?"

"We're not leaving you for dead, Dad," replied Sam. "We'll be back in a week or two."

"I'm sure you will," said Morris, feeling it was going to be more than that. Although Morris was pissed off at his family because they were leaving him in such a horrible place, he knew he would miss them and understood it was for the best.

The Grovers said their goodbyes to Morris and Cyndi and were on their way out of the nursing home. As they were exiting, Sam said, "I think Dad will have a whole new outlook on life."

Jude was starting to second-guess the decision of leaving Morris at the nursing home. "Do you think we did the right thing, Sam?"

"Jude, we went over this at the house. You were right. Listen, I had my doubts about bringing Dad to a home, too, but we have to do what's best for everyone."

"You're right, Sam. We decided on this nursing home for a reason - it's much nicer than all of the other ones we've looked at."

"Then I guess it's settled," concluded Sam.

"Well, Todd, it looks like we're gonna make it home on time for you to see your little rock group," Jude told her son.

JAMES J. MURPHY III

"Hopefully I do," said Todd, "but first, I need to take a shower. I thought I was going to puke in that place."

Sam agreed and said the place smelled like a garbage dump. "Jude, if this ever happens to me, please leave me for dead. I don't want to deal with what Dad is going through. How is he going to deal with that stink every day? God bless him."

— Chapter 3

It was only a few minutes after the Grovers left Morris in the care of the nursing home that he was alone and had time to think to himself. He was silent. This is a new beginning, he thought to himself. He looked around the small white room. Two beds, two TVs, two closets... Oh, great! Looks like I'm gonna have company, Morris complained to himself. Morris noticed what must be his roommate's family photo. I wonder what this chum is going to be like. I guess I'm going to have to get used to my new surroundings.

Morris glanced up at his room number. He had been assigned room 243. At least I'm on the second floor, he thought. I can actually wheel my ass to the window and look at the beautiful scenery and breathe the fresh air. How am I going to do this if I'm stuck in bed? he reminded himself. I can't even get into the wheelchair by myself. Hell, when I'm assisted to the bathroom, I'm lucky if I can hold my own dick or wipe my own ass.

JAMES J. MURPHY III

Morris was already embarrassed about wearing an adult diaper to bed. I'm going to have to depend on some dumb-ass nurse or aide, he realized, sitting in his wheelchair.

Morris began to worry. I'm supposed to be a man, damnit! It was bad enough when I had to depend on Sam and Jude and even my wise-ass grandson, Todd, but now I have to depend on complete strangers who don't give a fuck if I live or die, just as long as they get their paycheck at the end of the week. The more he thought about it, the more depressed he felt. When Sam told Morris he was going to go into a nursing home, it was all fun and games, but since Morris was there on his own, he saw it was a reality and he was scared, although he didn't show it.

Visiting hours were from 10:00am to 9:00pm on Monday through Friday and from 10:00am to 6:00pm on the weekends. There were always people on the clock. All of the patients were woken up between 7:00am and 8:00am for breakfast. If they slept in, tough luck – they would have a cold tray of breakfast waiting for them. They'd have one hour until their tray was collected. From 8:15am to 11:00am was where exercise, physical therapy, or other health appointments were fit in. Then they'd rest until 12:15pm, when lunch was served. After lunch, patients were brought back to their rooms or kept in the lounge room where a staff member would leave a random TV show on or have other activities going on. Every day there was something new. Patients could choose from Bingo, Checkers, Go Fish, and other card games. Sometimes the aides would sing to them, tell them stories,

THE NURSING HOME

or read something depressing, like the news. Dinner time was 6:00pm and after that, they were free to be put into bed with their TV on.

A few hours after Morris had gotten settled into his new room, Cyndi wheeled in who would be his roommate. His name was Felix and right away Morris could tell that he was British by his accent. Felix had been a patient at Rigg's for three years.

Felix also had bad legs, but what was worse was his forgetfulness. He couldn't remember a thing that he was told even a minute before. Just a simple conversation could be so frustrating. Morris thought, 'Great, a Blimey; and even worse, a forgetful Blimey.'

Felix was one of those people who'd talk in his sleep and jibberish would come out of his mouth. Morris always got aggravated because it kept him up at night. Morris was curious about what the hell Felix could be dreaming about. As soon as Felix woke up every morning, 'Who's this?' and 'Who's that?' would be the first things Morris would say. Who could Felix be referring to in these crazy dreams? Morris always thought. Felix would just give him a dumb, profound look and say: 'What, Marty?' Every morning it was the same reply. Morris would correct him by yelling, 'It's Morris, damnit!' Morris had learned to deal with it. After two weeks, Morris had gotten used to Felix's bad habits and thought to himself: *Is this what I put Sam and Jude through?*

Felix and Morris had an aide named Bill who treated them with total disrespect. He was impatient with both of them, but he was especially cruel to Felix. Whenever it was time to eat and Felix wasn't hungry, Bill would shout: 'Time to eat, you fucking idiot!' When Felix didn't listen, Bill would purposely spill the food on him and say: 'Enjoy!' Morris always watched, wishing he could help patients like Felix, but was too afraid. One time, the food stuck to Felix's skin like leeches and Felix helplessly tried to clean himself the best he could, but there was only so much he could've done. That was only one of the horrible ways that the staff treated their defenseless patients. Other than direct abuse, like Bill's spiteful behavior, some of the staff members were negligent. Sometimes it would be hours before anybody checked their rooms.

With each passing day, Morris became more skeptical. He tried to keep an eye out for himself and for Felix, especially when Bill was in the room. How could someone so disrespectful, who has no concern for others, be working at a place where you are supposed to take care of people? Morris really wanted to tell Bill off, but was worried that Bill would do something even worse. As for right now, I'm just trying to survive, he thought. Careless staff and shitty meals... Is this what I have to look forward to? Then what? I kick the bucket? Morris found himself actually looking forward to seeing his family just so he could tell them the stories about how the nurses and aides, especially Bill, really treated the patients.

Morris's curiosity about Bill increased every day that Bill was in charge of aiding them. He felt like a detective on a television show as he tried to gather information whenever he possibly could. Bill's usual schedule had him stationed for their hall on Mondays, Wednesdays, and Thursdays. Morris always had his eyes and ears open to learn more.

THE NURSING HOME

Bill was forty-three years old and born in Houston, Texas. He graduated from the University of Florida with all honors. Bill appeared to be just over six feet tall and a good two hundred pounds. His hairline was receding, his breath was repulsive, and everything about him disgusted Morris.

It seemed to Morris that Bill had a chip on his shoulder and was born with a silver spoon. Bill appeared to get off on belittling and degrading most of the patients on the second floor. If Bill's supervisors were aware of his behavior, they apparently didn't do anything about it; most likely because they didn't want to deal with him. It seemed like he wanted to intimidate everyone around him and Morris would be damned if he became one of his victims. Basically, because Bill was experienced, he walked around arrogantly and threw his weight around the elderly patients. Morris figured Bill had been doing that since Day One, which, as he learned, was three years ago.

When Bill was off duty, Marsha was in charge. She was new to the nursing home and did everything by the book. Morris didn't trust Marsha as far as he could throw her, but he'd take her services over Bill's any day. She was in her early thirties and was trying to do a good job. Although she seemed to be a little nervous, Morris favored her over the other staff members simply because she took her time to do things the right way. As for the patients, Morris didn't have a problem with any of them yet. Of course he could find a fault with each one, but he got along with them pretty well. It was just the staff that he didn't trust, especially Bill, only because of what he had witnessed.

— JAMES J. MURPHY III —

Down the hall was a patient who was probably the most vulnerable to Bill. Bill constantly provoked her. One time, he said: "Mrs. Douglas, I bet you were a hot piece of ass forty years ago. Too bad you are nothing but a wrinkled piece of shit now." Mrs. Douglas just looked at him and smiled as she stared into her own world. People like that infuriated Bill, which pissed him off even more. He kept trying for a reaction. "Do you think your family actually gives a flying fuck about you, Mrs. Douglas? You should have died twenty years ago."

Another incident was with Mr. Gothersorg. The old man couldn't walk without his cane, so Bill held out the cane while Mr. Gothersorg grabbed for it, and then continued teasing him by playing Keep-Away. After ten minutes, Bill finally threw it to him after the senior citizen defecated himself. Things like that happened every day. Patients didn't look forward to the day when Bill was working.

It was just another day of gossip in the lounge room with Pauly running his mouth, as usual. The only reason Pauly was at Rigg's was because his family couldn't take care of him, or at least they didn't want to. Thanks to Pauly, Morris was learning what went on behind the scenes at Rigg's. Pauly had been at the nursing home for five years and was probably the most reliable source of information. Pauly had been through so much over the years that there was not one staff member that he put his trust into. "If I had the choice of being here or being dead, I'd definitely choose death, just so I don't have to see that

THE NURSING HOME

no-good, lying, son-of-a-bitch Bill! He ain't nothing but a lying sack of shit and everybody knows it," Pauly said, raising his voice. "Wouldn't it be great if we all woke up one day and that creep, Bill, wasn't here anymore? Maybe he could magically disappear, but that would just be too good to be true."

"Pauly's going off his rocker!" interrupted Marlo, sitting at the window.

"Once our families drop us off, we all tend to jump off our rockers," said Morris. "But not me. Magically disappear? Next, poor Pauly is going to tell us the Boogyman's gonna jump out of the closet. God, I need to get out of this shit box."

"Hey, Morris, how long you been at this place? Five days?" asked Pauly.

"Try two weeks!" Morris yelled back.

"Well, I've been here five years and I've seen some sick shit and it's only gonna get worse. Unfortunately, our Lord, the Almighty God, hasn't taken me yet. Knowing me, I'll be here for another five years witnessing more disgusting acts. Has your family come to visit you, Morris?"

"They're coming tomorrow, as a matter of fact."

"If you tell them what you saw in the last two weeks, they won't even believe you."

"How do you know?" Morris asked in disbelief.

"Trust me, I know."

⟶ Chapter 4

The Grover family finally came to visit Morris for the first time since dropping him off two weeks prior. Morris was greeted with a big hug and kiss from Jude, a handshake from Sam, and a wave from Todd. Before Morris got a chance to yell at his family, Marsha immediately walked in and introduced herself. Morris was disappointed that everybody was being friendly with one another. Watching them laugh together felt like a nail going right through his toe. He felt the steam coming out of his ears. Marsha was raving about what a delight it was to have Morris at Rigg's.

"Are you sure you are not talking about one of your other patients?" kidded Sam.

"Oh, Sam, would you stop?" said Jude. Marsha laughed. Todd just smiled. More like a delightful pain in the ass, the teenager thought to himself.

"So, what have you all been up to since I have not been around?" asked Morris.

"We went to visit my mother in Hastings. She made us her famous lasagna," answered Jude.

– 29 –

— THE NURSING HOME —

"So, how are they treating you here, Dad?" Sam butted in.

"How would you feel about being in a place like this for two weeks?" Morris was being sarcastic. He couldn't help himself. Marsha said goodbye to Morris's family as she saw an argument beginning. Morris went on as he said, "Would you please get me out of this shit-infested place?!"

"Don't you like it here, Dad?"

"Like it here? Are you fucking kidding me, Sam? Why don't you try staying here for a while and tell me how much you like it?! You wouldn't last a day!"

"Aren't you overreacting just a little, Morris?" Jude asked politely, trying to calm him down.

"Overreacting, *my ass*, Jude! Boy, Sam, you sure know how to pick the winners."

"Knock it off, Dad!" Sam demanded. "You're way out of line." They both told each other to go fuck themselves.

"Todd, go get some candy from the machine," instructed Jude as she dug in her purse for money.

"But I'm not hung–"

"Just go, Todd!" she insisted, holding out the dollar. Todd knew his mother was serious. He took the money and left the room.

"Sam, within these past two weeks, I witnessed my roommate, Felix, being ridiculed and scolded like a dog. Our aide, Bill, got rough with him. The douche bag spilled Felix's dinner all over him on purpose. Would you get me the fuck out of here?!" Beads of sweat started pouring down Morris's wrinkled, pale face.

—30—

— JAMES J. MURPHY III —

"Relax! Cool down... Are you sure your not imagining things, Dad?"

"Damnit, Sam! Why don't you believe me? It's true what they do to people in these places. Just like in the movies..."

Todd strolled in with a chocolate bar. "Sounds like Grandpa needs to take his medicine," he joked while adjusting his cap.

"Not now, Todd." Sam had a stern look on his face.

"Shut up, you little bastard!" Morris said. "Fuckin' brat," Morris continued, although he was smart enough to keep it under his breath.

The argument continued for almost another ten minutes. Finally, the Grovers gave up. "That's it, Dad! We're leaving. See you in a few weeks. We're outta here!" Sam motioned his wife and son to the door. Everyone knew that when Sam got heated, there was no point in trying to reason with him. Morris watched as his family abandoned him again.

Morris sat in his room alone, feeling ashamed. Family is supposed to be the most important thing in a person's life. Then why doesn't mine believe me? wondered Morris. How could they just go on with their lives knowing how I feel?

Bill entered the room with Morris's medicine. "Hi Bill," Morris said, still feeling down.

"Take your medicine, old man," Bill replied with a mean look on his face.

"What did you call me?!"

"I ain't got all day! Take your medicine."

"You know, Bill, you could use a lesson in manners. Maybe try taking Manners 101."

— THE NURSING HOME —

"I don't need any lessons from you, you old fuck. Just take your Goddamn medicine or you'll end up like your buddy, Felix."

"What happened to Felix?" Morris questioned.

"Let's just say he had a little accident." The smirk on Bill's face made Morris sick to his stomach. He knew he had to get out of there.

The next day, Cyndi Gillian made an announcement over the loud speaker very early in the morning reporting that Felix Sumner had passed away. Morris was curious as to why she didn't announce the cause of death. Was it because Felix didn't take his medicine? He wondered. During lunchtime in the lounge room, some patients were discussing the mysterious incident involving Felix, while others just stared into space.

"Poor Felix," Ralph said. "How could this have happened to such a nice guy?"

"Hey, knock it off with the bullshit, Ralph!" yelled Pauly. "A lot of patients are here one day and gone the next. We all know Felix had problems, but I'll bet anything that Bill, Pearl, or one of those pieces of shit had something to do with it. I'll bet my life!"

"No need for that, Pauly," said Morris. "I believe you."

"Wising up a little, aye, Mori?"

"It's Morris, and yes. Bill threatened me; he said I'd end up like Felix, too, if I don't listen to him. I swore he wanted to kill me. Him and that arrogant sneer."

"If we all tell Cyndi, she'll believe us," Wade said enthusiastically.

— 32 —

"I don't think so, Wade," Morris told him. "I hate to admit it, but Pauly's been right one hundred percent this whole time. I tried telling my own family about Bill, but they just think I'm nuts." Morris stared down at his feet.

"I told all of you that these people don't give a fuck about us," said Pauly. "Cyndi just hired four people. To top it off, they are all kids. I saw Cyndi going around introducing them to everyone. They look about sixteen. It's bad enough that you can't trust an adult staff, but now we have to depend on teenagers to take care of us. Hell, when I was a teenager, all I cared about was getting some tail. Still do." Pauly smiled.

— Chapter 5

Jay, Jeff, Beth, and Ron were the four newest acquisitions to the staff. Usually Cyndi didn't hire people under twenty-one, but she was taking a chance and hoping that the four kids that she hired turn out to be responsible enough. Cyndi told the new employees that they could begin working the first week of December.

Jeff and Jay were good friends and both worked at Kirk's Video Store as well. They needed to take on a second job in order to satisfy their parents. The two of them were inseparable since the beginning of freshman year of high school, where they came together as outcasts, although it never bothered them. They were always known as screw-ups. Their friends and family didn't know who was worse. Jeff and Jay did everything together, from drinking and smoking to playing video games and watching horror movies. They were both lucky enough to graduate from high school and had no intentions of college. Two years after graduating, they still didn't care that they weren't

JAMES J. MURPHY III

accepted by society. Working in a nursing home sounded creepy and that intrigued them. Jeff Randle's mother got them the job through a friend. They didn't trust adults over forty, but senior citizens seemed harmless to them and they looked forward to filling their minds with their own interests, like classic zombie flicks. Even though some of the patients might end up considering them kids of the Grim Reaper, they did intend to go out of their way to take care of the elderly patients. They'd read and play games with them, talk to them about movies, and more importantly, listen to what they have to say.

Beth was nineteen years old and a student at the University of Miami, where she became a huge fan of the Miami Hurricanes. She planned to major in Astronomy and always wanted to become a scientist. In her spare time, she liked looking through microscopes and mixing chemicals together. In order to pay for her college tuition and get serious in her next year of college, she took the semester off to get a job. One of Beth's classmates suggested she apply at a nursing home or hospital.

Ron was also nineteen years old and originally from Florida. He went away to college in Denver, Colorado and was looking forward to becoming a history teacher. He took a huge interest in current events. Like Beth, Ron took the school year off to go back home and make more money. Ron didn't mind working because he liked to keep busy. He would just miss skiing and the cold, snowy weather. Ron was the shy and quiet type and was definitely a bookworm. Other than his interest in world history, he was a bit of a science fiction geek. Ron wasn't happy to be home, but he was going to make the best out of a bad

—— THE NURSING HOME ——

situation and work at Rigg's Nursing Home until he made enough money to pay for the next semester.

Chapter 6

Morris strolled into the lounge room and was not surprised when he saw the guys gathered at the same table. "Hey gang."

"Hey there, Mori, old boy!" Pauly had a big smile on his face.

"Hello Pauly, and it's Morris."

"He knows it is. He just loves busting your balls," Ralph said as the rest of the gang chuckled. "So, where you been the last week or so, Morris? We miss you here."

"Motormouth Pauly has been on a talking rampage since you've been gone. Nothing new," said Frank.

"If you two could stop asking questions for one minute, we will know where Mori's been," interrupted Pauly.

Morris shook his head. "Well, since you guys asked so nicely, I'll tell ya. I usually have physical therapy on Mondays and Wednesdays. I think I overdid it a couple of weeks ago. Last Sunday, I had a tickle in my throat, as if a cold was about to come on. When I woke up the next

THE NURSING HOME

morning, I was not feeling at my best. When do I ever?" he kidded. The gang laughed. "So now," continued Morris, "not feeling so good, I have to do physical therapy. Brian, my physical therapist, takes me out of my wheelchair and has me do these annoying stretches. I stretch here, I stretch there, I'm all stretched out. Usually, I can handle the stretches, but with me not at one hundred percent and Brian yelling in my ear, I got a headache. I'm shocked I'm not deaf."

"I know what that's like," Pauly butted in. "Last week, Brian worked me like a mother fucker. I'm still feeling the aches today."

"Brian's not a bad guy or anything; he is just so energized and pushes you to the limit so you feel the burn," added Frank, scratching the back of his bald head, which had nothing left but a few tiny gray hairs.

"For a guy in his forties, he's in great shape," replied Morris. "Maybe I should introduce him to my son, Sam. All Sam does is sit in front of the TV, watching a sporting event while stuffing his face with greasy chips and drinking soda." The gang was amused by Morris's story.

"Reminds me of my wife, Mary," interrupted Pauly. "I used to call her 'The Old Battle-Axe.' She just sat in front of the tube, watching that romance garbage."

"You're married?" asked Morris, jumping at the chance to ask about Pauly's personal life.

"Unfortunately, Mary passed away thirty years ago. She had lymphoma cancer." The gang paused for a brief moment, feeling for Pauly. He was actually being serious, talking about the death of his wife, instead of kidding around like he always did. However, everyone, including

-38-

Pauly, wanted to hear how Morris's story turned out.

"Continue, Morris," encouraged Frank.

"Also, Brian still has all of his hair – that lucky bastard. Do you believe that?" asked Morris.

"What?" Frank responded.

"Not one single white hair on his head or goatee."

"Hey, we are what we are. Even though my hair and sideburns are silver, at least it matches," Ralph joked.

"What are you guys complaining about?" asked Pauly, being nosey as usual. "Brian won't look like this forever. He may end up like me... Balding crew cut and fat as a hippo."

"Don't forget *grumpy*," added Frank.

"Well, are you sure you can trust your physical therapist?" asked Ralph, getting back to the subject.

"No," answered Morris. "He's part of the staff."

"Now you're catching on, Mori," cheered Pauly.

"So, after all this, all I did was go to my room and sleep," said Morris.

"So, what happened to you yesterday? We didn't see you at Bingo," said Ralph.

"I was too exhausted to think about Bingo. Hell, I didn't even get to do my word search. The only reason I go is to meet up with you guys, anyway," explained Morris. "Also, earlier today, Brian had me do hand exercises for my arthritis. Basically, I'm squeezing a rubber ball, moving my fingers, and doing writing practices. This guy does push you to the limit. Once again, after that, I just went to my room to relax. But this time, I got interrupted. Nurses Anne and Helen came in to see how I was doing. They took my temperature to see if I had a

— THE NURSING HOME —

fever. You know, the usual shit. They also checked my blood pressure and told me how to keep it down. They are a couple of Chatty Kathys."

"Anne and Helen have been here forever," said Pauly.

"Then I got my hair shampooed," Morris told the group. "You know, I looked in the mirror today and I realized my hairline is receding. Has this always been the case?" They all agreed, laughing together. Morris went on, "They also weighed me. I'm eight pounds less since I've come to Rigg's. I'm down to 152. Hopefully I'll gain it back."

"Oh, you will," reassured Pauly. "Just eat the shit this place serves you."

"After physical therapy, I feel weaker than usual. I'm sure as hell glad to see you guys," Morris said.

"Same here," Frank said as the others nodded in agreement.

"Even though this week I have been physically exhausted and weak, it's been such a relief to have Bill off my back. Where has he been? Not that I'm complaining, but I haven't seen him in days," Morris said. "Maybe Pauly's wish came true."

"Unfortunately, that's not the case. He's been in Vermont, skiing. He goes every year around this time," informed Frank.

"Wouldn't it be great if he didn't come back?" asked Ralph.

"It would be even better if he skied into a tree. That would be a Happy Thanksgiving!" exclaimed Pauly, followed by laughter from the group.

"Yeah, that's wishful thinking. But we all know that

Bill never misses a party," Frank said, delivering the bad news.

"He's always ruining our fun."

"Pauly, to get off the subject for a moment, is it true that Brian's leaving?" asked Morris.

"No, Mori. Physical therapists here just work in other nursing homes or change floors for a few weeks. Nothing permanent. Actually, to make you a little bit happier, Brian is taking a cruise to the Bahamas, so he's gonna be gone even longer. He'll have a replacement, so there is no getting out of physical therapy." Pauly chuckled, rubbing his big, round belly.

"I hate getting used to new routines. At least with Brian, I know what I'm getting myself into." Morris paused. "Torture."

Chapter 7

"Good morning, everyone! It's Thanksgiving! Up and at 'em!" Cyndi Gillian was very enthusiastic while reading the morning announcements, sounding as if someone spiked her apple cider with tequila. That was what Morris woke up to. All he wanted to do was sleep the day away, but Cyndi's loud mouth over the P.A. woke him and he couldn't go back to sleep. He kept imagining what his family was doing on Thanksgiving without him.

Jude usually woke up at eight o'clock in the morning to start preparing the big turkey dinner. It took hours for her to prepare all the food. Every year, the Grovers enjoyed a peaceful day of salad, beets, cranberry sauce, stuffing, yams, turkey, espresso, cake, and pumpkin pie. While Jude was busy cooking, Sam and Todd usually watched the Macy's Day Parade and pointed out the inflatable characters. The family always began eating between 1:30pm and 2:00pm at the dining room table, while the TV was blasting. Sam needed to hear the football game. They would always give

JAMES J. MURPHY III

thanks and praise. After dinner, Sam always continued watching the football game, announcing who was beating who and what the score was. He always kept up on his sports. Jude would then clean the dishes, while Todd disappeared into his room to work on model airplanes.

When Gertie was alive, she had been there with them, relaxing over coffee and a good conversation. Remembering the Thanksgivings with Gertie put a lump in Morris's throat. He could still picture her smile and hear her laugh, like the times when he'd try to use a one-liner and screw it up. To Gertie, Morris had always been her stick figure and to Morris, she had always been his round bunny. The holidays would never be the same without her, but without his family, he really felt alone. He'd be lucky if he even got a phone call wishing him a Happy Thanksgiving. Morris couldn't believe that he was trapped in a nursing home on such a so-called thankful holiday.

It wasn't until 10:45am that Morris got out of bed and that was only because Nurse Helen insisted on it. She told him that there were treats and festivities in the lounge room. As he was wheeled down the halls of the nursing home, he noticed pictures and cut-outs of turkeys, pilgrims, and Indians. Through the windows, he could see pumpkins and a scarecrow with a stack of hay outside. He was relieved to see the gang sitting at their usual table.

"Hey gang," greeted Morris.

"Well, well... Look who got out of bed," teased Pauly.

"Helen made me. It's either that or she probably would have reported that I am depressed, then make me go to therapy. That's all I need... to talk to some quack who tells

—43—

— THE NURSING HOME —

me what to do about my problems," described Morris.

"Who needs that shit?" replied Pauly as Ralph and Frank nodded in agreement.

"Are you guys ready for today's pilgrims and Indians play?" asked Ralph.

"I'd rather do the arts and crafts," said Frank. "A long time ago, I was an artist. I used to draw and paint everything from cartoon characters to environment and nature. Now I'm here." Frank's voice sunk down to a low and depressing monotone.

"Hopefully it's better than last year's event," said Pauly. "Seeing Bill dressed up as an Indian and Eddie dressed up as a pilgrim made me swallow my own vomit. Besides, every year it's the same old shit. After five years, you'd think that they would have a new event. Maybe, after God knows how many straight years, they will change the damn movie. I'm so sick of watching *Home Alone*," complained Pauly. "Family forgets kid. Kid defends his home. Come on! New movie!"

"At least we may see our families today." Frank tried to look on the bright side.

"Maybe I'll get a visit from my family for once," said Ralph.

"How about you, Mori?" asked Pauly. "Is your family coming?"

"I don't know... and it's Morris."

"How about your family, Pauly?" asked Ralph. "Come to think of it... I don't recall seeing your family here, either."

"Me neither. Not for the whole five years we've been here together," said Frank.

— 44 —

"Fuck family!" Pauly exclaimed. "You guys wanna know why my family doesn't visit? I'll tell ya. They dropped me off here five years ago because they considered me to be a useless and helpless gimp. They also thought that I was a pain in the ass, and vice-versa. Personally, they all could forget about me because it would be a cold day in hell before I ever talk to them again."

"We're sorry to hear this, Pauly," said Morris.

"Don't be, Mori," Pauly fumed. His dark brown eyes were boiling. "Who needs them? My real family are you lug-heads."

Later that evening, after dinner, Morris went back to his room. Thanksgiving dinner ended up being ham, potatoes, and stuffing that didn't even taste real. You call this Thanksgiving? Morris thought to himself.

At seven o'clock at night, there was a knock at the door. Who could it be at this hour? Morris wondered. "Come in!" It was the Grover family. They came to visit Morris and wished him a Happy Thanksgiving. "Does it look like I'm happy?" Morris mumbled.

"We brought you something, Dad," Sam said, handing him a present. "Well, aren't you gonna open it?" Morris opened it and found a turkey drumstick, stuffing, and a slice of pumpkin pie.

"Aren't you thrilled?" enthused Jude.

"Between your family dinner and the football game, you actually had time to visit little old me?" joked Morris.

Bill showed up and introduced himself to the family. The Grovers seemed delighted to meet him as he was busy

── THE NURSING HOME ──

kissing their asses. Too bad they don't know this guy is a real schmuck, Morris thought to himself.

"I'll heat this up for good ol' Mori after you all leave," Bill suggested. "Well, it was very nice meeting you."

"Same here, Bill," the Grovers responded.

"It's Morris!" He hated how spiteful Bill was, especially around his family.

"We'd better hit the road," said Sam, signaling to his family that it was time to leave. Todd waved goodbye to his grandfather.

"We'll see you soon, Morris." said Jude.

"What? In another four to six weeks?" replied Morris.

"Oh, Dad. Goodnight."

As the family was leaving, Bill returned with Morris's heated food. "Here you go, Morris," Bill said with arrogance. Bill obviously faked a slow stumble. "Oops... I dropped it." Bill grinned.

"You blundering idiot!" Morris screamed. "My family brought that for me. Do you know how long it took to make?!"

"Hey, old man... Your family thinks I'm a swell guy. I could have them eating out of the palm of my hand. Who would anyone believe? You, someone who can't even wipe his own ass, or me, the responsible caretaker?" Bill laughed. "Words of advice, Morris... Don't fuck with me. Happy Thanksgiving!"

Chapter 8

Cyndi Gillian gave Jeff, Jay, Beth, and Ron a tour of the nursing home and introduced them to one another so the new faces could get acquainted. They were also introduced to some of the staff that they'd probably be working with, as well as some of the patients. "If you have any questions, just ask for me," said Cyndi. "Most of the information should be in the handbook."

Jeff and Jay were assigned to work on the first floor. It was usually the quietest because that was where there were the least patients. Mainly on the first floor was a movie room, where the patients went every Wednesday night to watch an old black and white movie from the 1940s. Their job was to get the room ready and to make sure it stayed clean. Other tasks they were in charge of included vacuuming the rooms, mopping the patients' rooms and the long hallway, changing the garbage, and cleaning the bathrooms. Their job might be messier than Beth's and Ron's, but it was the least stressful. They didn't

—— THE NURSING HOME ——

have much interaction with the patients unless, on the rare occasion, they were assigned to bring patients their meals.

Beth worked on the second floor. She did have patient interaction. Her main job was working at the desk and greeting patients as they passed by, as well as their family members and other visitors. If someone needed to know what room a patient was in, she informed them. She was in charge of filing, updating data, and taking calls. When Beth wasn't doing that, she was assigned to give patients their meals and take away their trays when they were finished eating. Sometimes she fluffed their pillows and made them feel comfortable.

Unfortunate for Ron, he was assigned to the third floor. He had the most responsibility. He had to serve the patients their food, tend to their needs, and talk to them with care. On the third floor, most of the patients were incoherent. Ron didn't think every patient was 'all there.' One time, a patient asked Ron if he remembered when Ian got bit by a snake. Who's Ian? Ron thought, confused. He decided the best thing to do was to just agree with them. It was not as bad as the patients who cursed at him or called him names. Those were tough situations for Ron. He was the shy and quiet type, and felt intimidated by the senior citizens. Sometimes he left in tears. How am I going to become a history teacher if I can't handle these old geezers? he thought. What's worse? These old fucks I'm dealing with now or the young fucks I'm going to have to deal with in the future? Ron was going to have to pull himself together and fast.

— JAMES J. MURPHY III —

Monday, December 10, was Jeff and Jay's second week of work. Eddie made sure they were settled in and showed them where all of the maintenance equipment was. He gave them a brief list of things they had to complete before their shift ended. "Any questions?" Jeff and Jay shook their heads to assure Eddie that they knew what to do.

To get things done quicker, the two of them split up, starting at opposite ends of the hallway. Their plan was to meet in the middle. Their first mission was to change all of the garbage bags. Eddie gave them a few extra large bags so they could condense the smaller bags into one large one. Both youths couldn't believe how much garbage the hospital accumulated. Next, they had to sweep the hallways and the patients' rooms. After that, it was time to get a bucket of water and begin mopping the patients' rooms, as well as the bathrooms.

Jay held his breath when he entered John Crombert's room, thinking to himself: *Did this guy just drop some ass when I came in? I think I'm going to be sick.* It got worse as they passed each patient's room and bathroom. Jeff felt the same way. They were relieved to see each other when they finally met up.

"Dude, I'm gonna gag," complained Jeff.

"I wonder if the other floors are any worse."

"At least we only have to vacuum the movie room. Then we get to go to lunch."

"Let's get this over with." It was obvious that Jay was exhausted.

"Thank goodness we are only part time. When they hire us full time at the video store, we can forget this place," Jeff said with a smile on his face.

— THE NURSING HOME —

"I hear that," agreed Jay.

After they finished vacuuming, Eddie sent Jeff and Jay to lunch.

When the kids returned from their break, it was their job to bring lunch to the patients. "Hey, Jeff, do me a favor?" Jay asked.

"What is it?"

"You bring lunch to John Crombert and tell me if he smells like ass! Then you'll really gag!"

"Fine," said Jeff.

The boys started bringing lunches to the patients. They tried being friendly to the old, but it was tough. When you're a teenager, you shouldn't trust anybody over forty, they thought. When Jeff made it to John Crombert's room, he greeted him. No response. Jeff just put the tray of food on the table and was out of there. He continued going from room to room, delivering the patients their meals and hoping the other rooms didn't smell as bad as Mr. Crombert's.

Jeff informed Eddie that Mr. Crombert did not answer him and that the room smelled like shit. "He's probably just sleeping," Eddie explained, teasing his gelled, spiked hair, as if it was 1987 all over again. Then he reminded Jeff that they were working in a nursing home. "Expect the rooms to smell like shit," Eddie laughed.

The boys finished the day at one in the afternoon and were relieved as hell.

—50—

Later that evening, the night crew was bringing the patients their dinner. Gail, one of the evening nurses, noticed Mr. Crombert was not moving and thought he looked malnourished. She felt for a pulse. She freaked out when she couldn't find one. Immediately, she called Dr. Welling. He came in, examined the body, and informed the staff that there was nothing he could do. John Crombert was dead.

The very next day, Cyndi Gillian announced the death of John Crombert over the loud speaker. "Unfortunately, John Crombert died in his sleep at the age of seventy-eight. This is a terrible and unexpected tragedy. He will be gone, but not forgotten, here at Rigg's Nursing Home."

Cyndi informed Jeff and Jay of the death of John Crombert the next time they came in to work. The two friends looked at each other, not believing what they heard. As Cyndi walked away, Jeff said to Jay, "Whoa, I waited on a dead dude."

Chapter 9

By Tuesday, almost everybody in the building already knew about the death of John Crombert. News got around quickly to everyone from the staff to the patients. When Beth went in to work, she expressed to Cyndi how sorry she was to hear about Mr. Crombert. She was only trying to be professional, considering she had never met him before.

"Well, today's a new day, Beth," Cyndi said quickly. "We need you to file all of our patients' names in alphabetical order according to their last name. If there is an asterisk next to a name, that means the person is deceased. Move the file into another folder immediately. You'll see a separate folder for expired patients," addressed Cyndi. "For now, just bring breakfast to the patients."

Beth obeyed, while thinking that even though authority figures believed that people under them were capable of doing nothing on their own, the reality of the situation was that the more people thought they knew something, the more clueless they were in life. She managed to smile back at Cyndi.

The morning went by quickly for Beth as she did her duties. At lunchtime, Beth went to the breakroom on the second floor. She took a ham and cheese sandwich she brought from her home out of her bag. She also took out an astrology book and started reading to herself.

Jeff and Jay were floor-hopping on their break and were curious to see what it was like on the other floors. They checked out what the staff and patients were doing. When they came across Dr. Welling, they decided it would be interesting to ask him what it was like dealing with dead bodies.

The doctor rolled his eyes. "Maybe when somebody's about to kick the bucket, I'll make sure we page you two morons immediately so you witness what I go through every day firsthand."

"Nice talking to you, Doc," replied Jay. The two kids got out of Dr. Welling's sight and were soon snuck up on by Bill. Bill put his hands on their shoulders sternly and asked what they were doing on the second floor.

"We were just curious about the other floors... and also wondering if other floors smelled as bad as ours did yesterday," answered Jeff.

"Sometimes even worse," laughed Bill. "Especially when someone dies or when a patient pisses or shits themselves. The smell goes to your head; you breathe heavily or it feels like you're gasping for air." Bill enjoyed scaring the kids.

— THE NURSING HOME —

"Well, we gotta get back to work, Bill," the boys replied.

"Be good, boys." Bill headed in the other direction.

"I'm hungry, Jay. Let's see what goodies are in the breakroom," suggested Jeff. They went in and caught Beth reading her book.

"Hey, I remember you," said Jay. "You're the chick from orientation."

"Yes, I am," Beth said, amused. She decided to put down her astrology book and engage in conversation. She thought that the two guys seemed wild and probably had too much caffeine, but didn't see them as a threat. They asked her if she heard about the death of 'Old Man Crombert.' "I did," she said. "Isn't it a shame?"

"I guess. We didn't really know him," replied Jeff. "I waited on him yesterday and noticed his room smelled like ass. I told Eddie and he laughed at what I said. We thought he was sleeping. We never woulda thought he kicked the bucket."

"Do you know if Ron is working?" asked Beth.

"Not sure," they said, shaking their heads. "We gotta get back to work," said Jay. "See you later." It was time for Beth to get back as well.

When Morris was brought into the lounge room, he overheard Pauly discussing the sudden death of John Crombert with the usual gang.

"Do you believe this shit?" asked Pauly. "Not that long ago, Felix died mysteriously... and now Crombert."

"Well, he *was* seventy-eight years old."

"I know, Ralph, but dying in his sleep like Felix? Come on!" exclaimed Pauly.

"There has to be some explanation," Ralph replied.

"Explanation? I'll give you an explanation!" Pauly raised his voice. "The explanation is Crombert probably died a day or two prior to the announcement, but our staff is too Goddamn stupid to realize it. Word has it, even one of those teenagers who went into Crombert's room noticed something funny. What I hear is that Eddie laughed him off."

"Don't you mean 'shrugged?'" interrupted Morris.

"Point is, Mori, if these assholes were doing their jobs to begin with, these incidents would not have happened."

"You're right, Pauly, but do we have proof?"

"Your proof is Crombert's dead."

"Good point – and it's Morris."

Ron went in to work later that day. Before Beth left, she went to the third floor to talk to him. "Hey Ron. I was looking for you." She noticed Ron looked a little confused. "You don't remember me, do you? We had orientation together."

"Oh yeah, I remember you now," replied Ron. "How are you?"

"Before everyone comes to you, I'll give you the bad news. Mr. Crombert, a patient on the first floor, died last night."

"How?" asked Ron.

"A heart attack, supposedly. Well, maybe I'll see you around the premises."

"Alright, I'll see you around." Ron went to get the

THE NURSING HOME

laundry cart. He had to change all of the sheets in every room. Thank God I already ate dinner and I'm wearing gloves, he thought. He wished he could be in Beth's shoes and leave. Ron sighed. I signed up for this, I knew what I was getting myself into, and now I have to deal with it, he said to himself. He changed the urine and feces-infested sheets with a disgusted look on his face. After that, he began giving the patients their medicine and bringing their dinners to them. The meal of the evening was chicken noodle soup with mashed potatoes and a cup of apple juice. The last patient Ron served was an old lady named Diana.

"Did I ever tell you about my son, Erik? He loves chicken noodle soup," she told him.

"Oh, really?" Ron tried looking interested.

"You look just like him."

"Thank you."

"When is dinner?" Diana asked.

"I just gave you the chicken noodle soup. You said I look like your son, Erik."

"Erik? Who's Erik?" The old lady looked puzzled.

It's going to be a long night, Ron thought to himself as he slowly walked away. For the time being, he set up everyone's TV and did some filing. At about 11:30pm, he left the building, just to come back the next day.

Chapter 10

Early Wednesday morning, everyone heard Cyndi speaking firmly over the loud speaker. "Edward Reynolds, please report to my office at once."

What could I have done? Eddie thought to himself. When a boss calls you by your full name, it has to be serious. Eddie entered Cyndi's office. "You needed to speak to me."

"Yes, I do," she replied sharply. "What is this I hear about you being the reason that Mr. Crombert died?"

"What do you mean, Cyndi?" asked Eddie.

"All kinds of rumors are flying around this nursing home telling me that one of our new staff members informed you that Mr. Crombert wasn't responding and that you brushed him off."

"Just like you said, Cyndi, they are just rumors. We both know this place; once someone does something or once something happens, all of a sudden it's everybody's business. I'll even bet that when I leave your office after

── THE NURSING HOME ──

this meeting, everyone's gonna be gossiping about us. We'll be the talk of the day. Who said this, anyway?"

"Names aren't necessary."

"I checked on Mr. Crombert. He looked fine to me."

"I hope, for your sake, that you are telling me the truth, Eddie, so help me..."

"Cyndi, would you relax? Do you expect these patients to be singing and dancing?! These people already look like death, so it's my job to nurse them."

"If I ever witness you abusing or doing anything that you shouldn't be doing with these patients, I will fire you on the spot. Do I make myself clear, Eddie?"

"Got it."

"Now get out of my sight!"

Eddie left the office in a foul mood. Pearl approached him and asked him if everything was okay. "No, everything's *not* okay, Pearl. Cyndi's saying that I'm to blame for Crombert's death. I wish I knew how this rumor started."

"We both know that there are no secrets in this place, Eddie. It could have been those new burnout kids that Cyndi hired. You know, the ones who have been working with you as of late," Pearl suggested.

"Why didn't I think of this? It had to be them. Thank you, Pearl. Now I know who to take my anger out on."

Jeff and Jay entered the nursing home and clocked in. "Another day here at wonderful Rigg's," Jay said sarcastically.

– 58 –

"Hopefully we get that full time gig at Kirk's. I could care less what the hours will be. At least we will be enjoying ourselves," said Jeff. The boys were waiting in the movie room for Eddie, who had to give them the keys for the maintenance supplies. Eddie began to approach the boys as if he was about to rip their heads off.

"Did Eddie get up on the wrong side of the bed?" Jay whispered to Jeff. The boys acted more serious when Eddie actually confronted them.

"Which one of you little bastards are spreading rumors about me?" Eddie wanted answers. Jeff and Jay looked at one another, dumb-founded. "Don't give me that innocent routine," Eddie demanded, already heated up. "I know at least one, if not both, of you little pricks are going around saying that I didn't help or save Old Fuck Crombert. He's old; he deserved to die."

Jeff decided to take a stand. "First off, Eddie, you did laugh me off about it. You probably could have done something, but you are nothing but a selfish fuck who cares about nobody but yourself."

"Yeah, Eddie," chimed in Jay. "My bro is right about everything he said about you. Guess what, Eddie? You may be our boss, but you don't have enough power to fire us, so fuck you! This isn't exactly our dream job, so if Cyndi wants to fire us, fine; we really don't care. If she does fire us, you'd be looking for a new job, too, because we'll tell her how you really did ignore us when we came to you for help, so we have nothing to hide and nothing to lose," he stated. "Remember, Eddie, we're teenagers; we could easily find another job. What are you, in your forties?"

—— THE NURSING HOME ——

"Here are the keys," said Eddie. "Just do your job. This talk never happened. Got it?!"

The boys did agree because in reality, they did need a second job for income. "You're damn right! Today is a wonderful day," Jeff said to Jay with a smile on his face.

"Hey guys," greeted Morris as he wheeled himself into the lounge room.

Ralph and Frank said 'Hi' back, while Pauly blurted out: "How the fuck are you doing, Mori, old boy?!" He seemed very excited and hyper.

"I'm fine... and it's Morris. Why are you so peppered up today, Pauly?"

"You wanna know? Well, I'll tell you lug-heads. You know, I could care less about the staff, but I heard that those two teenagers, Jed and Joe, told off Cock-Sucking Eddie."

"I believe it's Jeff and Jay, if I'm not mistaken," interrupted Frank.

"You can call them anything you want, for all I care," Pauly replied. "The point is... I love these kids already. I wish they worked on our floor. We could use kids like this to tell off Bill."

"Pauly, where do you get your information?" questioned Morris.

"Oh, I have my sources."

"Pauly probably hired an electrician and had this place wired!" kidded Ralph.

"Where would Pauly or any of us get money for an electrician?" Frank chimed in. The gang had a great laugh.

–60–

JAMES J. MURPHY III

"I told you guys how staff members like Bill or Eddie are useless," Pauly continued.

"It's more than that." Morris got serious. "Look at what happened to poor Felix."

"Good ol' Felix was a snazzy dresser in those fine-looking suits he used to wear," butted in Wade.

"What are you talking about, Wade?" asked Frank.

"I saw a bunch of old pictures of him in his photo album," Wade answered.

"Well, do you guys think it was an accidental death?" Pauly asked the gang.

"I believe Bill left him to die intentionally," Morris responded.

"You're damn right, he did," insisted Pauly. "Mori hasn't been here long enough to remember, but I believe you guys have, as well as some others in this room. Who remembers White Witherspoon, John Hopkins, Fat Claire, Grouchy Larry?" Pauly was reading names off left and right.

"Your point is, Pauly?" asked Ralph.

"Point is, Ralph, that all these people I'm mentioning died mysteriously. Am I the only one who notices this?"

"It could be a coincidence," suggested Frank. "Besides, Cyndi has been really good to us. Even you, Pauly."

"I don't know about the rest of the staff, but you're right. Cyndi has been good to us. I'm telling you guys, if it's not Cyndi, then someone else is covering up past mistakes and I want to know what they are!" demanded Pauly.

"Staff alert! Act like we're talking about an old movie," Morris warned.

—— THE NURSING HOME ——

"I can't wait to see what the special movie is tonight," Frank said, pretending to sound interested.

Bill walked by, hearing them talking about the movie special. Pathetic, dumb fucks, Bill said to himself. He had a big smile on his face.

"What are you so happy about, Bill?" asked another aide.

"Nothing really, Margo. You notice that these old fucks have nothing better to look forward to except a Wednesday night movie."

"Well, Bill, you know these people have been alive since the dinosaur era. What do you want them to do? Go food shopping? Run a few laps around the track?"

"I'm just saying, Margo."

"Yeah, Bill, that's all you do is say."

"What's your problem?"

"You," responded Margo. "All you do is ridicule and put down the patients and talk behind everybody's back just to make yourself feel better. Just like these patients, Bill, you may also be helpless one day, too. I just wish it was sooner than later, so I can see how many people actually give a damn about you. I definitely won't be one of them."

"I knew it! It must be that time of the month," enthused Bill. Margo walked away with her middle finger up in the air.

"Finally, we get some real entertainment," Pauly commented to the gang after witnessing what happened.

"Another person who hates Bill... Why am I not surprised?" said Morris.

The patients were sent back to their rooms.

– 62 –

— JAMES J. MURPHY III —

Morris decided to take an afternoon catnap. Five minutes passed and Morris was out like a light. Soon after, he was greeted by special guests. The Grovers were hovering over him. Morris was startled. "Jesus Christ! Are you trying to give me a fucking heart attack?!"

"Would you calm down?!" Sam said.

"We've come to surprise you," interrupted Jude as she started putting her long, light brown hair into a scrunchy.

"I should have guessed." Morris sighed. "It's only been about six weeks since the last visit. Are you gonna actually grace me with fifteen minutes of your time instead of the usual ten? Boy, do I feel special..." Morris went on.

"Told ya he didn't want to see us," said Todd, adjusting his black cap.

"Mind your manners, Todd," instructed Jude.

"You didn't have to startle me," said Morris. "Ever hear of knocking?"

"Well, anything new since last time we visited, Dad?" asked Sam.

"Not really. Last time, I told you Felix died mysteriously; now another man named John Crombert is dead."

"How did he die?" Jude seemed interested.

"Supposedly, he died in his sleep," Morris told his daughter-in-law.

"It happens," said Jude.

"This is the second death since I've been here."

"It's a nursing home, Dad. These people unfortunately die of old age," Sam reminded his father.

"Sam, I told you two people are dead since I've arrived. When are you getting me the fuck out of here?!"

"It's coincidental, Dad! Calm down!"

–63–

THE NURSING HOME

"I think the staff is hiding something," said Morris.

"What could they be hiding? They seem very concerned. At least you're kept up to date on what's going on," said Sam. "We gotta go now. See you soon, Dad." The Grovers were making their exit.

"I know, probably in another month or two," Morris said, hoping they'd hear his remark.

Chapter 11

On Thursday night, Ron had to work the late shift. Ron would rather be any place but Rigg's. At least if he was working the morning shift, or even the afternoon shift, he'd have friends to see or eat lunch with. It was just him, Rita, who was the head supervisor for the night shift, a couple of nurses, aides, and a janitor. Ron did his usual routine of bringing patients their dinner and making conversation with them. He also changed their sheets and gave them their required pills.

After Ron accomplished his early tasks, he took his mandatory dinner break. He went into the breakroom and began heating up a frozen dinner of chicken, corn, and mashed potatoes. Ron studied the box. Oh cool, he thought, I get a dessert with this meal. He looked around for a set of plastic utensils, but all he could find was silverware. Ron took a fork, assuming that it was there for the employees. He was impressed to see all that was provided for the staff in the breakroom. They even

THE NURSING HOME

have a toaster, he noticed. Then he put a dollar into the vending machine and pushed the button for a can of soda. Ron opened up his science fiction book and read while he ate his dinner.

After dinner, Ron clocked back in and told Rita that he had some paperwork to do. She gave him the okay and said she had to put some records in order as well.

"Hey, Ron... At around nine, could you check on the patients to see how they are doing?" asked Rita. "You know, the usual shit... tuck them in, fix their pillows, and leave the TV on for them."

"Sure, Rita," agreed Ron as he was putting papers in order.

A few minutes later, he heard coughing from a distance. At first, he ignored it. Then it was getting louder. Ron followed the sound out into the hallway. It was coming from a patient's room. "Are you okay, Diana?" asked Ron, entering her room. She just smiled at him. Ron poured her a glass of water. He even stayed to make sure she drank it. She seemed fine, so he continued on with his duties. It was probably the smell in this place, he thought to himself. It makes me cough as well.

"Did I hear coughing?" asked Rita, passing by.

"Yeah," Ron responded. "It was Diana, one of the patients. I gave her some water. She seemed to be okay after that."

At around nine, Ron began to check on the patients. He went from room to room to make sure everyone was comfortable and to see if they needed assistance with anything. Finally, Ron got to Diana's room and couldn't believe what he was seeing. What he saw made him feel nauseous. It looked as if Diana had choked on her own vomit. It appeared as if blood was mixed in. Ron screamed Rita's name.

Rita bursted in. "What is it, Ron?" Then she saw for herself. "I'll get Dr. Owens." She ran down the hall.

After what felt like an eternity, Dr. Owens finally barged through the doors. He immediately cleared the workers out of the patient's room as he attempted to revive her. Apparently, it was too late and there was nothing that he could do.

"Who spoke to her last?" asked Dr. Owens.

"It was me," informed Ron. "It must have been two or three hours ago. She was coughing, so I gave her some water. She seemed to be fine."

"Unfortunately, she's not fine now," said the doctor. "Maybe she is in a better place."

"It looks like we've gotta give Cyndi a call," stated Rita.

This is the third patient in a short time span to pass away, Ron thought to himself. The second patient since I've started.

Cyndi arrived shortly after and started asking questions. "How did Diana die?"

"She must have choked after regurgitating," the doctor responded.

"I'd better give her family a call and report the bad news. Tomorrow I will make an announcement to inform all patients and employees," Cyndi said, obviously upset.

The very next day, Cyndi made the announcement regarding the death of Diana Roberts. Beth heard the

— THE NURSING HOME —

announcement and called Ron on her break. "Hey Ron, it's Beth."

"H-Hi Beth, what's up?" replied Ron.

"You tell me. Cyndi made an announcement saying that another patient died last night."

"Yeah, it was an awkward situation. It looked like she choked on her own puke. I called Rita and she called the doctor, but the old lady was already dead. Dr. Owens even questioned us about it. I still have that stench of puke envisioned in my head. I'm just gonna relax today."

"Alright. See you tomorrow, Ron."

"Bye Beth," he said, hanging up.

"Yo Beth," a voice said, causing Beth turn around. "Who were you on the phone with?"

"That was Ron. He's still having visions from last night," she told Jay.

"That sucks," said Jeff. "Now, just like us, he witnessed a dead body here at Rigg's. You're next, Beth," he kidded.

"Be serious, Jeff. Would ya?" said Beth.

"Sorry."

"With all seriousness," Jay interrupted, "would there be a police report?"

"Ron never said he was questioned by police; only by Dr. Owens," Beth informed.

"Never trust doctors," the boys said. "Yeah, man. They are the ones in charge of saving you or leaving you to die. It's all in their hands," added Jeff.

"They do what they can do," said Beth.

"If I'm dying, *let* me die," stated Jeff. "Besides, if a doctor looked at me, he'd probably agree," he laughed. "I gotta get back to work now."

– 68 –

— JAMES J. MURPHY III —

"Later, guys," said Beth.

Morris found himself looking more and more forward to meeting up with the gang in the lounge room. He wanted to catch up on what was going on. "I almost joined Felix the other night, guys... God bless his soul."

"How's that?" asked Pauly.

"My dumb-ass family decides to crowd around me while I'm sleeping. When I woke up, I thought I was under attack. I'm telling you guys... I nearly crapped my drawers." The gang was laughing hysterically at Morris's story.

"Next time that I smell shit, you're the first person I'm going to look at, Mori, old boy," teased Pauly.

"Doesn't my family know that I can kick the bucket at any time? And look... they're hovering over me like vultures. I figured Jude, as naive as she is, would have some common sense because we know my son and grandson sure don't."

"It could be worse," butted in Frank.

"Yeah," said Ralph. "It could have been Bill hovering over you."

"I know," said Morris. "Now *that* guy wants us to die."

A few minutes later, Bill pranced over, acting giddy. "Sorry, guys... Break's over."

Bill started wheeling Morris to his room. "Another patient died last night. Do you believe that, Morris?" He had the biggest grin on his face. If he smiled any bigger, his face would break.

"And your point is, Bill?" Morris responded.

–69–

—— THE NURSING HOME ——

"My point is that one day, you and your old-timer buddies are gonna join Diana, Old Man Crombert, and your good buddy, Felix. I didn't witness him dying, but seeing him lying there, dead as road-kill, and just seeing those hazel eyes staring back with no motion whatsoever, put a smile on my face."

"You know, Bill, if I was twenty years younger and not in a wheelchair, I would kick your ass. You are nothing but a cock-sucking yuppy who was givin' a silver spoon at birth and wouldn't know a hard day's work if it bit you on the ass!" Morris let him have it.

"Drop dead, old man!" Bill retaliated.

"I knew you played for the other team," Morris yelled back. "You're nothing but a male nurse. Where's your dress, faggot?!"

Bill was infuriated and bitch-slapped Morris so hard his ears were ringing. "I'm going to make your life a living hell, mother fucker!"

"We'll see," replied Morris. Could he just have outsmarted Bill? Cyndi just happened to be going from room to room checking on all of the patients. A lot of the patients were already in the state where they couldn't feed or take care of themselves. Cyndi accepted that. She also talked to patients to get a better idea on how they were doing.

When Cyndi got to Morris's room, she noticed his face was swelling and that he had a fat lip. "Morris, who did this to you?! What happened?" She seemed deeply concerned.

"It was Bill!" he blurted out. "He snapped on me for no apparent reason." Morris pretended to be nervous and frightened, but he was laughing deep down inside. Bill was passing by and noticed Cyndi in Morris's room. He walked in and began the ass-kissing act.

"Hi Cyndi," greeted Bill with a positive attitude. "I'll get your dinner for you, Morris."

"Enough with the act, Bill! You see Morris's face. What happened?" Cyndi demanded.

"I was helping Morris out of his wheelchair and he fell forward. I tried to catch him, but I was too late." Bill had a sympathetic look on his face.

"The truth, Bill!"

"Fine, I'll tell ya what happened, Cyndi. First off, he deserved it. You had to hear all the bad things he said about us Rigg's employees!" Bill explained. "I admit it; in the heat of the moment, I smacked him. I felt I had to defend our nursing home."

"That's all I wanted to hear, Bill. Isn't it great being honest?" asked Cyndi.

"It sure is," agreed Bill with confidence.

"By the way, Bill, get out of my sight – You're fired!"

"What? You can't fire me, you bitch!" Bill screamed.

"I just did!" she screamed back. With everything that was going on at Rigg's, she refused to tolerate any more nonsense. She was planning to keep a closer eye on things.

Bill packed his things and left. While he was leaving, Cyndi was smart enough to report what happened to the police. They were outside waiting and escorted Bill away from the premises in handcuffs.

Chapter 12

By Monday, the environment was still a little stressful at Rigg's Nursing Home, but not as intimidating since Bill was no longer around. There was one person to thank for that and his name was Morris Grover. The usual gang and other patients were chilling in the lounge room as they did every day.

"Isn't it great that the pansy-ass, no-good, son-of-a-bitch Bill is no longer working here at Rigg's? You notice everyone here seems a little bit calmer," commented Pauly.

"Yeah," Frank and Ralph agreed.

"I wish I witnessed Cyndi firing Bill firsthand," said Pauly. "I would have gotten out of my wheelchair and done The Charleston."

"You're nuts, Pauly." Ralph was amused.

Morris strolled into the lounge room in his wheelchair and everyone stared at the swelling on his face.

"Hey Mori! You look like shit today," teased Pauly.

"Thanks, Pauly, and it's Morris. The swelling should

JAMES J. MURPHY III

go down soon. Hell, I took harder hits from Gertie than from that low-life, Bill." The gang laughed. They were glad to see that Morris was being his usual self.

"You planned this shit out, old boy, didn't you?" asked Pauly.

"I overheard the staff mentioning Cyndi was going to visit everyone's room, so I knew this was a great opportunity to get Bill riled up. This was our chance to get back at him for all those times he ridiculed or abused all of us patients, past and present, in this Godforsaken place," explained Morris. "I knew exactly what buttons to push so he would hit me. It was perfect. Cyndi walked in and I pretended to be scared. I gave her the puppy dog eyes."

"Mori, you are a genius!" exclaimed Pauly.

Nurses Anne and Helen interrupted the party. "Sorry, everyone, but it's time for you all to go back to your rooms," said Helen. Before the patients were escorted back, Anne asked Morris how he was feeling.

"It could be worse; my son, Sam, could be cooking dinner for me," Morris joked. The nurses laughed. Morris's buddies were watching how much he was enjoying all of the attention.

"I'll get you an ice pack," Anne said. Morris thanked her. All of the patients were brought back to their rooms for an afternoon catnap.

Nurses Helen and Anne stepped out for a cigarette break.

"Do you believe what Bill has done to Morris?" Anne asked her co-worker.

"Between you and me, Anne, I always thought Bill was an asshole, but I never thought that he would stoop as low as striking a patient," replied Helen.

—— THE NURSING HOME ——

"Well, after a ten hour shift, even *I've* pictured going off on some of these patients."

"Same here," agreed Helen. "But this *is* our job. We get paid to do this. Maybe this is why we go on our cigarette breaks," she kidded. "It calms us down."

"I have a feeling it's going to be a long night."

"We'd better get back to work, girlie."

As nighttime approached, the late night staff checked on the patients to see if they were okay. They seemed fine. The staff brought dinner to all of the patients, left their TVs on for them, and tucked them in.

Around ten o'clock, Nurse Anne wandered into the breakroom for a cup of hot tea. At least I've been trying to cut down on coffee, she thought, pouring herself a cup. Anne walked over to the table and sat down. She felt relaxed as she sipped her hot tea. While staring at the bulletin board, she heard a noise. Assuming something fell behind her, she turned around and was startled to see one of the patients staring at her from the open doorway. Anne was so shocked that she almost dropped her tea. "How the hell did you get out of bed?" the nurse asked, in a panic.

The patient stared back at Anne, as if in a trance. Anne got up to bring the patient back to his room, not realizing that another patient had snuck in beforehand. The second patient picked up the tea kettle and cracked it right over the back of Anne's head. SMASH!!! Shards of glass splattered everywhere. Hot tea scorched her skin. Anne was lying unconscious, bleeding from her head.

JAMES J. MURPHY III

A few hours later, Nurse Helen went to the breakroom for a midnight snack. She found Anne lying on the floor, not moving, and started freaking out. She screamed for help. A few employees ran in from the hall. Helen immediately called the police.

Officers O'Conner and Conway rushed to the nursing home. They investigated the crime scene and found very little evidence to work with. The officers asked the employees who were on duty if they noticed anything strange or heard any noises.

"It was only us and the patients here all night," explained Helen. "We have maximum security here, making it hard for anybody to break in. I just saw Anne around nine o'clock. Who would do a thing like this?"

Officer O'Conner promised to have a sit-down and question everyone in the building. It was routine procedure. He also contacted Cyndi, the head of the nursing home, awakening her from a deep sleep.

Shortly after, Cyndi arrived with her hair a wreck. All she threw on was a pair of jeans and a jacket that was not even zipped. Officer O'Conner asked Cyndi if she noticed anything odd or if anybody was acting strange lately. "I don't believe so," she said. "Although, at this place, rumors tend to fly around a lot. Actually, one of our latest rumors was that one of our staff members, Eddie Reynolds, was asked to check on a patient and he didn't, and the patient ended up dying. I had a serious talk with him and he denies it. You can talk to him if you want; I have his number in the office."

"We'll talk to him just in case he knows something," the officer assured Cyndi. "In the meantime, we'll see

THE NURSING HOME

where the evidence takes us."

"Actually, I don't know if this is relevant, but I recently fired a male employee for assaulting one of our patients. As a matter of fact, I had him removed from the property by the police."

"Yes, we were the ones who handled that," O'Conner informed her. "Thank you, Ms. Gillian. Your cooperation is appreciated."

The very next day, a sad and gloomy Tuesday, Cyndi made an announcement over the loud speaker about the mysterious death of Nurse Anne Meyer. "Anne was a dedicated worker, team player, mother of two, and a very special person. She could light up anybody's dark day, but now, unfortunately, she is gone... So we, as a team, have to find that light ourselves. We'll miss you, Anne." Cyndi finally ended the speech, all shaken up.

During their lunch break, Jeff and Jay went looking for Beth and Ron. The four of them decided to go out to lunch together. They grabbed a quick bite at Moe's Diner. All four of them were puzzled about how to bring up the previous night's incident. Finally, Jeff broke the ice. "Do you guys believe what happened last night?"

"Yeah, man. I know," Jay butted in. "We've never worked at a place where people got murdered. This reminds me of a slasher movie, dude, but it looks like we're the stars."

"Hey, I want you two burnouts to wake the fuck up! This is no fucking horror movie; these are our lives you are talking about," Beth said, giving everyone a serious look.

–76–

"How could anyone do a horrible thing like this?" Ron asked, shy as a mouse.

"Who said someone? It looked more like some*thing*," Jay said.

"Yeah, man. I hear you," Jeff agreed. "Do you guys think the cops know more than what they are saying?"

"We can always ask them," suggested Beth.

"The older cop seemed like he was doing all of the talking," said Ron.

"So maybe we should talk to his partner instead," stated Jeff.

"Why's that?" asked Ron.

"Because people who do all the talking are all talk and no action. It's a fact," insisted Jeff.

"Yeah, man. Like when a teacher tries to teach a class a certain subject that they don't have a clue about," said Jay.

"This is the dumbest thing I've ever heard," Ron said with confidence. "Basically, what you guys are saying is that when I become a history teacher, nobody's gonna listen to me."

"Exactly," Jay said. "Because teachers go on and on about one subject, trying to drill it into students' heads until they don't give a fuck anymore. Hell, you were in high school, Ron. You know how the story goes."

"Ron, you may think it's dumb, but it's the truth," said Beth.

"Alright, guys," Jeff interrupted. "Enough talk; let's eat. We have to be back soon or else Cyndi will have our heads."

"Not like that!" Jay laughed. They all agreed. The kids ate a good lunch and had a great time.

Chapter 13

"Conway, I've been on the police force since about the time you were born and I've never seen anything as strange as this case. Hell, I was probably a rookie when you were popping out of your momma's belly and sucking her titty."

"What's your point, O'Conner?" Officer Conway snapped back, looking at himself in the side view mirror, playing with his hair and admiring his good looks.

"My point is this place is as tight as hell; you can't break in and if you did, you wouldn't get out in time because cops would be there in a jiffy."

"How do you explain the murder of that nurse?" asked Conway.

"That's what I'm trying to figure out," Officer O'Conner said, gathering the facts. "We interrogated every employee working that night and they all had alibis that checked out. Plus, to top it all off, there was no suspicious evidence left behind."

"Maybe we should interview the patients, as well," suggested Conway. "They may be senior citizens, but they are not all stupid."

"Conway! I know you're new to the force, but you are also a fucking idiot."

"No, I'm not!" said Conway sternly. "The fact that you have twenty-something years on the force doesn't mean shit to me."

"It should!"

"Why's that?"

"Because," was O'Conner's only defense. Conway stared at him, still waiting for an answer. "Conway, you're trying to tell me that one of these patients may have killed that nurse? First off, most of them can't walk. Also, a lot have already flown the coo coo's nest. And finally, you're telling me that a patient has the strength to overpower and kill a practicing nurse, hide the evidence, as if they're *really* that smart, and then return to their room and go back to sleep? I think you saw one too many episodes of *The Twilight Zone*," teased O'Conner.

"Well, you know, O'Conner, there is a lot of amazing technology out in the world today. If the pieces of the tea kettle are big enough, we can get it dusted for prints," Conway informed his older partner. "You've got to move forward with the times, because if you don't, you'll be left behind."

"You know something, Conway... I was left behind a long time ago. No use trying something new now. My routine got me where I am today and if I wasn't so stubborn, I would have never solved any of these cases."

"Try seeing things my way. I'm willing to do anything I can to help."

THE NURSING HOME

"Conway, you kinda remind me of *The Little Engine That Could*."

"What do you mean by that, O'Conner?"

"You think of everything. That's why I like you. Now just shut up and let's get some coffee. My treat."

"That's why I like you, too, O'Conner."

Chapter 14

On Friday morning, everyone at Rigg's was gathered in the cafeteria. Nobody looked happy to be there, but they didn't have a choice. The whole week, there were signs posted all over the building that read:

**All employees and patients must
attend the assembly meeting on
Friday, December 21st at 10:00AM.**

Even if employees were originally scheduled off, they had to show up. The meeting was mandatory due to the recent events that occurred at Rigg's.

At a quarter to ten, all of the employees and patients were waiting for the meeting to begin. Everybody could notice all of the cliques were sitting together; the kids on one side, Eddie with Pearl and Sue on the other side, Morris and the gang in the front, and so on.

"I thank you all for making it here for this morning's assembly under these circumstances," Cyndi began.

THE NURSING HOME

"I know some of you had the day off today and probably had plans with family or friends, or just intended to relax, so I do apologize and remind you that this time will be made up to you, I promise. As you all have noticed, a lot of mysterious things have been happening around here lately. For example, the death of John Crombert, one of our patients."

Just hearing the name 'John Crombert' infuriated Eddie. Listening to Cyndi lecture about it over and over again made him feel sick. He looked over at the kids, who he suspected ratted him out. To his surprise, they were staring back at him, smiling, and one of them even waved. He quickly looked away and focused back on Cyndi.

"I'm lead to believe that this accident may have been preventable. Of course, there are two sides to every story," Cyndi continued. "I can't prove who is right or wrong regarding this incident, but if any of our patients are being neglected or abused, or if I witness any patients being mistreated, I will have no problem firing the person, or people, at fault. Just last week, I had a former employee fired and escorted out in handcuffs for assaulting one of our patients."

"Mori," whispered Pauly with a giggle.

"Shush, Pauly... and it's Morris," he whispered back.

Cyndi went on with her speech. "All of us here at Rigg's Nursing Home work long hours and, even some of us, around the clock. With lack of sleep, we may not feel at a hundred percent and tempers may flare, but remember the number one reason why we are all here." 'Paycheck' was the word that came to every employee's mind. "For the ones here who need our help,"

– 82 –

Cyndi stated, turning her head to address the patients. "You are all important to us. Our job is to come here and serve you the best we can. Your comfort and your well-being are our top priorities." Cyndi paused for a moment, and then looked up and glanced around the room. "Let's be team players; look out for one another and please speak up if you notice anything strange going on. Also, if you don't want to be here, just leave, because I don't want you here. We are here to do our best and I expect nothing less. Thank you for your time and cooperation. Everyone have a Merry Christmas and let's look forward to a Happy New Year." Cyndi concluded the meeting. Everyone clapped like a flock of sheep; nobody wanted to look bad in front of Cyndi.

It was already lunchtime when the meeting had come to its end. The gang met in the lounge room, as usual. "Do you guys believe all of the crazy things that are happening here lately?" asked Morris.

"Nothing crazier than usual," said Pauly. "That assembly was a joke."

"I wish this meeting happened on a Monday so I wouldn't have to do my usual Monday routines. Then I wouldn't have to go to physical therapy until Wednesday."

"Don't think they will let you get away with missing a session, Mori, old boy. Brian or his sub will have you make up the session another day instead. That could mean back to back sessions."

"Never mind, I'd be thrown off track."

— THE NURSING HOME —

"When it comes to physical therapy, Brian has no sympathy," Ralph butted in.

"I know," agreed Pauly. "That guy really makes you work. Picture if you gave him a megaphone while you were doing your drills – forget about it," kidded Pauly.

"Sorry to interrupt, guys, but this is a serious situation," addressed Wade, wheeling over with his food tray on his lap. "There was a murder and Cyndi is very concerned."

"You're so gullible, Wade," laughed Pauly. "Actually, you all are if you believe this speech."

"Come on, Pauly," said Morris.

"Don't be sweet on her, Mori, just because she mentioned you at the meeting."

"I'm not, Pauly. And it's Morris."

"You all notice that when a patient here dies, Cyndi makes an announcement over the loud speaker and it's the talk of the day. Then the next day, everyone will go on with their lives... but when a *staff member* dies, it's a huge ordeal."

"She was murdered, Pauly," said Ralph.

"What about us patients, who are abused? What about Felix? Do you guys think he wanted to die?"

"I agree with you, Pauly, but this was a cold, bloody murder," insisted Morris.

"You know, Mori, I don't give a fuck about Nurse Anne's death. They could all drop dead, for all I care. See you guys tomorrow." Pauly wheeled himself to his room angrily. The rest of the gang could see how frustrated Pauly was.

"I hope he's not mad at us," said Ralph.

"You know Pauly; tomorrow he'll be his usual self,"

Frank assured everyone. "He always storms off when he gets this heated."

"Pauly does have a point about the patients not getting as much respect as the staff," Morris admitted. "But I do agree with everything Cyndi said in her speech today. Looks like the break's over, guys. Here comes Brian."

"Hey Morris," greeted Brian as he quickly approached. "I've been subbing at another nursing home and then went on vacation for a week and a half. Did you miss me?"

"Maybe," said Morris.

"How was my replacement, Mikey, while I was gone?"

"Mikey was good."

"Mikey's back on the third floor now. Are you up for a session today? I know it's a little late notice, but I think we'd both rather do it today. Monday is Christmas Eve."

"I might as well get it over with now," Morris said, remembering what Pauly said about the possible two straight days of physical labor. Brian wheeled Morris towards the physical therapy room, rambling on about the stretching, squeezing, and writing practices that they'd catch up on. Today's going to be a long day, Morris thought to himself.

When Morris finished his physical therapy, he wheeled himself back into his room. He put on the news while he rested in bed. He was tired, as always after a major workout, and decided to take a catnap. All of a sudden the phone started ringing. Morris didn't bother to pick it up. He was just getting into a deep sleep when the phone rang again a half an hour later. It woke him. Puzzled, he answered the phone. Sam was on the other end.

"Dad, we're getting you the fuck out of that place!"

— THE NURSING HOME —

"What the fuck are you talking about, Sam?"

"Cyndi Gillian, the head of the nursing home, called us earlier and said a staff member mangled your face."

"Pipe down, Sam. It was just a hard slap and it happened over a week ago. Anyway, Cyndi fired him. The prick deserved it. Besides, Sam, why do you give a shit about me all of a sudden?"

"We always care, Dad."

"How about all of those other times I tried telling you, Jude, and the brat what I was witnessing? You all thought that I was picturing things."

"We're sorry, Dad. We're gonna get you out of this place as soon as possible."

"Sam, I'm staying here whether you like it or not, so I suggest you leave me the fuck alone!" Morris slammed the phone down out of anger. Sam tried calling again and again throughout the day, but Morris refused to pick up. Morris felt bad about what he said to Sam, but he also meant it. After all, he had the gang to go to whenever he had a problem.

— Chapter 15

Later that same night, the kids decided to chill at a nearby park. Ron was going to meet up with them when he got out of work. When he arrived, Jeff and Jay were already smoking up and Beth had a beer in her hand. They all welcomed him and asked 'What's up?' and Ron greeted them back.

"Do you want a beer, Ron?" asked Beth.

"I'm not a heavy drinker, but I guess one won't hurt," he said, accepting the offer.

"Who ever said that you have to be a heavy drinker? I'm not," Beth told him. "We're just chilling."

"Yeah, man," jumped in Jay. "I just like seeing blurry pictures."

"You mean, like pink elephants?" chimed in Jeff.

"Dude, you're fucking stoned off your ass," joked Jay.

"I know, man, and we got work tomorrow."

"You guys are nuts," laughed Beth. "Speaking of work, I have to work with Sue tomorrow. This will be my third time working with her and I can tell that she hates my

THE NURSING HOME

guts." Just thinking about it made Beth grip her beer bottle tighter.

"Dude, Sue hates everyone's guts," butted in Jay.

"Maybe she needs to get laid," kidded Jeff, "but I ain't the one who's gonna give it to her."

"I think she looks down on me just because I'm young and I actually know what I'm doing," explained Beth. "Enough about Sue, time for me to drink up."

"Aren't you guys worried about the weird stuff going on at work?" asked Ron.

"We are," said Jeff, "but can't we escape reality for a little bit? There's a lot of fucked up shit going on at work, but now we're out of work, so let's have a good time. Pass me another beer, man."

"This person must be a pro," Jay said, handing his buddy another beer. "I hear the cops are having a hard time figuring this out."

"Yeah, man. Cyndi's been buggin' out lately," Jeff replied.

"Well, why don't you relax her, Romeo?" Beth laughed, starting on her second beer.

"Maybe I will."

"Seriously, guys... do you think it's one of the employees?" Ron looked nervous.

"No, dude. None of the Rigg's employees are that smart," joked Jay.

"Not even Eddie," laughed Jeff.

The kids were having a good time and were apparently getting a little too loud. There was a call to the police station about disturbing the peace. Officers O'Conner and Conway were on patrol. The kids saw the lights of the police car and immediately ditched the beer and pot.

"Just act cool." Beth saw the officers getting out of the vehicle.

"Let's arrest these no-good teenage hooligans." O'Conner slammed the door, ready for action.

"Settle down there, O'Conner. Let me talk to them, okay? Weren't you young at one time?" Conway teased.

"Yeah, Conway, at one time, but not now." O'Conner paused, and then reopened the car door. "I'll let you handle it... but if I see a struggle, I'm coming, too."

"You got it," Conway agreed. He walked over to the group of teens. "Hey guys, what's going on here?"

"Nothing, Officer Conway," answered Jeff, fearing that he reeked of beer and pot.

"I know there's some illegal activity going on in these woods. Don't worry, I'm not gonna tell on you guys." He leaned in and lowered his voice. "Listen, my partner's over there watching us. I don't want to give him a reason to come over here."

"Don't worry, Officer, there won't be a problem," assured Ron. The kids nodded their heads in agreement. Beth asked the officer if there were any leads on Nurse Anne's case.

"We're still working on that," Conway said. "I came up with some ideas that will hopefully lead to some evidence. My partner may think I'm crazy, but we have to try everything."

"We'd definitely be interested in helping, Officer," Jeff offered.

— THE NURSING HOME —

"From the way it looks, it seems like it has to be someone who knows the place well," Conway told them. "We questioned all of the employees, but not the patients."

"This is getting too strange for me," commented Ron. "I think I need to go home and clear my head. Maybe I'll pop in a *Star Trek* DVD. Captain Kirk always has the answer."

"Oh, would you relax, Ron?" said Beth. "No offense, Ron... you are my friend, but *Star Trek* got cancelled years ago because Captain Kirk ran out of answers."

"Well, kids, I gotta jet. My partner's waiting. If you have any information, call me. Here's my card." Officer Conway handed a card to each of them.

"Will do, Officer," Jeff said. As Conway was walking away, the kids decided to split, as well. Jeff and Jay had to wake up in a couple of hours, Ron was still stressed out about the Nurse Anne situation, and Beth was just tired.

Conway got into the car. "I'm sorry I took so long, O'Conner. I was just questioning what those kids were up to tonight."

"Questioning? More like socializing. Did you give them your card? Maybe next time, if they happen to call you, you could all plan a tea party or a picnic," O'Conner kidded. "I hear you make a mean ham and cheese sandwich."

"Knock it off, O'Conner."

"By the way, I just got a call from the Captain. Officers Myers and Thompson may need back up."

"Really? What's up?" Conway asked his partner.

$-90-$

JAMES J. MURPHY III

"Hopefully it's just a regular convenience store robbery. You know how this one ends: robber comes out with his hands up, we make arrest, case is over. We go home to sleep and then we do the same thing again tomorrow. It never ends."

Chapter 16

The next day at Rigg's was a rather uneventful one for Jeff and Jay. They were actually relieved to have a break from the recent chaotic situations. Their hangovers were so intense that they jokingly questioned if they could still handle partying when they had work the next day. Of course, they still thought it was worth it. To make matters worse, they had to work with Eddie. As the day dragged on, the boys looked forward to watching a horror movie. Instead, by the time their shift was over, all they could think about was sleep.

Ron enjoyed his day off. It was a weight off his shoulders that he didn't have to serve patients while overhearing the constant gossip regarding the deaths of the patients or Nurse Anne. Sometimes he asked himself why he continued to work at a nursing home. Ron ended up doing what he had hoped to do, which was to watch a science fiction DVD. Watching movies like that always took his mind off of reality. He felt good being in his old room; it hadn't changed a bit. It was wall to wall collector's items and movie memorabilia. After watching the DVD, he put on one of the history channels, which reminded him that he had to keep his job in order to afford tuition. He wanted to be a history teacher more than anything, even if it meant working at Rigg's for the time being.

Beth was in a deep sleep until the ringing of her cell phone woke her up. Cyndi was on the other end. Someone had apparently gone home sick and Cyndi wanted to know if she would be able to come in a few hours early. Beth agreed, seeing it as an opportunity to make some extra money.

After Beth clocked in, she went straight to her desk, which was piled with paperwork. Beth started entering data into the computer right away. Today is going to be an exhausting day, she thought to herself. After only five minutes, Sue walked over and dropped off even more paperwork for Beth and said 'Have fun, dearie,' in a sarcastic tone. Beth just looked up at her, as if to say 'Whatever.' Beth continued typing, answering phones, and greeting guests for two hours and then decided to stretch and take a walk. On her way back, she visited some patients to see how they were doing. As far as she could tell, each one was doing fine. When Beth returned to her desk, she saw Sue waiting for her.

"Where the hell were you?!" Sue raised her voice. "This paperwork is not going to get done by itself."

"I went to see how the patients were doing," answered Beth.

"You've got more important things ahead of you."

"Sitting at this desk is not my only task. I also have to check up on our patients," Beth defended herself.

—— THE NURSING HOME ——

"You listen to me, you little bitch. I can have you fired at any time, so do what I say. Got it?!"

"No, I don't. You listen to *me*, Sue. I didn't need to come in early. I could have done other things today, but I did this as a favor to Cyndi, not you. Instead of bitching at me, you should be thanking me for the help."

"I don't need to thank you for nothin', Beth, because I'm the one in charge, not you."

"Actually, Cyndi's the one in charge, Sue! At least I know one thing for sure. I'm not going to end up working in a place like this in my forties and smelling like a Goddamn chimney, like you. If you keep on threatening me, you may end up just like Bill."

Sue was so heated that she wanted to claw out Beth's eyes, but instead, she just walked away. She wanted to take her anger out on somebody. At least the innocent patients couldn't fight back. They had no way of defending themselves.

Around five o'clock, Beth was in the breakroom reading her astrology book. She was eating take-out that she picked up from a nearby Chinese restaurant. Sue entered the breakroom to get some coffee. At first, neither of them acknowledged each other. Then Sue told Beth that she was sorry and that she thought they both overreacted. Beth accepted the apology, although she knew Sue didn't mean it.

"So, whatcha reading?" asked Sue.

"A book on astrology," answered Beth.

How pathetic, Sue thought to herself, but replied to Beth, "I don't think I've read that one yet. I'll let you get back to your break. See you later."

Beth waved as her face was buried in the book. She got the feeling that Sue was up to something, but she continued reading. Beth put her book back down and decided to put money into the soda machine for a cold beverage. She opened the can, sipped the cold, sweet cola, and took a deep breath. She began wandering around the breakroom and noticed that there was a word search book lying around. She opened the booklet to see what kind of interesting puzzles there would be. The inner cover of the booklet had a name that she recognized as one of the patients on the floor she worked on. How the hell did Morris Grover's word search book end up in here? she thought to herself. Beth assumed that Bill or another staff member must have misplaced it or forgot to give it back. Beth's dinner break was coming to an end, so she returned to work. Before going back to her desk, she knocked on Morris's door.

"Who's there?" asked Morris.

"It's me, Beth."

"Come in."

"I'm sorry to bother you, Mr. Grover, but I found your word search book in the breakroom. I thought you'd like it back."

"Why, thank you," Morris said gratefully. "Beth, you said?"

"That's right."

"I've been wondering what happened to this! I carry it everywhere I go. How did it end up in there? Oh, well. At least now I can continue my word searches."

"I have to get back to work, otherwise Sue will be on my case for the whole night. I told her off once already."

—— THE NURSING HOME ——

"To be honest with you, I don't trust this staff. Too many unexplainable things are happening."

"I know," agreed Beth. She said goodnight to Morris and then headed back to her desk to continue with her paperwork. As she continued her duties, Morris popped into her head. She was still puzzled about the whole word search book, but had to get back to work. Beth's next task was to assist the patients in rooms 226 through 250, while Sue did the first half.

Meanwhile, Sue began taking care of the patients that she was in charge of for the night. She usually went from room to room fluffing their pillows, tucking them in, and making sure their TVs were on. She started with room 225, where Lillian was staring up at the ceiling talking her usual jibberish. I need a new job, Sue said to herself as drool dripped down Lillian's face. Sue dabbed her mouth with a paper towel. "There, there, you old bag." No response from Lillian. She didn't even know what day it was. Sue couldn't wait until her tasks were over. It seemed to get worse as the room numbers went down.

When Sue entered room 216, Nelson Levar was lying in bed, watching TV. The room smelled like shit. Sue felt as if she was about to throw up. She noticed where the smell was coming from. "You old fuck," Sue muttered. "I want to get out of this place sometime tonight, but patients like you don't care. You don't know if you're dead or alive. Because of you, I have to lower myself and clean your mess." What Sue saw when she changed the old man's diaper almost made her vomit on the floor. The smell went straight up her nose until it hit her brain. Sue hadn't even finished checking on all of the patients that she was supposed to and she already wanted to give up on them.

By the time she got to room 214, Sue just couldn't take it anymore. Lying in bed, sleeping peacefully, was Mr. Gothersorg. He'd been having trouble breathing the last couple of months and was hooked up to a ventilator. Sue cleaned his room and tucked him in. The thought of her and Beth arguing crept into her mind and got her even angrier. *Who the hell does she think she is?* Sue said to herself. Beth thinks that because she is young and bright that she has a future and that I'm a good-for-nothing staff member working here to make ends meet. Sue realized what Bill went through after he was fired. It was all because of these no-good patients. They are a waste of space and life, she thought. Mr. Gothersorg may not be bothering me tonight, but who's to say he won't be annoying me tomorrow? Then a sinister smile came across Sue's face. She imagined putting on a pair of latex gloves and pulling the plug on innocent Mr. Gothersorg. She pictured watching his vitals drop until he flat-lined. Someone needs to put this old wind-bag out of his misery, she thought. Sue stopped daydreaming and got back to work. She leaned in and whispered, "Pleasant dreams, old man." She put the news on low for him and went to shut off the light. As she was leaving, Sue tripped on what she thought was her shoe. Goddamn heels, she said to herself. Little did she know that her dreams were about to become a reality. Mr. Gothersorg wouldn't be bothering anybody ever again.

Sue returned to her desk. "Hey Beth, I finished checking on the patients."

— THE NURSING HOME —

"Cool," said Beth. "I'm done, too. I think I just got carpel tunnel syndrome after typing all those papers today."

"Well, tomorrow's another day." They left the building and went their separate ways.

Early the next morning, Cyndi came in unusually early. One of the ways she planned on keeping the staff on their toes was with unexpected visits. She decided to see how good a job the employees were doing and figured that it would reflect on the patients. Therefore, she chose to go from room to room to see how the patients were doing. All of the patients seemed to be sound asleep. Cyndi was relieved to be almost done with the second floor without any problems until she got down to room 214. She knew from the moment she entered the room that there was something wrong. It was too quiet. She didn't hear the usual hum of the ventilator. Her first reaction was to check his vitals on the computer screen. The screen had been turned off. She immediately looked at the plug outlet. Both the ventilator and the vital machine were unplugged. Nervously, she felt for his pulse and his cold body showed no sign of life. "Oh my God!" Cyndi screamed, beginning to panic.

A janitor ran in. "Ev'thin 'ight, Cyndi?"

"No!" she yelled loudly. "Who was on staff last night?"

"I don't member ev'ron," he replied. "Wutt's her name? Suzi wuz in charge. Why? Wuzzup?"

"I have to call an ambulance. Another patient is dead."

"Say wutt?"

– 98 –

A few hours later, Cyndi informed everyone that Mr. Gothersorg was found dead earlier in the morning. "Hopefully we get to the bottom of this," Cyndi said in a serious manner.

All day, there was silence throughout the nursing home, including the lounge room, due to the unfortunate incident involving Mr. Gothersorg. Everyone felt bad because the useless old man didn't even see it coming. Out of the blue, breaking the silence, Morris screamed: "BINGO! Ha-ha, I finally got it." Everyone seemed to come to.

"What did you finally get, Mori, old boy?" asked Pauly. "Why are you so happy?"

"I just completed another word search. And it's *Morris*."

"Hey fellas, there was another death at this dump and Mori's as happy as a pig in shit because he found all the words," announced Pauly.

"Hey... I feel bad about Gothersorg, but maybe it was his time, Pauly. He was nearly ninety, you know."

"Morris does have a point," added Ralph.

"Yeah," agreed Frank. "The guy's been here for nearly twenty years."

"Maybe it is for the best that Gothersorg ain't here. At least he doesn't have to deal with the incompetent bullshit here anymore," declared Pauly. "Word got around that Cyndi noticed his breathing tube wire was unplugged. Tell me, guys... How did his breathing tube get unplugged?" The gang looked at one another, puzzled, and then back at Pauly and shrugged. "Don't you guys get it by now?" Pauly continued. "It had to be one of the staff

THE NURSING HOME

members. They're singling us out, one by one."

"That's absolutely ridiculous," said Morris. "I know that I had problems with Bill and I distrust the staff as much as you do, Pauly, but singling us out? Come on!"

"How do you explain it then, Mori?" Pauly wouldn't let it go.

"If we are being singled out, Cyndi has nothing to do with it," announced Morris.

"Or does she? She's probably behind all of this and covering all her tracks."

"Pauly, I know it's been a rough day, but we need to cool our jets," suggested Frank, trying to calm his friend down.

"I give up," submitted Pauly. "I'm too tired to argue with you lug-heads."

"A catnap is in need," said Ralph with a yawn. The rest of the group agreed.

"You notice every time we come to work, it seems like there's a new adventure. We deal with moronomy, stupidity, and death," Jeff said to Jay.

"Dude, is moronomy even a word?"

"I don't know, man, but it sounds funny."

"The more you smoke, the weirder words sound," joked Jay.

"I know, man, just like in high school."

Ron approached the laughing boys. "Hey guys."

"Hey Ron," they responded back.

"Have you guys seen Beth yet?"

"Can't say we have, Ronny, my man," answered Jay.

"We were talking about how every day something new happens here," said Jeff.

"I guess you guys heard about poor old Mr. Gothersorg," said Ron.

"Yeah, man. Everybody here's really freaked out about it."

"I know that it sucks that he died, man, but the dude's been in this joint for, like, twenty years. It was gonna happen sooner or later," concluded Jay.

"Man, if I was in this place for that long, I'd wanna die, too," responded Jeff. "Hell, I hate coming to this place now, and I get paid to be here."

"I agree with you guys," said Ron, "but whoever killed him couldn't have had a care in the world. Who would do something like that? How could someone be so cruel?" Ron ranted on to his friends.

"Relax, Ron," said Jay. "Just take a deep breath and chill."

"Yeah, man. Have you been living in a cave all your life?" Jeff jumped in. "Ron, you have to wake up, man. Dude, with your whining, you sound like a fifteen year old high school girl on her period." Ron was trying to get a word in, but Jeff was putting him in his place.

"Settle down, dude," said Jay. "You're getting too loud." Even Jay was trying to calm Jeff down, but to no avail.

"No! I won't settle down," screamed Jeff. "This guy's gonna be a fucking history teacher. What a joke! All we are witnessing here are a few deaths and Ron's crying like a baby. How the fuck are you gonna explain what Hitler or Stalin did when they had power? These seem to be a

THE NURSING HOME

few simple deaths – What Hitler and Stalin did was much worse," he vented.

"Don't you think I know that?" retaliated Ron. "What do you want me to do, Jeff? Smoke as much reefer as I can so I can hallucinate and not see the real picture? I admit that I'm scared as hell, but at the same time, I'm facing the reality of it."

"Fuck you, man!" yelled back Jeff. "Do what you do best... ask your precious space hero for advice." Jeff stormed off, leaving the nursing home. He didn't even bother punching out.

Jay apologized to Ron. "He must be having a bad day or something, but he'll be fine later."

"I've never seen him like that," reacted Ron nervously. "I just hope he doesn't hate me, because I consider you guys my friends."

"He doesn't hate you, Ron. You're a friend to us, too. He's having family issues with the parents. By tomorrow, everything will be alright." Jay cleared everything up.

Beth entered the building, clocked in, and then approached Jay and Ron. Before Beth could greet them, Ron blurted out: "Did you hear what happened here?!"

"What now?" she asked.

"Mr. Gothersorg is dead!"

"Are you kidding me?" asked Beth. "I worked last night and we checked on the patients, as usual, to see if everyone was okay." Everyone seemed fine, thought Beth. She kept thinking to herself.

"What is it, Beth?" asked Ron.

"You guys know something? Come to think of it, Sue was the one who checked on Mr. Gothersorg last night, not me."

JAMES J. MURPHY III

"What are you trying to say, Beth?" questioned Jay.

Right before Beth was going to speak, Ron actually overcame his shyness and shouted out: "Sue killed Gothersorg!? Are you fucking kidding me?!" Beth and Jay couldn't help but laugh at Ron's outburst. Ron was always so quiet and nervous, so for him to say one curse word seemed like a big step.

After the laughter died down, Beth got back on topic. "Sue seemed pretty steamed at me because we had an argument earlier in the day. It looked as if she wanted to kill me, but when I was on my dinner break, she tried talking to me all nice in a fake, girlie voice."

"I hate when bitches do that," interrupted Jay.

"Go on, Beth." Ron was getting antsy. He couldn't wait to hear the remainder of Beth's night.

"Sue *could* have killed Gothersorg... but not even she, I believe, has it in her to commit a cold, bloody murder."

"At least not face to face, anyway," added Jay.

"I better get to work before someone has my neck. I'll see you guys later," said Beth. The boys waved. Everyone went to do their jobs.

Chapter 17

It was a wonderful bright and sunny day. The birds were chirping and everybody was singing Christmas carols. Morris sat alone in his room, looking out his window at the beautiful scenery. God, I wish I could walk my ass outside and take in that fresh air, he thought to himself. Unfortunately, he was confined to a miserable thing on wheels known as a wheelchair.

The one sad thing in Hampton was that there was not a single snowflake in sight. As a matter of fact, there wasn't a single snowflake in all of Florida. That always caused the little kids to worry. They'd wonder if Rudolph was going to even bother guiding Santa's sleigh or if Santa was going to bring them any presents. The parents would explain that there was a blizzard at the North Pole and that by the time Santa made his way to Florida, it would be easier for him to coast from house to house and he wouldn't have to worry about slipping on top of a roof. The children would smile because they'd be getting a Christmas present after all.

Morris reflected on the great memories he had with Gertie. He remembered all the times he gave thanks to the Lord by attending midnight mass and singing the same carols that he'd been hearing all week at Rigg's, and having a great time doing so. Then he pictured when Ben was six, opening his present on Christmas day and being so happy to get a monster truck. It was no ordinary truck; it was the truck with the handle on the side. The back would drop when the handle was turned. Ben was the happiest kid in the world that day and Morris knew it. A tear dropped very slowly from his left eye as he smiled. He even pictured when Sam was a kid. Before he could get a very special thought, the head of staff barged in and yelled, "Merry Christmas, Morris!"

"Merry Christmas," Morris said back in a low voice.

"Let me wheel you to the lounge room, where all of the activities are happening." Morris didn't bother responding. As long as he could see his friends, that would make his day. "Oh look, Morris, I'll wheel you over to Pauly, Ralph, Frank, and the rest of the guys." After Cyndi wheeled Morris over, she greeted other patients, their family members, and the staff. Everyone seemed to be enjoying themselves.

"I think the arts and crafts look pretty good this year," mentioned Frank. "What do you think, Morris?"

"Not bad," Morris replied.

"Did your daughter come to visit, Frank?" asked Ralph.

"Yeah, she came with her husband. They gave me a nice card and some art supplies. They know I have arthritis in my hand, but they believe I can pull through, in their hearts. How about you, Ralph? Your family visiting?"

— THE NURSING HOME —

"Doubt it," said Ralph. "How about your family, Morris?"

"Hopefully not," he responded. "That would be the best Christmas gift ever, but knowing them, Jude may twist Sam's arm into coming."

"Come on, guys. Christmas is just another day here. Nothing special," Pauly went on.

"I'm guessing your family won't be visiting. Right, Pauly?" asked Morris.

"You got that right, Mori, old boy. Seriously, I thought it was bad enough on Thanksgiving when Bill dressed up as a pilgrim and Eddie dressed up as an Indian, but things just got worse."

"What do you mean, Pauly?" questioned Morris.

"Now Eddie and some other dick-heads are dressed up as elves. Yeah, this turned out to be a Merry Christmas." Everyone was able to sense the sarcasm in Pauly's voice.

"You have to admit, the decorations don't look as bad this year as they did other years," commented Frank. "If I didn't have this damn arthritis, I'd show you guys what *real* holiday decorations are supposed to look like."

"We know you would, Frank," Ralph encouraged his buddy.

"We might as well take advantage of the free food, guys," added Morris.

"You call this food?! It all looks like crap to me," Pauly said with bitterness.

"Do you enjoy *anything*, Pauly?"

"Yes, I do, Mori, old boy. I just don't enjoy anything that comes out of this place."

"Merry Christmas, Pauly," kidded Wade.

— JAMES J. MURPHY III —

"Merry Christmas, my ass. Bah Humbug!" said Pauly. The gang laughed. They all managed to have fun for the remainder of the afternoon, even Pauly.

Around seven in the evening, Morris was lying in his bed, watching *A Christmas Story* on television; part of the twenty-four hour marathon. He wished he could be watching *Miracle on 34th Street* or *It's A Wonderful Life*. He then thought to himself: *It's a wonderful life, my ass.* What's so wonderful about it? I'm stuck in this place until I die, thanks to my family.

Just then, there was a knock at the door. "Go away!" yelled Morris. "I'm watching a movie."

The doorknob turned and the door opened. "Merry Christmas!!!" echoed the Grovers. Jude gave Morris a hug and kiss.

"Here ya go, Dad," greeted Sam as he handed his father a Christmas card. "Thought we'd stop by to wish you a Merry Christmas." Todd left a wrapped gift on his grandfather's bed table.

"I was having a Merry Christmas until you barged in here like raving lunatics. I was watching a movie."

"Oh, Morris, the movie can wait," said Jude, grabbing the remote and turning off his television.

"Are you going to open your gift, Grandpa?" asked Todd. Sam and Jude also encouraged him to open his gift.

Morris opened his card. It was red with a green trim and had Christmas tree designs on it. The card read:

— THE NURSING HOME —

Grandpa,

Wishing you happiness all year round.
Merry Christmas and Happy New Year!

Love,
Sam, Jude, and Todd

Morris could tell that Jude signed the card. It had a woman's touch. He then opened the present. Inside was a container of lasagna. It looked delicious. Hard work was put into the meal, but all Morris could say was, "Oh, wow. Even though it's Christmas, you had time to stop at a 7-11 and a Walgreen's just to get me a gift."

"For your information, Dad, we went to Jude's mother's today and she baked that herself. Then we drove here to deliver this to you, so show some appreciation."

"Appreciation for what, Sam? You bringing me something on a holiday? You're somebody special..."

Sam rolled his eyes, shaking his head at his wife. "I told you this was a waste of time, Jude. My only day off this week, and look how we spent it."

"Calm down, Sam," she said, trying to relax him.

"Just leave!" yelled Morris.

"Jude! Todd! You heard the man," Sam told his family.

– 108 –

JAMES J. MURPHY III

"Sam!" Jude begged him.

"We're leaving! Now!" Sam screamed, heading towards the door. Jude and Todd followed like soldiers.

Morris was able to squeeze out one final comment. "See you in a month or two!" he shouted, pissed off. The Grovers were gone and Morris's movie had already ended. He didn't want to watch it from the beginning again. He channel-surfed and eventually fell asleep.

Chapter 18

It was Friday, March 21, the beginning of spring, and all Rigg's had seen for days was nothing but rain. "I hate these Goddamn dead zones!!" screamed Eddie, out of anger, when he noticed his cell phone had lost service. He looked around, concerned that Cyndi might have heard him. Phew, the coast is clear, Eddie said to himself. Finally, I get some damn service in this place.

Scrolling through his numbers, he wondered who he should call. Delicious Debbie? I wouldn't mind having some fun with her tonight. Eddie pictured all the kink-o-rama they'd experienced in the past. Tonight would be perfect for this, he thought, smiling. What a gloomy day... Nothing but thunderstorms all night. This would mean after work I'd have to pick her up, take her to the movies, and then hopefully go back to her place. Would any of this even happen tonight, considering it would probably take her an hour just to put on fucking makeup? Is it even worth wasting my time and good hair gel?

Eddie reconsidered. He continued skimming through his cell phone and paused when he saw the name 'Mark.' Don't wanna shoot pool, thought Eddie, shaking his head.

Finally, Eddie saw a name of interest. His eyes lit up at the sight of the person's name for what seemed like a whole minute long. He had a sinister grin on his face that wouldn't disappear. One would have thought that he was a predator who had just caught his prey. Eddie pushed the button with the green telephone symbol on it. The cell phone began dialing. After three rings, the party on the other line picked up.

The voice said, "Hello?"

"Hey, what's up, Bill?"

"Ed-ster, is that you, you fuck-head?! How the fuck are ya?"

"Doin' fine, and yourself?"

"Could be better, could be worse. I'm still unemployed, thanks to that old fuck, Morris Grover."

"Are you collecting off the government?"

"You better believe it, Eddie. Can you believe it's already been three months? How is it at Rigg's?"

"Dude, you don't wanna know. Death after death. Remember when Old Man Crombert kicked the bucket? I was blamed for that by some burnout kids. Whatever. Nurse Anne died, too. Did I tell you that Gothersorg died?"

"No, you didn't. How did that old dinosaur die?"

"That's just it... Nobody knows. The cable from his breathing machine was found unplugged."

"Who gives a fuck about these old bags, anyway?" said Bill. "Speaking of old bags, is that no-good, douche bag Morris still alive?"

—— THE NURSING HOME ——

"Unfortunately," replied Eddie.

"What I wouldn't give to have five minutes with that wrinkled prune, just to beat the fuck out of him. I could hear him now... gasping for air... begging for mercy, 'Please, Bill! No more!' as he whimpers into the night, praying for his life to end."

"I may be able to help you there, Barbaric Bill."

"How, pray tell, could you do that, Eddie?"

"What if you come to the nursing home tonight? I'll sneak you in."

"Dude, that place is sealed tight. Not even a bug could sneak by security."

"How long have you known me, Bill?"

"Too long," he laughed.

"Larry is the main security guard tonight. Let's just say he owes me from last week's poker game. I'll talk to him later. I think he'd rather do me this favor than pay me the money he owes."

"You're twisted, Ed-ster!"

"That's why they call me 'Twisted Eddie.' Stop by here around ten tonight."

"You know if Cyndi catches me there, I'm dead," replied Bill.

"Cyndi gets out at six tonight, so don't worry. She's so stressed out that she is not gonna want to be here."

"Tell my girls, Sue and Pearl, that I say 'Hi'... and that I'm gonna give 'em a big hug and kiss and something else, if you know what I mean."

"Later, Bill."

"Later," he responded back.

Eddie hit the button with the red telephone symbol before he closed the phone shut.

"What's going on?" questioned Cyndi as she approached Eddie from behind.

"Damnit! You startled me, Cyndi."

"Were you making a phone call, Eddie?"

"Yeah, so?"

"What part of *'No using cell phones in the nursing home'* don't you understand? If you want to use your cell phone so bad, I suggest you walk your lazy body outside on your break and do so. Got it?!"

"Okay, okay," responded Eddie as it went in one ear and out the other.

"Give me time, Eddie. You're on really thin ice and, personally, I hope you sink. Now get back to work and out of my sight." Cyndi was irritated. Why can't anybody follow simple rules? she thought to herself. You don't need a bachelor's degree to understand how to follow directions or read a sign. She felt even more flustered just thinking about it.

Eddie walked away feeling pissed, but then his evil grin reappeared, remembering he had one up on Cyndi because of what he had just master-minded involving Bill.

"Do you guys think the rain's gonna stop anytime today?" asked Morris.

Frank and Ralph shook their heads and Pauly added 'No' to the conversation. "How much fucking rain could one state get?"

"I don't know, Pauly," answered Ralph.

"I would sure like for the rain to stop," contributed Frank. "Those poor plants are drowning and dying."

THE NURSING HOME

"*Poor plants!*" exclaimed Pauly, mocking Frank. "Next, you're gonna be saying: 'Save the rain forest; Save the children; blah, blah, blah...' What are you, a fucking environmentalist now?"

"No," responded Frank, defending himself. "I just like seeing nature develop. When I was an artist, I used to draw all of this. Hopefully when I'm gone, I will have the ability to do so once again."

"Yeah, and hopefully Rigg's gets a good staff one day, too, but there's no chance of that ever happening," Pauly said with his usual grumpy attitude.

"I heard the amount of rain we get here, in Florida, is just the tip of the iceberg of what other states or countries get," Morris went on.

"First we have an environmentalist and now we have a weatherman," said Pauly. "Do you have any input as well, Ralph, along with these other two lug-heads?"

"Not at the moment," he responded. "Come to think of it, Morris is right."

"Right about what?" Pauly seemed interested.

"The weather. Do you know how much it rains in London?"

"No, why don't you tell me?"

"A lot," was Ralph's response.

"It rains every day in Seattle, as well," added Morris. "What a depressing town, huh?"

"Who cares where else it's raining? It could be raining in Albuquerque, New Mexico, for all I care," said Pauly. "All I know is that it's raining here. I'm sorry I brought up this subject."

"On a day like this, who would want to leave the

— 114 —

house? I wish I could sit by the warm fireplace and do my word searches," Morris told everyone. "It looks like I'm stuck here or in my room now."

"Isn't that too bad, Mori, old boy?" teased Pauly.

"Not really, Pauly, just as long as I can do the word searches... and it's Morris. I bring these damn word searches everywhere I go."

"How could we not notice? Your word searches are stuck to you like glue."

"Did I ever tell you guys what my dumb-ass son, Sam, did a few years ago?" Morris changed the subject.

The gang shook their heads for 'No.'

"It was in the middle of summer and the Marlins were playing the Mets. It was dreary that day and it looked like it was going to rain cats and dogs. Sam took Jude and Todd to the game. When it comes to baseball, Jude doesn't know her ass from a hole in the wall and Todd was too young to understand the sport."

The gang laughed.

"The score is zero-zero by the second inning. The torrential downpour begins... The family gets drenched and there's a rain delay. A lot of the people were getting up to leave, but my dumb-ass son decides the family stays. The game begins again as the rain clears. The stadium actually has puddles on the field. The players don't even want to play. By the fifth inning, there was another delay because of the rain. Once again, they sit there like a bunch of morons. Finally, the game is called due to the storm and my family is drenched, then have to sit in traffic. Sam was pissed, and I laughed at them when they came home. To be honest with you guys, I don't know what could be

THE NURSING HOME

funnier: seeing Sam and the family going to a rainy game or seeing Sam get so excited about one of those stupid bands he liked in high school."

The gang couldn't stop laughing.

"I gotta admit, you got some good stories, Mori, old boy," said Pauly.

"This afternoon went by so quick," commented Ralph.

"I know," agreed Frank.

"Soon it will be dinner, then bedtime," Morris told everyone. "Who's on staff tonight?"

"Eddie, the moron," answered Pauly. "It stinks... none of those kids are working tonight."

"Aye, they deserve to have some fun," said Ralph.

"I know," said Pauly, "but they are better workers than all the other staff members combined."

"You're right about that. Did I tell you guys about the time when Beth brought me my word search book? It must have been lost for days or even a week. I can't remember."

"For the hundredth time, yes, Mori, old boy," answered Pauly. "How many more times do we have to hear the word search story?" Ralph and Frank laughed.

"Sorry, Mr. Cranky Pants," teased Morris. The gang looked at each other and laughed.

"I'm not even gonna bother, old boy," said Pauly, shaking his head with the biggest smile. All Pauly said afterwards was: "At least you didn't use a quote from *Dennis the Menace*. Then I'd have to smack ya."

"Well, guys, dinner time has come upon us," announced Morris.

"What kind of slop are we gonna get tonight?" asked Pauly sarcastically.

JAMES J. MURPHY III

"Ham, peas, and, unfortunately, potatoes," said Frank.

"I'm not a fan of peas." Ralph sounded disappointed.

"I hate it all," complained Pauly. "Asking Cock-Sucking Eddie to actually reheat this shit is completely useless. I'm not sure what I hate more about Eddie: talking to him or seeing him tease his hair like a little fairy. Eddie's not so popular here; sometimes he'll fake being your friend and other times he'll act exactly like Bill, except he'll be playing with his hair the whole time." Nobody at the table disagreed. Soon after, all of the patients were taken back to their respective rooms to be served their meals.

Throughout the evening, the patients had their pillows fluffed, beds adjusted for them to see the TV, and were tucked in. The storm was getting worse. *Why would anyone want to drive or go out in these weather conditions?* Eddie thought. After walking around, he decided to go to the breakroom. He put money into the vending machine for a chocolate bar. According to his cell phone, it was 9:57pm. A minute later, his phone started ringing. He saw Bill's name flashing as the incoming call. The ringing made Eddie so anxious that he almost came in his pants from the excitement. He picked up.

"Ed-ster!" the voice said. "I'm outside; parked. Let me in. It's raining like a mother fucker out here."

"I'll be right down." On his way down, Eddie was all smiles.

"Hey, Eddie, this guy says he knows you," said the security guard.

— THE NURSING HOME —

"Yeah, he's cool, Larry. Let him in."

"Didn't Cyndi say that no one except the employees and the cops are allowed on the premises?"

"She did, but she's not here and I'm in charge. Besides, if you do this, we'll forget about that large sum of money you owe me from the card game."

"Works for me." Larry was eager to get rid of the debt. He gladly let Bill in the building.

While walking down the hall, Eddie and Bill were talking to each other like a couple of high school kids. "You owe me one," said Eddie.

"I know," Bill said. The two of them entered the elevator and Bill hit the number '2' button. It lit up in orange and the doors closed very slowly. "I forgot how long it takes for these damn doors to close."

"Tell me about it," agreed Eddie. "This is what I deal with every day."

"Maybe it's good that bitch, Cyndi, fired me," Bill told him. "I wouldn't have minded going a few rounds with that fucking bitch, in the ring *and* in bed. You know what I mean, Ed-ster?"

"Oh, yeah! I do, I do, Bill. Trust me, I do."

As the elevator doors opened for floor number '2,' their voices lowered. No longer sounding like a bunch of tenth graders going to the history museum, they were getting down to business. Eddie and Bill walked to room 243.

"Well, this is the end of the ride, Bill."

"Thanks, Eddie." The two gave a handshake and a manly hug.

"Give that old fuck a right hook for me, as well, Bill," Eddie said with encouragement.

"You got it, Ed-ster!"

Eddie walked away with an evil smirk, touching up his hair, which was soaked from the rain. He headed back to finish his paperwork as if nothing was happening.

Bill stood outside of Morris's room and took a deep breath. He entered room number 243 with the most malicious intentions. Morris was sound asleep. Bill turned on the light and walked towards Morris's bed. Looking over him, he had his fists clenched as if he was going to bash Morris's brains in right then and there. Instead, Bill said: "I've wanted to do this for so long." He started shaking Morris to wake him up, as if he was having a bad dream.

Morris, all sandy-eyed, was in a daze. "What's going on?" he asked, startled.

"You were having a bad dream," said Bill, "but now I'll make sure you have a horrible nightmare."

"What the fuck are you doing here, Bill?" Morris was confused. He was breathing heavily and his heart was beating what felt like a thousand miles per hour. He felt trapped. Morris tried screaming for help, but the words wouldn't come out. Bill knew he overpowered him and he thrived on it. He took his first swing and nailed Morris right in the jaw. It gave him an adrenaline rush, making him feel like he just hit a game-winning home run.

"Now shut the fuck up, old man, or I'll have no problem killing you right here, right now. Got it?!"

Morris was shaky and helpless and even quivering, like a wounded pup who was abused at the pound. Bill physically got Morris out of his bed and flung him into his wheelchair. If the wheelchair had not been against the wall, Morris would have done a complete somersault,

—— THE NURSING HOME ——

backwards. At that point, Morris was in excruciating pain. Bill wheeled him to the breakroom. He had to hold Morris's mouth shut so nobody could hear his crying. As they entered the breakroom, Bill put Morris's wheelchair against the wall.

"Bill!!! You're gonna go to jail, you bastard!"

"If I do, I do, Mori. Just as long as I get to bash your brains in before I go. I want to see you suffer like the old dinosaur that you are. Thanks to you, I'm still unemployed." After saying that, Bill gave Morris a right hook to the mouth, and then a left, followed by another right. "How does that feel, old man?" Morris was too slow to block himself. Bill put his face close to Morris's and said, "Hit me, you old fuck!" Morris was defenseless. Bill continued with onslaughts of slaps and punches. Finally, Morris was just lying on the side of his wheelchair unconscious. Bill was all grins and giggles.

Bill walked towards the soda machine, oozing with confidence. I deserve a cold drink after a good workout, he bragged to himself. He inserted seventy-five cents into the coin slot and reached down for the cola. Bill opened up the cold can and began drinking. After a few gulps and a loud belch, he was stunned at what he saw in front of him. "Am I seeing things?" he said aloud. Bill rubbed his eyes as if he was hallucinating. "No, this can't be."

Standing at the door of the breakroom were about ten patients. "Get out of here!" Bill yelled at them. They just stared towards him. "What are ya, stupid?!" They started walking closer to him. "This is going to be as much fun as bashing Mori's brains in. Now I get to have open season on ten more useless pieces of shit."

JAMES J. MURPHY III

When they got closer to Bill, he went into a boxing stance. He was going to strike at any moment. He was so preoccupied about beating up the group of patients that he didn't realize that Morris came to.

Slowly, Morris got out of his wheelchair, as if he was sleepwalking, and grabbed the knife closest to him. He stabbed Bill hard in the back. Bill fell to one knee and turned around. "You old fuck! How the fuck are you walking!? Answer me!" Bill screamed. Morris and the rest of the patients had Bill surrounded. "Eddie! Help! Help me, Eddie! Please! Help me! Eddie!!!" Eddie was nowhere in sight. The patients cornered Bill like a pack of wolves and attacked. Bill tried to defend himself, but it was hopeless. He was outnumbered by the same wrinkled and smelly bunch of old-aged patients he used to pick on just months ago. Over and over again, Bill was stabbed with the knife. The patients didn't back off until Bill could no longer fight back. Blood seeped out of the wounds, soaking up his shirt, as he lie motionless on the breakroom floor. Little did he know that a number had been carved into his chest. All of the patients walked back to their respective rooms without making a sound, as if in a trance.

Just after eleven, it was time to do one final check on the patients before the graveyard shift was expected to take over. The staff members went from room to room in their designated halls and saw that the patients were sound asleep.

"Alright, Eddie. I'm done. Everyone's out like a light," reported Sue. "Is it okay to punch out?"

THE NURSING HOME

"I'm ready to go." Eddie was relieved. "I want to get out of this dump tonight."

"Wait, I think I left my cigarettes in the breakroom," said Sue.

"Okay, go get 'em," he said, "and hurry."

"Okay, okay." Sue started walking down the hall.

The only thing Eddie could say was: "Women." The other staff members faked smiles to be on Eddie's good side. The few employees that stay overnight were just starting to come in to work. All Eddie did was roll his eyes because he knew nothing would get done. They basically get paid to sit on their asses, he thought. All of a sudden, Eddie heard a scream coming from the breakroom.

"Help! Call 911!" exclaimed Sue.

"What the fuck is going on?" Eddie ran towards the breakroom.

Sue was beyond ecstatic and almost catatonic at what she saw.

"Oh, God!" yelled Eddie, surprised at how he was seeing his friend. He rushed over to help him. "Get a doctor, somebody! How the fuck did this happen?"

"What is Bill doing here?" Sue asked as she got her voice back.

"Don't worry about it," said Eddie. "He's dead now." The staff couldn't believe the amount of blood on the floor.

Sue asked: "What the fuck does 1843 mean?"

Chapter 19

Officers O'Conner and Conway got an emergency call to come to Rigg's as soon as possible. They had already been driving in the opposite direction. Conway put on the siren lights and did a one-eighty in the middle of oncoming traffic, causing everyone on the road to break or slow down. O'Conner held on to the ceiling handle for dear life, hoping that the car wouldn't flip.

"God, I love being a cop!" screamed Conway.

"What the fuck are you doing, you Goddamn rookie-lunatic?!" O'Conner yelled at his partner.

"Sorry, O'Conner. Guess who was on the phone?" Conway had a big grin on his face.

"Who?"

"That was the Captain. Guess where we get to go for the five-hundredth time?" Conway said jokingly.

"Are you fucking kidding me? Rigg's again?!"

"You better believe it."

"I got an idea, Conway. Why don't we vacate at Rigg's for a week or even move into the damn place?"

THE NURSING HOME

"Now you are being just plain old stupid, O'Conner."

"Think about it, Conway. It seems like we're at this nursing home all the time; they all know us by now. All they have to do is provide us with food and coffee. It beats wasting money at the doughnut shop. Besides, with that one-eighty you pulled before, you owe me a coffee."

"Alright, O'Conner. Next doughnut-stop is on me."

"You're a good kid, Conway." Conway smiled as he was reminded of the days when his father gave him a speech after breaking curfew.

Soon after, they pulled up to the Rigg's building and parked in front. Larry, the security guard, was standing right outside and greeted the officers. "Right this way," he said as he guided them towards Eddie. He went back outside and stood guard.

"Hi Officers," said Eddie.

"Who's in charge tonight?" asked Conway.

"I am." Eddie tried to stay cool.

"What's going on here?" asked O'Conner.

"Well, Officer..."

Before Eddie could explain, Sue jumped in and screamed: "Bill's dead! Hurry!" Sue was trembling as she lead the officers to the breakroom. Eddie started getting nervous, knowing that when Cyndi found out about what was going on, he'd be in deep, deep trouble.

"Holy shit!" shouted O'Conner.

"What the hell happened here?" asked Conway. "This is a fucking bloodbath."

"We can see that, Conway."

"I was just going to get my cigarettes," explained Sue, "and I see Bill lying on the breakroom floor, dead.

−124−

— JAMES J. MURPHY III —

I screamed, told Eddie, and called you. I'm still wondering how or why Bill was here." Eddie wished he could hit a mute button on her because she was giving out too much information.

"What do you mean by that, Ma'am?" questioned Officer O'Conner.

"I mean-"

Eddie cut her off. "Bill was my guest, Officer. I let him in here because we were supposed to have a double date later tonight. The storm was much worse before, so I told him to park his car and I let him stay. I didn't want him to get into a car accident, but unfortunately, he was involved in a much worse accident here instead." Eddie was talking like a kid who lost his dog. He actually felt more pissed off at Bill than sad because it was his hide when Cyndi found out, not Bill's.

Conway walked over to the body to get a closer look. "O'Conner! Get over here!"

"In a minute."

"Now!"

"What is it, Conway?"

"Doesn't this guy look familiar?"

"Can't tell with all the blood," replied O'Conner as he walked over and glanced at the motionless corpse.

"Look closer," said Conway sternly. "This guy used to work here. We arrested him for abusing one of the patients a few months ago."

"What is the meaning of this?" O'Conner eye-balled Eddie.

"So now I'm not allowed to be friends with people who used to work here?" Eddie said, defending himself.

—— THE NURSING HOME ——

"We could care less who you're friends with, but when someone is banned from the premises and they turn up here, dead, it just seems kinda fishy to me," retaliated O'Conner.

"I don't know what to tell ya, Officer." Eddie touched up his hair, acting like everything was cool.

"Well, Eddie, since you're the one in charge here tonight, you're the lucky winner," announced O'Conner.

"And what does he win, O'Conner?" Conway was interested in what his partner had up his sleeve.

"The lucky winner gets to make the phone call to Cyndi."

After hearing that, Eddie felt a huge lump in his throat. "Well, guys, you know... it's really late right now. I don't need to bother Cyndi." Eddie was trying to stall. "She needs her beauty rest. I'll make sure she gets the message in the morning."

"No, Eddie, you'll call her *now* and tell her to get here as soon as possible. Besides, we think you're a real prick and we can't wait for Cyndi's reaction," said O'Conner.

"If you don't tell her, we will," added Conway.

Eddie was stuck between a rock and a hard place. Either way, he was fucked. The officers leaned over Eddie's shoulders as he called Cyndi's home from the office using speed dial. Hoping Cyndi wouldn't pick up, the fingers on his left hand were crossed for good luck. Not even a four-leaf clover could help him.

The phone rang numerous times and Eddie thought that he was in the clear. He was relieved to hear Cyndi's message. "*You've reached Cyndi Gillian. I am away from my*

—126—

— JAMES J. MURPHY III —

phone at the moment. Please leave your name and number and I'll call you back."

"Hello Cyndi, it's–" Eddie didn't even get to finish leaving his name. Cyndi picked up and asked what he wanted. "You'd better come down here right away," he said in a serious tone. "Officers Conway and O'Conner need to talk to you."

"Damnit! I'll be right down." Her tone was unprofessional. Lately, it seems like I'm always on call to come to this place, Cyndi thought to herself. All Cyndi did was button her jacket back up. She just got home from the twenty-four hour supermarket a few minutes earlier and hadn't even finished unpacking. "Can't I sit down for one minute?" she said aloud, grabbing her keys and heading back to her car once again. "Why don't I just sleep at the nursing home?" What in God's name could Eddie have done now? Cyndi wondered. Did another patient die? It could be anything. All of those thoughts were racing through her mind as she was fidgeting with her CD player while keeping her eyes on the road.

Finally, Cyndi arrived at the nursing home. She shut off her lights and turned off her car, while her CD was still in playing-mode, and didn't bother to lock her doors. Larry, the security guard, was the first person Cyndi saw. The only communication the two had was Cyndi saying: "Where's Eddie?" and Larry pointing her in the appropriate direction. Cyndi entered the nursing home and didn't even greet Eddie. The first words that came out of her mouth were: "What happened?"

"Well, Cyndi," began Eddie, "I was running the show, as usual, making sure everything was kept intact.

– 127 –

— THE NURSING HOME —

I had all of our Rigg's employees, including myself, check on and take care of all the patients and see if they needed anything."

"Get to the point, Eddie," Cyndi insisted, getting more and more annoyed at his delaying.

"All of the patients were sound asleep and I asked if everybody was ready to go. We were, but Sue left something in the breakroom... and... she found a dead body."

"What are we waiting for?" asked Cyndi impatiently. "Who was it?"

"Yeah, Eddie, who was it?" O'Conner egged him on. "That was an interesting story, Eddie, but it ain't the one you told us."

"What's going on?" demanded Cyndi. "Stop playing games, Eddie! Damnit! Just tell me."

"Alright, alright. It was Bill."

"Let's see this cock-sucker weasel his way out of this one," O'Conner whispered to Conway.

"Bill!!! It was Bill?! Are you fucking kidding me?!" Cyndi was definitely going off the deep-end. "That can't be. Bill's not allowed on the premises, Eddie."

"I know, Cyndi."

"If you knew, he wouldn't have been here. The reason he's banned from here is because of what he did to one of the patients. Oh, God!" she yelled. "Go to room 243. Check on Morris Grover to see if he's okay." Conway went to check on Mr. Grover as Cyndi grew more nervous. "How did Bill get in here?" she asked. "He couldn't have gotten past security."

"I ordered Larry to let him in, Cyndi. I'm the one in charge tonight."

– 128 –

JAMES J. MURPHY III

"Is this all fun and games to you, Eddie? And by the way, I'm your boss."

"The only reason you fired Bill is because of that old fuck. I was just helping out a friend. All Bill wanted to do was shake Morris up a little. I just wish *I* could've done it," Eddie explained arrogantly, touching up his hair.

"Shake him up?!" she screamed. "He's in his eighties. What's wrong with you?!"

"This doesn't explain Bill ending up dead in the breakroom," Sue spoke up.

"Morris had to have killed him," Eddie told her.

"Morris?!" exclaimed Cyndi. "He's a senior citizen and in a wheelchair. What did he do? Ride over him a hundred times?" Officer O'Conner laughed, finding what Cyndi said quite amusing.

Officer Conway returned and informed everyone that Morris looked fine and was sleeping peacefully. "Does Morris have a wheelchair, Cyndi?"

"Yes, Officer," Cyndi responded.

"Just checking. There was no wheelchair in his room."

"Wait! Whose wheelchair is that against the wall?" asked O'Conner. The officers walked over to it.

"M. Grover?" Conway read the name on the back of the wheelchair.

"What?!" Cyndi exclaimed.

O'Conner walked over to Eddie and got in his face. "Okay, what the fuck's going on here, Eddie?!"

"I told you what happened. Now leave me alone, okay?" Eddie said with an attitude.

"I'm not getting anywhere with this moron. Is there anything else you need, Cyndi?" asked O'Conner, finishing up his notes.

THE NURSING HOME

"Yes, as a matter of fact, there is. Call an ambulance to get rid of Bill's body and please arrest Eddie – this piece of crap."

"Arrest me?" asked Eddie. "On what charge?"

Cyndi's response was: "Accomplice to: abuse of a patient, letting someone in who is banned from the premises, murder... Should I go on?"

"I didn't murder anyone," Eddie said defensively.

"Don't bother coming back here ever again, Eddie, because first, I don't want you here, and second, you're fired!"

"What?!" shouted Eddie. "You can't fire me!"

What pushed his buttons even more was when she had the nerve to say: "You sound just like Bill. Or, actually, should I say 'sounded?'" Cyndi knew she could of handled the situation better, but she just couldn't hold in her anger.

"Fuck you! You bitch! I'm gonna kill you!"

"Another threat," said Cyndi. "Officers, please arrest this piece of garbage. Now!"

"We've been waiting to do this all night, Cyndi," O'Conner said with confidence. Conway held Eddie down as O'Conner cuffed him and read him his rights. Cyndi followed them outside. To add insult to injury, Conway messed up Eddie's hair when he ducked his head into the police car.

"Thank you," said Cyndi. "Before you guys leave, please arrest Larry, the security guard, as well. Also, tell him that he's fired. You'd be saving me some trouble."

"It will be our pleasure," the officers said in unison. "I love this job," Conway added.

"You don't have to remind me," O'Conner replied with a smile.

⟞ Chapter 20

"Sam, would you like to visit your father today?" Jude gave him that warm, southern smile.

Sam gave her his usual response of: "What did I do now?"

"You didn't do anything, dear. It's just been a few months, now, since we've last seen him."

"So?"

"So?!" Jude repeated. "He's your father; you have to see him. It's been since Christmas! Besides, it would be good for Todd to pay a visit." Todd shot his dad a look that said 'Please don't make me go.' "Wouldn't you like to visit Grandpa, Todd?" Jude continued.

"I can't, Mom. I have homework."

"It's spring break. There is no school."

"Then I'll look for a job," Todd said, trying anything to get out of going to the nursing home.

"That's my boy," encouraged Sam.

"Get off it, Sam. We both know he doesn't *want* to visit his grandfather."

— THE NURSING HOME —

"Do you blame him, Jude? The place smells like piss and shit. He's going on fifteen. These people are four or five times his age. He's at the stage, now, that it's even embarrassing to be seen with *us*, his own parents. Picture how he feels being seen with his grandfather. He'll be teased out of the town." Todd was relieved that he and his father were on the same page. Visiting his grandfather was the last thing Todd wanted to do on a Sunday.

"You're being ridiculous, Sam."

"Jude, if you'd remember correctly, I told Dad we wanted to get him out of Rigg's. We had that huge argument and I was man-enough to give that bastard a phone call. I kept trying to call him that day, but he refused to pick up. I even called on more than one occasion, you know. You tell him to get off *his* ass and give *me* a call sometime," Sam vented. His face was turning a pink-flustered color and it looked like he was about to burst like a balloon.

"I just hope that he's okay, Sam."

"He's fine, Jude. Having the time of his life!" kidded Sam. "He already had his chance, anyway, and he blew it. Besides, if he *wasn't* fine, we would have had a call from... what's her name? Cynda."

"It's Cyndi," Jude corrected him.

"You know what I meant, Jude. No need to be a smart ass," he teased. Jude laughed. "By the way, guess who has a week off from work?" Sam said enthusiastically.

"The florist," guessed Jude.

"Oh, you're a riot today, Jude. No, it's me!" Sam exclaimed.

Oh great, Todd thought, as his father made the announcement. I need this like I need a hole in the wall.

Sam was the type of person who, after working a five or six-day week, just wanted peace and quiet, and to be left alone to watch a sporting event. But when he got vacation time, he loved spending it with his family, either traveling or going on weekend getaways, such as camping. Jude basically went for Sam, and enjoyed herself when it was something of her interest. Todd looked forward to it more when he was younger, but being a teenager, the only things that interested him were girls and music. "I have a surprise for you two! Do you guys want to know where we're going for a whole week?" Sam asked the two of them excitedly.

"Where, dear?" His wife was interested.

"Orlando!" Sam screamed out. "I know it's still Florida, but there's so much to do in Orlando, like seeing Disney, Universal, and then some. Of course, we'll have to take in one Marlins game, even though it's Spring Training."

"That's wonderful, dear," Jude bursted out. Everything except for the sporting event, she thought to herself.

"Could we also go to the water parks?" asked Todd.

"I don't see why not," Sam replied.

Todd was beginning to think that he was actually going to enjoy the vacation. "Since you're in a good mood, Dad, could I drive?"

"Sorry, Champ," Sam responded.

"I have a learner's permit and the more practicing I do, the quicker I can get a license... and the quicker I get a license, the sooner you can lend me the car so I can get a job and be out of the house. Besides, you guys are always telling me to go out."

—— THE NURSING HOME ——

Sam thought his son made a good point and he was sold. "I'll let you drive in Orlando, but not when it's dark outside."

The biggest smile came on Todd's face, as if he just won the lottery. "You're the best, Dad!"

"Sam, you can't let him drive yet," complained Jude. "He's only fourteen!"

"Jude, he has to learn sooner or later. I don't want to treat Todd like my father treated me."

All Jude could say was: "Fine."

"Jude, Todd... the only thing I ask of you for this getaway is that you leave everything at home."

"What are you talking about, Sam? I need my clothes and makeup."

"I don't mean that. I mean our electronic stuff, like our cell phones or the laptop. I don't want any contacts."

"Sam, what if our family or friends call?"

"We'll call them when we get home. The point of vacation is *not* to hear or see these people."

"I agree with Dad," Todd spoke up.

"But, Sam, what if something happens to Morris while we're away?" Jude worried.

"What could possibly happen, Jude? Don't worry about it. Everything will be fine. Now let's get packing," he said with encouragement. "Also, we can bring two CDs each for the trip," Sam said, "and I got mine." The mother and son looked at one another and thought: *This is gonna be a long trip.* The family packed and left the following morning.

— JAMES J. MURPHY III —

Meanwhile, back at the nursing home, the gang were sitting at their usual table in the lounge room. "What kind of place are we living at?!" demanded Pauly.

"I know it looks bad," said Ralph, trying to calm him down.

"Looks bad!?" screamed Pauly. "It is bad! It's horrible! It's pathetic! Do I need to go on?"

"You're right, Pauly," said Frank, "but what can we do? We are elderly."

"Absolutely nothing!" he shouted back. "Mori, here, gets attacked by that fucking psychopath, Bill, in the middle of the night. Wasn't that dick-head fired? We have an incompetent staff and, now, dumb-ass security."

"Calm down, Pauly," Morris said, trying to simmer him down. "Cyndi might hear us or even the rest of the staff might."

"Good, I hope these scum bags do hear us! What? We can't even go to sleep anymore without being attacked?"

"The only reason I was attacked Friday night was because, as word has it, Eddie bribed the security guard to let Bill into the building to kick my ass. Remember, I got that son-of-a-bitch fired."

"So, you're blaming yourself, Mori, old boy. Bill must have scrambled your brains in real good because, right now, you're definitely talking out of your ass."

"All I know, Pauly, is I'm lucky to still be alive. The only thing I remember was being awoken by Bill. His breath reeked of a dead mouse."

"That's Bill, alright," added Ralph.

"I yelled for help, but nobody responded."

"Maybe you didn't yell loud enough," insisted Frank.

—— THE NURSING HOME ——

"I tried, Frank, but Bill said he'd kill me if I kept yelling. Plus, his hand covered my mouth as we were going to the employee breakroom. I'm shocked I didn't pass out with the stench of his hand. I think he took a dump and forgot to wash afterwards." The gang laughed. "Then I was brought to that damn breakroom to get my ass kicked. I never felt so defenseless and pathetic in my entire life. I feel like a rape victim, without actually being raped... or even worse, I don't feel like a man anymore," Morris told the gang as tears started building up in his eyes.

"Mori, old boy, you're as much of a man as any of us here. If you keep blaming yourself, I'm gonna bash your brains in myself," Pauly promised, "and that goes for all of you lugheads." Ralph and Frank nodded their heads in agreement.

"Pardon me, guys, but I couldn't help but overhear what happened to Morris and I do feel bad," interrupted Wade, sounding like an intellect.

"Enough of the bullshit, Wade," Pauly snapped at him.

"Yeah, Wade," jumped in Morris. "If you have something to ask, just ask it."

"Very well, then. We know you got a good butt-kicking, while Bill got beaten to a bloody pulp, and I use that term loosely. My question is, how did you end up back in your room and how did Bill end up dead?" Everyone, including Morris, all looked at one another, puzzled, because none of them expected a question like that coming out of Wade's mouth.

"Wade, I don't have an answer for you," replied Morris. "All I know is I got pummeled and blacked out."

"Even the cops don't have an answer," jumped in Pauly.

— JAMES J. MURPHY III —

A few staff members came to bring the patients back to their rooms. Before doing so, Cyndi went around and checked on everyone, including Morris, to see if they were feeling okay or if they needed anything. "Are you feeling better, Morris?"

"I'm fine," he answered back.

"I'm sorry about what happened to you. I just want you to know that I fired Larry, the security guard, and that sleeze-ball, Eddie."

"You shouldn't have hired them to begin with," he growled back. "You shoulda fired the dirt-bag after what happened to Old Man Crombert. I just want you to know, Cyndi, that I don't trust any of you, especially after what happened to me."

"Please believe me, Morris. I truly am sorry and I don't blame you."

"The only people that I like here are the friends I've made and that kid, Beth, who is really nice, and I hate to admit it, but I even believe that you are a good person, Cyndi. You have taken action and you have been fair."

"Thank you." Cyndi paused. She went on to say, "I'll take you to your room now. I'm in charge tonight, so feel free to ask me anything. Also, Beth is here tonight as well."

As Morris finally got settled into his room, there was a knock at the door. He thought to himself, if someone like that son-of-a-bitch, Bill, wanted to kick my ass or wanted me dead, they sure as hell wouldn't be knocking on my door. At last, Morris said, "Enter."

It was the nineteen year old girl, Beth. She turned the knob and entered slowly and nervously; almost as nervous as Ron was on a daily basis. She saw Morris

THE NURSING HOME

in bed, watching the news. "I hope I'm not disturbing you, Mr. Grover."

"I don't think that I could be any more disturbed than I was on Friday night." Morris tried to refrain himself from cursing because there was a lady present. "Tell me something, Beth."

"Yes, Mr. Grover."

"Have you ever been sound asleep and been woken in the middle of the night to see that the person you most despise is there trying to kill you?"

"I'm very fortunate that something like that has never happened to me."

"Do me a favor, Beth."

"Yes, Mr. Grover."

"When you get old, or if you do, never let your family send you to a nursing home. I never wanted to come here, but now, the only reason I don't wanna leave is because that would mean I'd have to go back to living with my stupid son and his family."

"Whatever you say, Mr. Grover. I have to get back to work now. Oh, by the way, this might come in handy."

"My word search book!"

"I keep finding this in the breakroom."

"How could I ever thank you, Beth?"

"Don't worry about it." She began to make her exit. "See you later."

"Goodnight," he said back.

Beth went back to her desk to continue filing and answering phone calls. She was scheduled to leave work at nine-thirty, instead of the usual eleven-thirty or midnight. Beth had plans to meet her friends after work and just

– 138 –

chill. Beth was so intrigued by her work that she didn't realize Cyndi was standing behind her. As she looked up from her studies, she gasped. "You almost gave me a heart attack, Cyndi," she said jokingly.

"I'm sorry, Beth. That's the last thing we need with everything going on here lately."

"You can say that again," agreed Beth.

"If you get a chance tonight, Beth, could you enter this information into the system for me?" Cyndi handed Beth a couple of papers.

"What's on here, Cyndi?"

"Nothing important; only Eddie's and Larry's termination forms. I hate being cynical, Beth, but after the stunt they pulled on Friday night, I hope nobody else is stupid enough to hire them, like I was."

"You're definitely not stupid, Cyndi." After a few months of working at Rigg's, Beth grew quite fond of Cyndi, especially since the first week or two.

"One thing I do know, Beth, is that they won't be allowed to use this place as a reference. Let's see that hot-shot, Eddie, explain how he lost this job at a future interview. I could see it now: him fidgeting, playing with his stupid hair, thinking it's 1987 and he's trying to act like David Coverdale. Trust me, Beth, he's no David Coverdale." They both laughed, even though Beth hadn't been born by 1987 and had no idea who Cyndi was referring to. "Well, it looks like your time is up, Beth. It's nine-thirty; time to go," Cyndi reminded her.

"Cool," she responded.

"I'd schedule you later, Beth, but three times a year, we hire someone from the outside to clean this place.

—— THE NURSING HOME ——

I know we have a maintenance team, but these people clean places where it's almost impossible, from the ceiling to the floor and even underneath the refrigerators."

"That's crazy," said Beth.

"Tell me about it. This is why they only come three times a year. It's really expensive; if they came all the time, we'd be out of business. Besides, we spend enough as it is to make this place look good. Now, get going. Enjoy the night... You're young."

"Goodnight, Cyndi. And thanks." Beth left the building and drove to the park to meet the rest of the kids.

Five minutes later, when Beth arrived, Jeff and Jay were already smoking and drinking and Ron was just standing there. "Hey guys. Looks like the party started already."

"You're *damn* right, Beth!" said Jeff.

"Weren't you supposed to close tonight?" asked Ron.

"I did," said Beth.

"But it's not even ten yet," Ron told her.

"I know. Cyndi let me out early tonight."

"She didn't fire you, did she, Beth?"

"No, the floors are getting done tonight."

"Me and Jay just did the floors the other day," Jeff explained to her.

"I know you guys did. Maybe that's why Cyndi hired outside help," she joked.

"Oh, real funny, Beth," Jay responded, entering the conversation.

"Cyndi said she hires outside help three times a year to clean from the ceiling to the floor and even underneath the refrigerators."

"Holy shit, Beth! I understood everything you just told me. I'd better smoke some more of this stuff," said Jeff. They all laughed.

"How crazy has Rigg's been lately?" asked Jay. "Did you hear about Bill beating up that old dude?"

"Yeah," replied Ron. "I heard Bill was found in a pool of his own blood. If I was there, I would have fainted, I think."

"I'm pretty sure you would have, Ron," said Jeff. "Me and Jay knew Eddie was an asshole since Day One. He should have been fired a long time ago."

"My bro is absolutely right," Jay agreed.

"The question still stands," said Ron.

"What question is that?" Beth looked at him.

"Who killed Bill?"

"Who cares who killed Bill?" interrupted Jeff, grabbing another beer. "He was an asshole from the beginning and everybody knew it, then got his ass fired... then got his ass killed. I'm glad the jerk's dead. He shoulda died sooner," Jeff vented, and then chugged his beer. "Hopefully Eddie is next."

"That's cold, man," replied Jay. "Of course we didn't like them, but to be stabbed to death..."

"I agree with Jay," said Beth. "That's just going a little extreme."

"More like too extreme," commented Ron.

"Why don't we stop talking about work and concentrate on having fun?" said Jeff, changing the subject. "Hopefully me and Jay could open up our own video store one day."

"That would be awesome, dude," agreed Jay.

— THE NURSING HOME —

"Yeah, that would be cool," said Beth, "but don't you need a little thing called *money?*"

"We'll get it," said Jeff.

"How much money do you guys have now?" she asked. Jeff and Jay looked at each other, clueless. "Exactly."

"Well, how 'bout you, Beth?" retorted Jeff.

"What about me?"

"You wanna be a scientist... How are you gonna be a scientist working at Rigg's?"

"Well, Jeff, I see that you're stoned off your ass right now and not meaning to act the way you are, so I'll explain it in the simplest terms possible, so even *your* fried brain can comprehend it. I'm going to college to learn. I'm working at Rigg's to make money to go back to school and accomplish a goal that I have my mind set on. Saying and doing are two different things."

Jeff tried retaliating, but failed by saying: "Oh, I guess we're going to have the next Neil Armstrong." They all couldn't help but laugh because not even Jeff knew what he was talking about at that point.

"Actually, Jeff, Neil Armstrong was the first man to walk on the moon," Ron pointed out, trying to educate his friend with his knowledge of history. The gang laughed as Jeff told Ron to go fuck himself.

"Let's get some food," interrupted Jay. "I'm hungry." The kids were about to leave the park when the cops pulled up.

"Everyone, just chill," advised Beth.

Officers O'Conner and Conway were patrolling the neighborhood, as usual. Checking the park was part of their nightly routine because that was when all of the teenagers came out. "Damn teenage hooligans," O'Conner said from inside the car.

"Settle down, O'Conner. Oh, those are just the kids from the nursing home. Let me talk to them."

"Fine." O'Conner decided to read his newspaper while Conway went out to approach the kids.

"What's everyone up to tonight?" asked Conway.

"Just chillin'," replied Jay.

"It looks like your boy, here, can't even drag his own feet," replied Conway, referring to Jeff. "Make sure he doesn't drive tonight or I'll personally arrest all of your asses. Understood?"

They all nodded, except for Jeff, who was in his own world. Jeff looked up. "Yo, Officer, tell me something! What the fuck is going on at the nursing home?"

"Never thought a drunk kid would ask a good question. First time for everything, I guess," said Conway as he scratched the side of his head. "Keep it on the down-low, okay?" The kids nodded in unison. "O'Conner and I examined the whole breakroom area and the only evidence we found was a kitchen knife. The knife had blood on it. I wonder, because it was so bloody, could it have washed off the fingerprints? We also found Grover's wheelchair in the breakroom."

"No way, man!" Jay sounded amazed.

"I know," Conway said. "This is even freaking out me and my partner. Eddie admitted that he let Bill into the building to harass the senior citizen. He last saw Bill when

— THE NURSING HOME —

he escorted him to room 243. When I went to Morris's room, he didn't look too banged up. What I mean to say is that it could have been worse. I was expecting a massacre. He took some good punches for a man in his eighties. I wouldn't have expected someone of that age to make it."

"That's impossible!" interrupted Ron.

"Go on, Officer," Beth said to the man in blue.

"The next day, Cyndi asked Grover about the wheelchair and he told her that he was awakened by Bill that night and remembers being wheeled to the breakroom, where Bill gave him a beating."

"Dude..." was the only thing Jay could say.

"How could an eighty-four year old man be pummeled in the breakroom and then be sound asleep in bed... and not one staff member knowing or hearing a damn thing?" Conway questioned. "There's no way Grover could have walked back to his room."

"Maybe the old man's really a zombie," Jeff slurred.

"A zombie?!" questioned Beth loudly. The kids started bickering.

"Well, I've got to go. I'm sure O'Conner's giving me that eye. Besides, we have to tell Cyndi that there's no new evidence. I want you all to get home safely." They all agreed. "Goodnight," he said, "and if you have any news, please let me know." They nodded and decided it was time to get going. Conway rushed back to his car, knowing he gave the kids a long speech and expected an even longer one from O'Conner.

"Did someone die in the family, Conway?" O'Conner asked as Conway got into the car.

"No, why?"

— 144 —

JAMES J. MURPHY III

"Because whenever you talk to those kids, you talk forever."

"Give it a rest, O'Conner."

"Last time it was tea. What was it this time? Dress up?" O'Conner loved teasing Conway and vice-versa.

"Let's just break the news to Cyndi." Away they went.

Chapter 21

Thursday night was dark and dreary. The staff were taking care of the patients, as usual, and dreading it, especially since there was a severe thunderstorm among them. Pearl stepped outside for a smoke. Standing underneath the rooftop, she opened up her purse and pulled out her pack of cigarettes. If these patients don't kill me, my bad habits will, she thought to herself. Pearl was several inches away from a sky shower, literally. She knew she should quit smoking, but working at a place like Rigg's, she figured it was either smoking or drinking. Right when I'm out, my old friend, Mr. Nicotine, gives me a call and I always answer, welcoming him with open arms, she said to herself. Fidgeting through her purse, she tried to locate her lighter. "No-good, Goddamn purse," she complained out loud. Just like every woman, Pearl knew she had to clean her handbag one day. Everything from gum and candy bar wrappers to lipstick and even a losing lottery ticket from 2006 was in there. At last, she found her shiny black lighter. She flicked her lighter with her right thumb and admired the orangey flame. Pearl lit her cigarette and began puffing away.

"Hey bitch!" addressed Sue.

"Who you calling 'bitch,' bitch?" Pearl kidded back.

"What a horrible night..." Sue was looking at the rain.

"Tell me about it."

"It was exactly a night like this when... when..." Sue couldn't finish the sentence.

"What, Sue? When Bill died and Eddie got arrested?"

"Yeah." She looked down at the ground, envisioning what happened that night.

"Sue, you know I always cared about Bill, but he did a lot of stupid things in his life and got caught. And what you saw that night, I can't imagine. Just move forward," urged Pearl with her Connecticut rich-bitch attitude.

"I was *kinda* referring to that, but not really."

"Then what?"

"Do you remember the night that old fossil, Gothersorg, died?"

"I think everyone's trying to forget that, Sue. It seems like that old prune is more popular dead than alive. Still, months later, all I hear is that old bag's name over and over again."

"Well, you might hear it again after what I have to tell you."

"Go on," Pearl said, wanting to hear the story.

"I was working late that night, just like tonight. I was checking on all of the patients to see if they needed anything... blah, blah, blah."

"Yeah, so, what's your point?"

— THE NURSING HOME —

"I checked on Gothersorg the night he died. I was looking over him after having a bad day. Pictures started popping into my head. I was thinking: *What if I take a pillow and suffocate him? Or strangle him? Or even unplug his oxygen tank, so he dies in his sleep?*"

"So, what you're saying is that you killed the old bag?"

Tears started pouring down Sue's face, just like the heavy rain outside. "I think I did; I don't know. All I know is that I wanted to get out of this place, as usual. I did my job and started to walk away. There wasn't that much light in the room. As I was walking, I tripped and my shoe came off. I don't know if I tripped over Gothersorg's wire, causing him to stop breathing, or what. The only thing I know is that Cyndi noticed the wires unplugged and flipped out. I wanted no part of that. I hate this job, but it pays the bills."

"You're absolutely right, Sue," agreed Pearl. "If I were in your shoes, I'd do the same thing, but on purpose."

Sue was beginning to notice that Pearl was a bigger bitch than she was. Even worse, a bitch with no conscience. Sue was going to say something back to Pearl, but they got interrupted by Nurse Helen. "What is this, Cigarette Break Central?" Helen joked. "You two are having fun on this miserable day while I'm dealing with these annoying patients. Please finish your smoke and help me after I finish mine," Helen said as she lit up.

Sue and Pearl started to head inside to see what was next on the agenda. They headed towards Cyndi's office to look at the schedule. "It's going to be a long night," said Pearl.

"And the fun has just begun," replied Sue.

– 148 –

"If Cyndi thinks I'm gonna get all of these reports done, she's fucking crazy. First of all, we're short-staffed and second, there's too much work."

"What's the point of complaining about it, Pearl? Let's just deal with it."

"Fine, but I still think when Cyndi was doing the schedule, she may have eaten one too many shrooms, taking her back to a time of innocence."

"Listen, Pearl! Less complaining and more focusing," snapped Sue. "If we focus and take no more cigarette breaks, we'll get everything done."

"Fine," said Pearl, "but you know something, Sue?"

"What?"

"You sound like a fucking infomercial."

Sue saw no point to comment.

Throughout the night, the staff were able to accomplish all of their paperwork and look over the patients. Everyone seemed fine. Pearl was about to page everyone to the office. The ringing of the telephone startled her. "Who the fuck is calling at this hour?" Pearl asked herself out loud, while Helen laughed. "Good evening. Rigg's Nursing Home. This is Pearl speaking. How may I help you?" she said with her rich-bitch accent.

"Pearl, it's Cyndi."

"Hi Cyndi."

"What's up?"

"Nothing much. I was just about to page the troops and punch out. We finished entering in all of the new data and checked on all of the patients."

"Excellent! I'm glad to hear that." Cyndi sounded enthused. "May I speak to Sue?"

— THE NURSING HOME —

"Sure, I'll get her for you, Cyndi." Pearl hit the 'Hold' button, and then paged Sue. "Sue, Line 1!" Pearl said into the phone, loud and clear.

"I'm right here," said Sue as she entered the office. "I want to get out of here," she complained.

"Just take Line 1... It's Cyndi. I wanna get out of here sometime tonight, too, you know."

"What the fuck does Cyndi want now... for me to work another ten hour shift?" Sue picked up the phone and hit 'Line 1.' "Hi Cyndi."

"Hey Sue," Cyndi replied back. "Sorry to bother you so late, but I was wondering if you could do me a favor."

"What's the favor, Cyndi?"

"Would you be able to switch shifts tomorrow with Rita? She has a personal issue she has to take care of tomorrow night. Could you work for her if she covers your morning hours?"

Under normal circumstances, Sue wouldn't have agreed to it, but due to the fact that she was so tired, she'd agree to anything. "I'll do it."

"Thanks, Sue. I owe you one." They said goodnight to each other.

"What was that about?" asked Pearl.

"I don't have to come in early tomorrow. Rita and I switched shifts."

"She should have called earlier," complained Pearl.

"Someone needs another cigarette," teased Sue. "Let's get out of here. All I want to do is take a nice bubble bath and go to sleep."

"Too bad you'll be taking it without a man. Manless, again..."

"You know, Pearl, you're a real bitch, bitch."

"I know." They both laughed. It was time to leave and let the overnight crew take over. The employees got their belongings and Pearl gave the keys to the next staff member on duty.

The following morning, Rita came in at seven o'clock, relieved that Sue was able to swap hours with her. "It looks like we're the first two here this morning, aye, Ron?" she said to her younger co-worker with a friendly tap on the shoulder.

Ron was absolutely speechless. His body was so tense that if a bucket of water was poured over his head, he wouldn't flinch. The only word he could manage to say in response was: "Yup." Rita felt such energy early on the sunny Friday morning, while Ron was still trying to shake the cobwebs.

"Cyndi should be arriving in a half hour or so to check up on everything," Rita told him.

"Okay. What do you want me to start with?" Ron was fidgeting nervously.

"First, let's check on all of the patients and serve them the breakfast they selected from the menu last night. You're not used to working the early shift, are ya, Ron?"

"Not really," he replied, as if he was about to be scolded.

"Ron, you're a good kid. Relax... I'm not gonna bite you. You've just got to chill. What are ya? Nineteen? Twenty? Hopefully you don't act like this around your girlfriend."

── THE NURSING HOME ──

"I don't have a girlfriend." Ron was speaking in a sad voice, feeling pathetic.

"Don't worry... Your time will come. Look at me; I'm thirty-five and not even married yet. How sad is that?"

Ron was thinking that an older woman wanted him. He stood there, blushing and about to explode in his pants, wondering if he should make a move on her, but all he could say was, "Don't worry, Rita. Your time will come, too." They both went and checked on the patients.

After months of working at the nursing home, Ron finally got used to patients speaking jibberish to him and cursing at him. Ron glanced at the menu that the patients had ordered from. Today's breakfast: *Oatmeal with Rye Toast* or *Scrambled Eggs with Grits*. How could anyone be satisfied with this slop? he thought to himself. Then Ron remembered that he was going to be a history teacher. How did people survive on food centuries ago? They hunted and fished, he thought. It's the twenty-first century; us kids don't realize how easy we have things. Everything is just a click away. Years ago, there were pen pals. Today, you can instant message anybody. Years ago, people hunted. Today, they go to the supermarkets... and if they don't want to go to the supermarkets, they go online and add food to the cart and have it delivered. Ron was aware of the laziness and the impatience of his generation, but at the same time, he liked having things done quickly, as well. He didn't want to be spoiled like his peers. Ron was taught to earn and save, not to take or waste.

By the time Ron finished serving all of the patients their breakfast, it was after eight. He knocked on Cyndi's door, looking for Rita. Cyndi opened the door with a smile. She was going over the day's agenda with Rita.

"I'm ready for the next assignment, Rita," Ron said.

"I'll meet ya outside in a minute, Ron." As Ron stepped outside, he put a breath mint into his mouth and then ran his hands through his hair, slicking it back with some water from the water fountain. "Sorry for the delay, Ron," Rita apologized, coming back from Cyndi's office. "I had to talk to the head honcho, if you know what I mean." Ron had no idea what she meant, but he nodded his head. All Ron knew was that he was in love with his supervisor. She was thirty-five years old and single. She was about five foot five, around 130 pounds, had long, dark brown hair, and green eyes. His dream girl was the girl in *Star Trek II*, but he knew he had no chance of getting her. A hot, mature woman was right in front of him and he hoped he could get her, but still didn't feel confident. "Today's going to be a long day," Rita preached. "So much paperwork, it's unbelievable. By the way, Ron, did you wet your hair? The A.C. is always on, you know."

Ron's quick response was, "I felt hot going from room to room. I started sweating." After hearing Rita's comment, Ron thought it was going to be a long day, too. Rita handed Ron a stack of papers. The stack was so big, he figured he'd be done by next Christmas.

"I'll be making some phone calls. Give me a holler if you need help with anything."

Ron nodded and began the paperwork. Basically, that was all he did until lunchtime.

During lunch, Ron sat in the breakroom, reading a science fiction book, as usual, while enjoying his

— THE NURSING HOME —

microwavable meal. When Ron approached the soda machine, he said, "Will I ever learn?" and fed the machine three quarters, like always, and pushed the button for a cola. He bent down to pick up his soda and heard a voice.

"You'll never learn, will ya?" the voice said.

Ron turned around and saw Beth standing behind him. "Hi Beth. What's up?"

"I'm working an afternoon shift," Beth told him. "Hopefully we could all chill tonight or tomorrow. Jeff and Jay are scheduled to work at Kirk's Video Store tonight."

"I know," said Ron. "What do you think Jeff and Jay are doing now?"

"Probably getting stoned," Beth kidded. Ron laughed. "Well, I gotta get to work and see if Cyndi needs anything."

"See you later."

"By the way, Ron... did you wet the sides of your hair?" Beth sounded happy.

"Why is everyone asking me this? First Rita, now you. Who's next, Cyndi?"

"You're working with Rita today?"

"Yeah, so?"

"Somebody's got a girlfriend," Beth teased him.

"She's just my supervisor."

"Wait 'til Jeff and Jay hear about this."

"Please don't, Beth. I'll never hear the end of it."

"I'm just teasing you, Ron. It's normal for a young guy to like an older woman. Besides, isn't your dream girl the girl in *Star Trek II*?"

"Yes, she is, Beth. Obviously, I would never be able to be with her; she's in another galaxy."

— 154 —

"Stop setting such high standards for yourself," she said, shaking her head.

"I'll talk to you later, Beth."

"Later." When the two of them went back to work, they did what they were instructed to do and finished for the day.

When nighttime approached, Sue was in charge. There were not as many staff members on duty. There was Sue, Pearl, a maintenance guy, Dr. Owens, and a few other around-the-clock employees. "What's up with this damn weather?" complained Sue to Pearl, standing under the roof outside on their cigarette break.

"Dé-jà-vu."

"You know, Pearl... at times, I hate living in Florida, but I do get a decent salary and it pays the bills."

"You always say this, Sue."

"I know I do... but don't you ever get tired of working at the same place, seeing the same damn patients day after day and night after night?"

"Of course, I do, Sue, but what am I going to do? Go back to Connecticut and pay outrageous taxes? Even the rent is high. Look at me, Sue. I'm in my forties. There's nothing out there for me."

"I just wish I could move to Vegas, win millions, and see live entertainment every night."

"Keep dreaming, girlie."

Sue finally jumped back into reality. "Seriously, Pearl, can't we go more than five days without rain?"

"That's what we would call a 'drought' here in

— THE NURSING HOME —

Florida, Sue. Nothing would grow. No trees, no grass, no fruit or vegetables."

"When did you become an expert on nature?" asked Sue.

"It's common sense, bitch."

"You, common sense? When did you start caring about the trees or plants?"

"I don't," said Pearl, "but I enjoy drinking water and eating vegetables. By the way, how was your bubble bath last night... being manless, as usual?"

"It was soothing... and who said I was manless?" A smirk came across Sue's face.

"Get off it, Sue. The last time you had a man was when the rotary telephone was invented."

"Do you not have anything better going on in your life that you have to look into my apartment window to see if I'm bathing with anyone?"

"No, I don't," Pearl laughed.

"You're pathetic, Pearl," Sue snapped back. "Let's get back to work." They both went back inside.

Throughout the night, Sue and Pearl did a lot of catching up on paperwork and updated a lot of files. There would always be work at Rigg's because it was impossible to keep up on everything. Dr. Owens had his own work to do; if not examining a patient, then write-ups. Other employees that were on duty checked on all of the patients. They fed them, changed them, made sure that they were comfortable, and left the television on for them.

At 11:10pm, Sue went into the breakroom for some iced tea. When she entered, her pack of cigarettes was right on the table, where she had left them. She wished she could light one up right there in the breakroom, but she wasn't allowed to because there was no smoking permitted in the building. "Oh, boy, what an exhausting night..." Sue complained aloud to herself. "I need a new job. My body is aching from these ten hour days." She sighed, looking up at the clock. Only twenty minutes to spare before the new shift comes in, she thought. As Sue began pouring the iced tea from the pitcher, she pictured herself clocking out, going straight home, and taking another hot bubble bath. The soap would be sudsy and the water wouldn't be too hot, but at a toasty, warm temperature. All Sue would need was a glass of wine to be set for a night of relaxation.

Sue sat down, stared at the microwave, and drank her iced tea. After Sue finished her drink, she threw away the foam cup and opened the refrigerator door. While placing the pitcher on the top shelf, something caught her eye. There sat a Boston Creme doughnut. Sue's mouth began watering, seeing the chocolate on the outside and envisioning the creaminess on the inside. One doughnut left, she thought to herself. Oh, well, you owe me one, Cyndi. She swiped the doughnut from the fridge and took a big bite. Tasting the chocolate and cream made her feel like she was in heaven.

Right before Sue took another bite, she froze and gripped the doughnut so suddenly that the cream shot out of it. She looked up to see a mob of patients blocking the breakroom door. "What the fuck is this?" she said out loud. "Aren't you all supposed to be sleeping? When did you all begin to walk?!" No response came from the patients as they began inching their way towards Sue. For a second,

—— THE NURSING HOME ——

Sue closed her eyes, hoping that she was hallucinating, but that was not the case. When she opened her eyes, the mob appeared even closer. They were dragging their old, decrepit bodies inch by inch closer to Sue.

Sue screamed for help. "PEARL!!! Help! Dr. Owens! Somebody! *Anybody!* Please help me! Please! Help!" Nobody responded. Sue hoped she could fight off the patients because of their old age, but quickly found out that with a mob of ten to twenty patients, the chances weren't good. She was trapped – screaming, kicking, and throwing punches, but to no avail. One of the patients snuck up behind her with a handful of cooking twine and wrapped it tightly around Sue's neck. Sue started to struggle. She kept kicking, but there were too many of them. Finally, she tried reaching behind herself to loosen the patient's hands and to grab the twine, but couldn't.

The struggle continued. Sue dropped to one knee. She was desperately gasping for air. Her face turned a bright pink. The more she struggled, the worse it got. Within seconds, her face turned from pink to red. Blue veins appeared darker by her eyes. Sue was flat on the floor, fighting and fighting, but getting nowhere. Her heart was racing. She couldn't breathe. All of a sudden, her face began turning pale. Finally, Sue became motionless. She was lying unconscious on the breakroom floor, while the elderly dragged their bodies back into their rooms.

When 11:30pm approached, a bunch of staff members were ready to leave. Pearl looked around to see if anyone was missing. "Where the fuck is Sue?" she asked the group of employees. "And where's that damn maintenance guy?"

"Maybe Sue left her cigarettes behind again," Helen suggested. "She has a habit of doing that, you know."

"Oh, we know Sue's bad habits," kidded Pearl. "At least *most* of us have our shit ready ahead of time. Every time I work the late shift, there's always someone who forgets their stuff. Why can't we all leave on time for once?"

The maintenance guy was still cleaning and hadn't realized the time as he was mopping away, listening to music on his earphones. He looked at his watch. "Oh, shit. 11:40?!" he shrieked. "Pearl's goin' ta kill me." He left the mop and bucket against the wall and ran to the breakroom to get his stuff. When he entered the breakroom, he saw Sue's motionless body, and then took two steps back and started breathing heavily. "Suzi! Get up, girl!" Plenty of thoughts rushed through his mind. His adrenaline was running rapidly. "Who dun it? Who dun it?" He ran to the office.

"We've been waiting forever for you and Sue, Clevon," said Pearl impatiently.

"Pearl, call da po-lice!"

"Why?"

"Suzi ain't movin'. She in da breakroom."

"Damnit!" She ran to the breakroom. "Sue! Sue!" Pearl screamed in a panic. "Get up! Please, God. Get up! Fuck!" Pearl quickly pulled out her cell phone from her pocket to call the police, but saw she had no reception.

— THE NURSING HOME —

"Of all the fucking nights for no reception!" She went into Cyndi's office to use the office phone.

Pearl dialed 911. On the fourth ring, there was a voice on the other line. It was the operator. "You have dialed 911. What is your emergency?"

"I need the police to come to Rigg's Nursing Home in Hampton as soon as possible!"

"We'll send them right now. They should arrive in ten minutes."

"We don't have ten minutes!" Pearl yelled.

"That's the best we can do. Please try to stay calm. Can you describe your situation?"

"There's been another murder!" Out of frustration, Pearl slammed down the office phone. Even Pearl was shocked that the phone didn't break, but looking at the circumstances, the phone was the last thing on her mind.

While Pearl was busy contacting the police, Clevon, the maintenance guy, got Dr. Owens and the two of them attended to Sue's body. Dr. Owens felt no pulse. He tried CPR. He did everything he possibly could, but unfortunately, Sue couldn't be saved.

Pearl returned to the breakroom and Dr. Owens broke the bad news to her. Tears started pouring down Pearl's face. "Only you can make me cry, bitch," she said in a sad voice.

Once again, the same two cops arrived. The guard on duty lead them to the breakroom. "What happened?" asked Officer O'Conner.

— 160 —

"Sue was found on the breakroom floor, unconscious," Pearl told the officers.

Dr. Owens elaborated. "Well, Officers, I just examined her and it looks like she was strangled with cooking twine."

"Cooking twine?! Oh, fuck," commented Officer Conway. "You know how thin that stuff is? Shit."

"We know, Conway, but if you wrap that around the throat and apply pressure, you'll fall no matter what," added O'Conner.

"It definitely looks like there was a struggle involved," Conway suggested, looking over at the strangled victim. "How long do you think you'd last when twine is tied around your neck? Five, ten minutes, tops?"

"Yeah," replied O'Conner, "but the more you struggle, the worse it is."

"Officers, I did everything in my power, but it was too late," Dr. Owens confirmed.

"We hear dat," interrupted Clevon. "When I's sees Suzi layin', her cigz wuzn't far from her. Da cigz looked like it's sayin' '1843.' Wutt dat mean? 1843? Wutt da fuck?" he babbled on. The staff and officers looked at one another and then at the maintenance guy, thinking that the guy was a nut case, but realized that the nut case was not so crazy after all.

Chapter 22

The following morning, Cyndi announced over the loud speaker, perfectly clear, that everybody must be at Monday's meeting at 7:00am sharp. All week there had been bulletins posted all over the nursing home that Cyndi printed herself. "If you don't attend, you will no longer be employed at Rigg's and you will be under investigation for murder. Officers O'Conner and Conway, two of Florida's best, will be here talking to every single person: staff members and patients. Unfortunately, Sue Cobb was found strangled in the breakroom. Over the last few months, we've lost some valuable employees *and* patients. I don't know about all of you, but I, for one, want this to end right now. Rigg's is supposed to be our home away from home, not a funeral parlor. Hopefully we catch the S.O.B. who's behind this and give him or her a taste of their own medicine." Cyndi paused, taking a deep breath as she gathered her thoughts. She continued, "Let's take a couple of seconds to bow our heads in a moment of silence to remember the employees and patients that we have lost." Bringing her speech to an end, she said, "Let's be positive and just do our jobs as usual. Once again, because of what's happened, we have to be alert and on our toes. Have a nice day." Cyndi concluded her speech on a positive note, hoping that she got through to everybody.

Everyone went back to their usual routine. Throughout the morning, the nursing home was pretty quiet. There wasn't a lot of talking, joking, or laughing; and nobody took a time-out for doughnuts or coffee. The staff just concentrated on their duties at hand. Some were trying to block out images of what they'd witnessed at Rigg's during the last few months.

When lunchtime approached, Morris was still in his room. "Same old shit on every single day," he complained out loud, surfing through the channels. "How much news can I watch? It's all depressing. I have a VCR now, thanks to Felix, God bless his soul, but no tape to play. How could I have been so stupid? Those two boys, Jeff and Jay, work at a video store, I overheard. Maybe I can ask them to rent me out some movies. I know we get the Wednesday night movie in the movie room, but other patients get to watch movies in their own room. Why can't I? Even my buddy, Pauly, has a thing called a 'DVD player.' Maybe somebody can help me. I have to be a man, damnit! But I still feel like a three-legged dog. Today's one of those days where I just want to stay in my room and do nothing."

Nurse Helen entered the room. "Good afternoon, sleepy head," she addressed Morris. "Who are you talking to?"

—— THE NURSING HOME ——

"Nobody. Well, actually, myself," he responded. "I was saying I've had a VCR in here for months, but no tapes to watch." Morris thought it would be nice to get a list of movies to choose from, but apparently that was not the case.

"Why didn't you tell us?"

All Morris could say was: "I don't know." In the back of his mind, he knew that they already knew, but wouldn't admit it. Basically, people couldn't admit anything because it made them look bad.

"Since you don't know, how about I wheel you to the lounge room, so you can see your friends?"

"Fine," Morris responded. Helen seemed to be in a better mood than usual, considering what had taken place over the last couple of months. Maybe she's forgotten what happened to her friend, Nurse Anne, Morris thought, or maybe she's in denial and blocks it out for the best. Could you blame her?

Helen wheeled Morris to the lounge room where he could be in the comfort of other patients and mingle with his friends.

Pauly was already yammering away, like always. "Hey there, Mori, old boy!"

"Hello Pauly... and for the thousandth time, it's Morris."

"You believe that bullshit announcement Cyndi made over the loud speaker? What a joke! Heh!"

"Which one?" asked Ralph inquisitively.

"Yeah, Pauly. Which one?" joined in Frank. "I started falling asleep again when Cyndi was rambling on. I feel bad because I couldn't sleep the night before because of what's been happening. I like Cyndi, you know?"

JAMES J. MURPHY III

"Oh, we know, Frankie boy, we know," teased Pauly.

"Not like that, Pauly, you old pervert."

"Well, back to what I was saying..." Pauly continued. "Cyndi said we have to attend this stupid meeting at seven o'clock on Monday morning. Are you fucking kidding me? What a crock of shit!"

"What's the matter, Pauly? You need your beauty sleep?"

"No, Mori, but I see you do. You look like shit today and I think your receding hairline moved back another inch."

"Real funny, Pauly. And it's Morris to you."

"Whatever. My point is, besides waking up early on a Monday, we're under investigation for murder. Yeah, like a seventy-five year old fat man, like myself, in a wheelchair, is capable of doing this. Has Cyndi been experimenting with these teenage kids in the parking lot after hours?"

"Experimenting...? What do you mean 'experimenting?'" asked Morris.

"You old horn-dog! I mean dropping some LSD, because her brain is definitely not functioning up to par. If she was experimenting with those teenage kids in other ways, I'd have to take my hat off to them."

"Good old Pauly," joked Frank. "You always have to throw one wise crack in."

"Damn right, I do. Seriously, guys... don't you think it's absurd that us patients are gonna be questioned about these murders?"

"I do, Pauly," agreed Morris, "but what can we do?"

"Absolutely nothing," muttered Pauly.

–165–

─── THE NURSING HOME ───

"We're all pissed off, but maybe it is for the best that everyone shows up for this meeting. Maybe the officers can narrow down the suspects." Morris tried looking on the bright side.

"Those officers couldn't find their asses even if they sat down. That's how stupid these guys are." Pauly had a smirk on his face. The gang laughed.

"Let's see, guys," said Morris. "We'll narrow down the list of suspects. First, there's Bill. I got his ass fired *and* arrested, then he kicked mine, then kicked, if you know what I mean." The gang liked Morris's sense of humor. He always wondered why Sam and the family never got the jokes. Different generation, he guessed.

"Then we have Cock-Sucking Eddie. The weasel was trouble since Day One," said Pauly. "He left Old Man Crombert to die, then he snuck Bill into the building to do a number on Mori, old boy, here. Plus, he's always touching up his hair like a faggot... and probably became one after being arrested."

"Also, there's Sue," said Ralph. "She is malicious and evil and a bitch... or shall I say *was*..." Everyone looked at each other, and then all eyes turned towards Ralph, knowing that he was right. "She was probably the one who killed Gothersorg, but we can't accuse her as the murderer anymore because she's the latest victim."

"Final member of their clique is Pearl," announced Frank. "I believe she is even more evil than Sue. Maybe she was the one who orchestrated all of these murders."

"Okay, Frank," said Pauly. "I think somebody here's watching too much *Matlock*."

— 166 —

"Real funny, Pauly," Frank said, standing up for himself.

"I know I am, but you may be on to something, Frank."

"Maybe it could be Nurse Helen," said Ralph.

"Or my physical therapist, Brian," jumped in Morris.

"Or maybe Dr. Owens!" Pauly shouted excitedly. The guys were shooting out names left and right.

"Hold on," said Morris. "What the hell are we doing? We're acting like a bunch of kids. Let the police deal with it. It's *their* job, not ours. Besides, they're the ones who are getting paid to do this."

"Even if they don't do anything, they still get paid." Pauly always had to have the last word. All the gang could do was agree.

A few minutes later, Brian, the physical therapist, entered the lounge room. "Speaking of suspects, Mori, old boy, there's your buddy, Brian," Pauly started up.

"Shut up, Pauly. He's not my buddy. Simmer down, guys. Here he comes," warned Morris.

"Hey everyone," greeted Brian. "How are you all doing?"

The gang mumbled, "Fine."

"Did you guys hear what happened to Sue?"

"I think all of Florida's heard about it," said Pauly, being a wise-ass. "It's Saturday. Why are you here, Bri?" he complained.

"I just wanted to see if any of you wanted to do some physical therapy today." They all looked at each other nervously. "God, you guys can't take a joke, can you? All I came here for was my paycheck. By the way, Mr. Wise Guy, it's Brian."

—— THE NURSING HOME ——

"Whatever, Bri. Deal with me during the week, and better off, report me to Cyndi. I might get detention," he kidded.

"I don't know how you guys deal with him." Brian had a huge smile on his face because he actually did like Pauly's smart-ass attitude. "See you guys during the week." They all said goodbye.

"Can you guys say 'Killer,' or what?" said Pauly.

"Oh, would you stop?" said Morris. "It could be anyone."

The remainder of the weekend was quiet at Rigg's. As Saturday evening crept upon them, Jeff Randle was trying to get ready to meet his friends. As usual, he had tuned in to the horror movie playing on his DVD player. "How you could find anything in this pigsty of a room is beyond me," his father said to him.

"Can't you knock?" Jeff responded back.

"Look at his place! Beer bottles, dirty clothes, movies everywhere... How many movies does one person need to watch? Besides that, you don't even bother hiding the beer bottles anymore and it smells like smoke in here! Would you please clean your fucking room, you waste of space?!" As Jeff's father went on and on, it was easier to tune him out.

"Whatever, Dad. Can you leave now?"

"Why can't you be like your older sister? She had a clean room and didn't look or act like a slob."

"Too bad you don't know what went on behind those closed doors, Dad."

"What is that supposed to mean?"

– 168 –

JAMES J. MURPHY III

"Look at Becky, Dad. She was popular, she was a cheerleader, and she was, and still is, fake."

"What was wrong with her being a cheerleader? She had a lot of friends. All the girls and boys always came over to study, make brownies, and go to the mall. What's wrong with that?"

"Dad, first off, are you a guy?"

"I'd better be or you definitely wouldn't be here."

"What you are saying is that you hate the way I live my life."

"You definitely ain't 'Son-of-the-Year.' At times, I'd say 'son-of-a-bitch.'"

"I got an idea, Dad. Why don't I go back to high school and be a stupid football-playing jock? Or, even better yet, why don't I join the Baking Team and sell cookies and cupcakes? I'll be accepted into a cooking university and be 'Baker of the Year,' so you'll actually like me."

"Now you're just being a moron, Jeff."

"Me, a moron? What about you? You probably think Becky hasn't been deflowered."

"Fuck you, Jeff! She's my little girl."

"She hasn't been your little girl since she's been, like, fifteen."

"I'm gonna bash your head in, you little bastard!"

"Try it! Truth hurts, doesn't it? Those asshole football players who came over to study definitely didn't come here to study algebra; they came over to study Becky's anatomy and she let those fuckers get the touchdown every time. Now you know why I hate jocks or any kind of sport."

Mr. Randle didn't know if he wanted to thank his son or kill him. All he said was, "Son, you know how I don't

— THE NURSING HOME —

like this road you're on and I really wish you'd clean your room, but the fact of the matter is that your mom and I only want the best for you. And, we, you know..." Jeff's father figured he got the point.

"Same here, Dad, but I gotta go."

"Stay out of trouble."

"Sure, Dad." They left the room and Jeff closed the door behind them.

When Jeff was out of sight and on his way to the park, his father asked aloud, "Where have I gone wrong?" Normally, it would have been directed towards Jeff, but he was having second thoughts about it.

Beth, Jay, and Ron were already at the park. "Thank God for Saturday night!" screamed Jay. "Whoooo!"

"Boy, somebody's in a good mood," commented Beth.

"Why shouldn't I be? I don't have work at either job for three days. That rarely happens." Jay opened his first beer of the night and started gulping away. "This definitely hits the spot."

"Sorry to burst your bubble..." Ron shyly interrupted.

"What bubble are you talking about, Ronny boy?" Jay asked.

"Oh, he didn't hear the announcement, Beth." Ron put her on the spot.

"What announcement is he talking about, Beth?" asked Jay as his high came down to a crash-landing.

"The announcement that Cyndi made this morning. Plus, bulletins have been posted everywhere. Didn't she call you?"

— 170 —

"Yeah, she did. I thought she wanted me to work today, so I was like, 'Fuck that.'"

"Maybe you should listen to what Cyndi has to say," suggested Beth. "After hearing her voicemail, you're going to want to drink her message away."

Jay put down his beer bottle on the side of a rock. He put his hand into the pocket of his baggy, black cargo pants and pulled out his cell phone. Jay checked his voicemail to hear all of the messages. When he got to Cyndi's message, he listened carefully. "*Hey Jay, it's Cyndi. I know you are not scheduled to work on Monday, but we need everyone, including you, to come in at 7am sharp. Officers Conway and O'Conner are coming in to question everybody about the death of Sue Cobb. I'll make it up to you, Jay. Thank you.*"

"Long-ass message," Jay responded. "Yeah, she'd better make it up to me. Tee Hee."

"Jay, get your head out of the gutter," Beth reprimanded.

"I'm tired of going to these stupid meetings," he complained.

"We all are," Beth agreed.

"Hopefully the police will catch the culprit," added Ron.

"Culprit!? Have you been giving up space shows for a detective series, Ron?" asked Jay. "Culprit..." he said again as he took another gulp of his beer. All Beth did was laugh. Ron was speechless. Jay saw Jeff arriving with a six-pack. "Where the fuck were you, bro?"

"My father had another one of his famous talks with me. You know how it is: 'Clean your room,' 'You're a waste of space,' 'We care for and love you, son.' And this time I decided to add 'Becky's a whore' to the routine."

— THE NURSING HOME —

"She did get around," agreed Jay.

"Who's Becky?" asked Beth. Beth and Ron looked at each other, puzzled.

"My older sister, who was a cheerleading slut back in high school," responded Jeff.

"You know, that's not very nice to say," said Beth.

"I know it's not very nice to say, but it's the truth," said Jeff. "She is my sister, though, and I will always be there for her."

"My bro tells the truth," agreed Jay. "You hadda see how many times Jeff got his ass handed to him because of his sister."

"Enough about my sister and my family. Let's have fun tonight because you know it ain't happening on Monday."

"So everyone knew about this except me," Jay continued whining. "By the way, Ron used the word 'culprit.'"

"Are you watching detective shows now?" asked Jeff.

Ron grabbed himself a beer and said, "It's gonna be a long night." As the night went on, the shocking thing was that the kids didn't drink that much and they did more talking to one another and enjoyed each other's company.

Later that night, the youths went to Moe's Diner. The manager at the diner approached Jeff and asked if he was okay. She was used to seeing him stumbling in drunk. "I'm fine tonight, Dee," assured Jeff.

"I'll get somebody to seat you guys."

"Thanks," Jeff responded.

When the kids sat down, Ron asked, "How many people do you guys know?"

"Oh, Dee?"

"Yeah, Dee," Ron repeated.

"Dude, she's like my second mother. Personally, I wish she was my real mother. She's always been there for me, even when I screw up big-time." Jeff paused, looking around the table. "Man, I can eat a horse," he said, changing the subject.

The kids were handed menus by a Mexican waiter named Perez. He was about five foot six with slicked back, greasy black hair of average length and had a skinny, greasy mustache. It looked and smelt like he hadn't showered for days. His shirt was tucked in, but that didn't hide the potbelly hanging over his waist. "Would you like anything to drink?"

All four responded, "Water." He said he'd be back shortly in his heavy accent.

Five minutes later, Perez came back with the four glasses of water. "Would you like to order?"

Prior to him returning, the kids had breezed through their menus and discussed amongst themselves what they wanted.

Beth responded, "I would like a bagel with cream cheese."

"May I have French Onion soup?" asked Ron politely. The waiter said, "Si."

"Dude, I'll have chocolate chip pancakes," Jeff told him.

At last, it was Jay's turn. "I'll have a B.E.C." The waiter looked at him as if he was a Martian from another planet. "Bacon, Egg, and Cheese sandwich," Jay informed him.

Once again, the waiter said, "Si." He collected the menus from the kids and walked away.

—— THE NURSING HOME ——

"Monday's a big day for us all, aye?" asked Ron, trying to make conversation.

"Don't remind me," bitched Jay.

"Guys, you know, I have every single deceased patient's data on file," Beth told them.

"Yeah, so, what's your point?" asked Jeff.

"Point is, Rigg's opened in 1841."

"What are you getting at, Beth?" Ron was curious.

"What I'm trying to say is, I made a copy of the disc and brought it home. It has everyone's profile and the deaths don't begin until 1893. The rest of the data must be missing."

"Maybe nobody died during that time period. So what?" It was obvious that Jeff thought it was no big deal.

"Are you trying to tell me that nobody died in fifty-two years?!" exclaimed Beth.

"Who knows... It was a long time ago."

"If the 1893 files were on the disc, there's no reason that the earlier ones shouldn't be," Ron added.

"Maybe all of the written work from that time got burned in a fire. Then they wouldn't be able to save it to a disc when they started using computers. Ever think of that?"

"Speaking of getting burnt... Are you okay, Jay?"

"Yeah, I'm a-okay, Beth."

"Ever since you found out that you have to go to work on Monday, you haven't been acting the same."

"Sorry, Beth. I just had to let out some steam."

"Let me get back to what I was saying," Beth continued. "So, the profiles don't begin until 1893. It just seems a little strange to me."

— JAMES J. MURPHY III —

"Fine, maybe something actually did happen to the data," said Jeff. "Besides, who cares about data that old, anyway?"

"What *I* think is that someone is trying to keep information from us and I'm determined to find out who." She saw Perez coming back with their orders. "Food's here. We'll continue this conversation after everyone gets interrogated. Deal?" compromised Beth.

They all said, "Deal."

"Now, let's dig in!" suggested Jeff, and that was what everyone did.

Officers O'Conner and Conway didn't bother patrolling the parks that Saturday night because there were no reported disturbances. All O'Conner and Conway did was drive around, as they were instructed to by their captain. The topic of discussion was Sue's murder. "Do you believe that we have to waste our time going to Rigg's at seven o'clock on Monday morning?" complained O'Conner.

"I know it's a pain, but somebody's gotta do it," stated Conway.

"Why us?"

"Captain's orders." Just then, they got interrupted by the captain. A robbery was in progress at Daily's Supermarket.

"We're on it, Captain," responded O'Conner, loud and clear. Conway pulled a one-eighty, once again, into on-coming traffic. "Oh, shit!" screamed O'Conner, trying to hold his balance without spilling his coffee. "Why do I bother letting you drive?"

–175–

— THE NURSING HOME —

"Because you live for that rush, O'Conner!"

The officers arrived at the scene of the crime and arrested a sixteen year old kid who was stealing cigarettes. "Kid, you're a fucking idiot," said Conway.

"Yeah, punk," added O'Conner, "at least go down for something big, like a bank robbery. Thanks to you, my partner did a one-eighty and made me hold on for dear life, driving like an asshole, just so we can arrest one."

"What my partner is trying to say," explained Conway, "is that you are under arrest and have the right to remain silent." He continued to read the kid his rights. They put the sixteen year old kid into the back of the police car and closed the door. The kid was speechless because O'Conner kept rambling.

As they drove away, O'Conner added, "Also, thanks to you, I have to buy another coffee." The kid would never make the same mistake again; sitting through O'Conner's bitching was punishment enough.

— Chapter 23

Monday morning arrived. Officers O'Conner and Conway had been scheduled to do the overnight shift the night before. They began working at ten at night and were originally going to get off at six in the morning. However, because of the recent incidents occurring at Rigg's Nursing Home, their captain told them that they still had to interrogate every single patient and employee, including the head herself, Cyndi Gillian.

Just a little after six o'clock, O'Conner and Conway were about to head to the nursing home. "What a waste of time!" bitched O'Conner.

"Oh, what's the matter, O'Conner? Is it past somebody's bedtime?"

"Don't worry about anybody's bedtime, Conway. You'll get to play tea-party with your kiddie-friends when you interrogate them. I could see it now: you'll be asking a serious question, while one of the kids are asking, 'Was that one lump or two?'"

—— THE NURSING HOME ——

"Fuck you, O'Conner."

"Right back at you, rookie. Conway, we're getting paid overtime. We don't want to show up too early at this fucking place. Besides, I'm hungry."

"I guess you want to go to the usual coffee shop."

"Why not?" said O'Conner. "Yeah, I'm craving a chocolate-glazed doughnut and a hot coffee."

"You're always craving that," replied Conway.

"Especially since last night because of that no-good, dumb-ass kid and your driving skills."

"Don't blame my driving skills on you having butterfingers. By the way, O'Conner, right now, you're just clumsy. Give it twenty years or so and you'll become senile, forgetful, and deaf, just like those senior citizens at Rigg's."

"Great, I can't wait until I see what my future holds," he said. "According to you, I'm 'clumsy.' Let me also add that I'm overweight, got bags under my eyes, and my wife, Muriel, is already asking me to quit the force."

"Oh, would you relax, O'Conner? Your breakfast is on me. Now stop the bitching."

"Thanks, rookie."

"With the weight... can't help you there, big man."

"Real funny, pretty boy. If you're still my partner in five years, you won't be so pretty."

"We'll see about that." They both laughed.

They headed to the coffee shop, got their breakfast, and made it to Rigg's at a quarter past seven. All of the patients and employees were seated in the cafeteria. They sat with their respective cliques. The kids were sitting together; Morris sat with his senior citizen buddies;

– 178 –

JAMES J. MURPHY III

and Pearl was by herself, since her clique was no longer alive, with the exception of Eddie, who was God-knows-where... probably unemployed, jailed, or maybe even dead. Everyone was talking amongst themselves, trying to figure out what was going on.

Finally, Cyndi approached the podium. She looked into the audience and acknowledged all who were present. "First of all, good morning to you all." Everyone greeted her back with 'Good morning, Cyndi.' Cyndi went on with her speech. "I know some of you were supposed to be off today and I assume you had plans, so I'm grateful that you came in. But, as I look into the audience, I notice some of you, names shall not be mentioned, are wearing pajamas. I called this meeting this morning to try to get to the bottom of things. In return, I wish you could have shown me some respect. At least wear a T-shirt and pants. This isn't a damn slumber party. There will be no popcorn or toe-nail coloring. Since I got that off my chest now, and have everybody's attention, let's proceed with the interrogation. I am proud to present to you two of Florida's finest: Officer Conway and Officer O'Conner."

The officers both stepped up and shook her hand. "Thank you, Cyndi," Conway said over the microphone. "We have a list of every Rigg's employee and patient. Everybody will be questioned." Everyone in the audience looked at one another thinking, 'Oh, great.'

O'Conner believed Conway had enough mic-time and grabbed the microphone and the list of names from him. The first name on the list was Pearl Adams. O'Conner called her down enthusiastically, imitating Bob Barker from *The Price Is Right*. At first, Pearl seemed embarrassed,

−179−

THE NURSING HOME

but then the blush disappeared from her face as she realized that since she'd be the first one questioned, it meant she'd be the first one done. Pearl followed the officers to Cyndi's office. The interrogation began. She answered all of the questions honestly, according to the best of her knowledge.

As Pearl was being questioned, the staff members and patients in the cafeteria bitched to one another, complaining about what a waste of time the interrogation was. Throughout the morning and into the afternoon, they were called one by one over the loud speaker to report to and speak with the officers.

The officers finally finished their interrogations. They might not have been satisfied with some of the people answering the questions. For instance, Pearl, who was as cold as ice; or Ron, who was as stiff as a board; or even good old Pauly, the wise-ass that he was. Even though the cops were not pleased with them, there was no evidence pointing towards them. They were in the clear for the time being.

"Cyndi, please come to your office," O'Conner demanded over the loud speaker in a strict, yet professional manner. Slowly and silently, Cyndi got up from her seat at the podium, trying not to draw attention to herself, but it was already too late. After hearing her name over the loud speaker, all eyes went directly on her, as if she was the perpetrator. Cyndi left the cafeteria and headed towards her office.

After she made her exit, the cliques started exchanging negative comments about her. "What did I tell you lug-heads?" Pauly said confidently. "You can't trust anybody here, not even Cyndi."

"Maybe the officers have to tell her something about today's investigation." Morris tried to clear it up.

"Morris is right," said Frank. "Or maybe the officers are saying their goodbyes."

Ralph also agreed, adding, "I can't see her doing anything like this."

"Now you've done it, Mori, old boy," grouched Pauly. "Add your two cents and these other two lug-heads go along with you."

"It's Morris to you," Morris said, shaking his head. Ralph and Frank remained speechless as they waited to hear another announcement. Pauly smiled, proud that he got the last word in, for the most part.

Meanwhile, on the other side of the room, Pearl was questioning Dr. Owens. "Well, do you think she did it?"

"No, I don't," responded Dr. Owens.

"What do you think, Brian?" Pearl asked the physical therapist.

"We'll find out. I'm accusing nobody."

"Well, maybe it was you, Brian!" attacked Nurse Helen.

"Me?! I didn't even work that night," he snapped back.

The kids overheard their nearby co-workers accusing each other. "At least we know it was none of us," said Ron in his mousey voice. His friends agreed.

"Maybe it was one of you stupid kids!" Helen shot a dirty look at the teenagers.

"Maybe your smoke killed her." Everyone looked at Ron, thinking that that had to be the stupidest comeback in history, but his friends backed him up, anyway. Ron felt

—— THE NURSING HOME ——

just a little embarrassed because Rita was in attendance. Everybody in the room started bickering at each other back and forth, left and right.

At last, Beth inched her way to the podium. She grabbed the microphone and screamed: "SHUT UP!!!" Everybody looked up towards the podium, startled. "Look at ourselves," she said. "Why are we arguing with each other? For all we know, the killer... or killers... may not even be in this room," she stated, even though in her gut, she knew he or she was. "Why don't we wait for Cyndi or the officers to make an announcement?" Immediately following Beth's little speech, the room seemed much calmer.

When Cyndi made it to her office, she greeted the cops. "Well, Officers, what's the good word?"

"There's no easy way to tell you this." The way Officer Conway was talking, it seemed like he was about to announce that her mother died. In Cyndi's case, she wouldn't have to worry about that because her mother died in a boating accident when she was twenty-one. Her father left when she was ten, and she couldn't care any less what happened to him. Cyndi took a big gulp, as if the cops were about to arrest her.

"Cyndi, just to make things clear, my partner is an idiot," stated Officer O'Conner.

Conway gave O'Conner the biggest, angriest stare-down. "Why, you no-good, lousy, coffee-drinking, doughnut-munching son-of-a-bitch! How dare you make me look bad!" Conway loosened his collar roughly, as if he was about to ring O'Conner's neck. He was steaming.

– 182 –

"Calm down, wouldcha, rookie?"

"Don't you tell me to calm down! You're lucky that we're in uniform right now, O'Conner, because if we weren't, your teeth would be all over the floor."

All Cyndi could do was observe the two officers, who were supposed to be doing the people justice, deteriorate and breakdown in front of her very eyes. She assumed the case was getting to them, as it would anybody. She witnessed that type of behavior among staff in the past, while she was working at Gerald's Rehabilitation Center.

"Conway, would you please relax? We are in front of a lady; let's act professional," insisted O'Conner. He turned to Cyndi. "I'm very sorry about our behavior, Ms. Gillian. Would you please forgive us?" Conway looked at him, thinking: 'You're such a suck-up,' and then smiled to himself. O'Conner, keeping his presentation professional in front of Cyndi, winked at Conway, thinking: 'I got you.'

"Fine, since you apologized to Cyndi and got everything out of your system, I also apologize. We both got a little hasty, but now we have to get down to business. O'Conner, if you don't tell her, then I will."

"Conway! Don't! I'm warning you right now."

"Tell her!" yelled Conway.

"Tell me what?!" demanded Cyndi as her hands went up in offense. "I want to know! And I want to know *now*!!! I could have other officers solve this, you know. You guys are a dime a dozen, so don't flatter yourselves for working this case. So, once again, either tell me what the fuck's going on in my nursing home or I'll ask the department for two other officers. Don't waste any more of my time!" Cyndi yelled unpleasantly, huffing away.

THE NURSING HOME

"Fuck it, O'Conner. I'm telling her."

"You're an asshole, Conway."

"Cyndi, we think our killer is Morris Grover."

"Morris Grover?! Did somebody spike your coffee, Officer?"

"Yes, Cyndi," the officer responded. "To Morris Grover being the killer, not the spiked coffee."

"This is asinine," replied O'Conner. "We are not in total agreement. But so far, the evidence is pointing towards him. I think he was framed. Besides, Conway, what real evidence do we have, anyway? No fingerprints, no proof, no *nothing*. The man is in his eighties for God's sake!"

"I know he did it!" demanded Conway. "But not alone. Somebody's been whispering into his ear."

"Whispering into his ear? Are you shitting me? Personally, I think you're insane, Conway. Have you been watching the midnight movies again, starring Vincent Price?"

"Vincent Price? Who's that? A talk show host or something?"

"You young kids..." said O'Conner, shaking his head in shame. "All you know about is what's current."

"Enough of this crap," snapped Conway. He grabbed the office microphone in an aggressive manner. "Would somebody please bring Morris Grover to Cyndi's office immediately?"

"You're nuts, rookie!"

"What do you want to do, O'Conner? Wait for another murder?" Conway turned towards Cyndi. "Well, what do you want to do, Ms. Gillian?"

– 184 –

Cyndi tried speaking, but couldn't get the words out.

O'Conner spoke up. "Conway, listen to me for one minute. Mr. Grover is in his eighties. There is no fucking way he committed these murders. What is the squad gonna think of us when we arrest a crippled old man?"

"Who cares?" said Conway.

"Great, I can see it now: Jackson and O'Leary laughing their asses off at us. How the hell are we going to explain this one to the Captain?"

"We'll just have to," replied Conway.

"It looks like I'll have to call Sam Grover, Morris's son, again," explained Cyndi. "What am I supposed to say to him this time? 'Hi, Mr. Grover. How are you today? By the way, your looney, old father's a killer and got arrested.' He'll throw the biggest lawsuit against us and we'll all be out of jobs."

"You'll get another job," Conway told her. "Listen, guys... You are absolutely right. Do you think I want to arrest Mr. Grover? Of course not. But what choice do we have? I obviously know that an eighty-something year old man couldn't have done this without help, so help me out here. I'm running out of options."

"We all are," agreed O'Conner, "but I just can't throw cuffs on this old man." There was a brief silence.

Meanwhile, Nurse Helen volunteered to wheel Morris Grover from the cafeteria to Cyndi's office. "What are you doing?" asked Morris. "Get your damn hands off me!"

"It's okay, Mr. Grover. Just calm down," the nurse told him as she gripped the back of his wheelchair.

THE NURSING HOME

"Don't tell me to calm down! Why are you taking me to Cyndi's office?"

"That's what we're going to find out, so please stop starting a ruckus and quiet down."

"You can't tell me what to do, lady!"

"Let him go!" Frank wished that he could do more to help his friend, but he was stuck in a wheelchair.

"Get off him!" Ralph said in a loud voice.

"We'll get you out of this, Mori, old boy," said Pauly. "I told you; you can't trust the staff."

"Keep your mouth shut, Mr. Gardener," the nurse scolded him.

"Or what, Nurse Whore? You're gonna report me to Cyndi?" Nurse Helen ignored the nasty comment and the room, once again, got rowdy.

The nurse wheeled Morris out the door. "You were right, Pauly! And it's Morris!" He was able to squeeze out one last line before the door closed completely.

Wheeling Morris down the hall, Helen attempted to make small talk. "You sure have made some friends here since you've arrived."

"Don't try making conversation with me, lady. It's not gonna work. Let's just see what this is about. You made me look like an ass in front of everyone, so don't do it again." Helen wheeled Morris the rest of the way in silence. She knocked on the door twice when she got to Cyndi's office.

"Come in," called Cyndi from inside. Helen wheeled Morris in and stood behind him, assuming she'd have to wheel him right back after the conversation. She saw the serious expressions on the faces of the people in the office

– 186 –

and, before a minute passed, Cyndi excused her by saying, "Thank you, Nurse. You may leave now."

"Get outta here!" Morris screamed at the nurse. "My life doesn't involve you."

Helen walked out slowly, closing the door behind her. She was angered because she couldn't retaliate on the old man's harsh words with the officers and Cyndi present. She didn't want to lose her job.

Once Helen had made her exit, Cyndi greeted Morris.

"Hello Mr. Grover," the officers said simultaneously. "Do you know why you were summoned to the office?" asked Conway.

"I have no idea. Why don't you explain this to me, Officer?" asked Morris.

"Here we go," began O'Conner.

"Well, Mr. Grover, do you realize that the number of deaths here increased significantly since you've arrived?"

"So what?" responded Mr. Grover defensively. "You think I had something to do with it?"

"I never said that," said Conway.

"Since Day One, I knew this place was no good. I never wanted to come here, but my dumb-ass son and his family didn't want me around anymore, so I had no choice. Then after that jerk, Bill, threatened and pummeled me, my son all of a sudden gives a damn about me. I told him to fuck off and stay out of my life. I wish you people would do the same thing. I have no options... either ask my son to take me back or stay here. Either way, I'm screwed, but at least I have friends here." Morris explained the scenario and continued to vent in frustration. The anger must have been building up since he arrived at Rigg's. "You only

— THE NURSING HOME —

seem to give a damn when a useless, no-good staff member dies, but when one of us patients die, all you people say is: 'It must have been old age,' just to cover yourselves."

"That's not true, Morris," said Conway.

"It's Mr. Grover to you, Officer."

"I care about you, Morris," butted in Cyndi. Morris didn't respond.

"Shush," warned O'Conner as he turned to Cyndi.

"We've been here for patients, as well, Mr. Grover." Conway tried informing the old man.

"Yeah, it only took ten deaths for you guys to make it over here. When Bill beat the hell out of me, where were you? Going on your doughnut break, I bet."

"You're way out of line, Mr. Grover!" Conway began getting louder.

"You people called me here; I didn't call you."

"This is a very serious matter, Mr. Grover, so I suggest you cooperate. Got it?" threatened Conway.

"Or what, Officer? You're going to arrest me? Where would I rather be: here or in jail? Either way, it's the same to me. I'm not going anywhere."

"You leave me no choice. Morris Grover, I'm placing you under arrest for the murders that have recently occurred." Conway began reading him his rights. Morris screamed in agony because Conway put the cuffs so tightly on his boney, wrinkled wrists.

"Conway, what the fuck are you doing? This has gone far enough," insisted O'Conner. "We don't have enough evidence to book him."

"What do you mean, O'Conner?"

"I mean, just because you don't like this guy, we can't

– 188 –

arrest him until we catch him in the act."

"Fine," a disappointed Conway agreed.

"We apologize, Mr. Grover," said O'Conner as Conway uncuffed him.

"Damn right! You should apologize," barked Morris. "You're lucky I don't sue your asses for assault."

"Assault?!" yelled Conway.

"Let it go, Conway," O'Conner said.

"I can see it now," said Morris. "I sue and the lawsuit goes on for years. I either lose because you cops stick together... or I win, only to have a heart attack and die. So, do I really win?"

"Cyndi, please wheel your patient out of here. My partner and I have to talk," O'Conner said, not so happily, looking directly at Conway.

"You got it, Officer," replied Cyndi. As Cyndi was about to leave her office, O'Conner suggested that she update Morris's family. Cyndi wheeled him out. "I'm sorry about what happened in there, Morris," Cyndi told him once they were in the corridor.

"You didn't do anything, Cyndi. That asshole cop should apologize to me."

"I doubt that will ever happen."

"I hope I didn't offend you in your office, Cyndi. Everything that I said was true. Personally, to be honest, I don't hate you... I don't like you... I don't trust you... I don't really know you as a person, but I do respect you."

"Thank you, Mr. Grover. I appreciate your honesty and hopefully everything here gets resolved."

They returned to the cafeteria. Questions were being asked left and right. *'Well, who did it?' 'Who's the killer?'*

—— THE NURSING HOME ——

'Was it you?' 'Was it him?' Everyone was jumping to conclusions.

Cyndi went back to the podium. "If today was your day off, thank you for coming in. Now you may go home. As for the rest of you, I think you've abused your break long enough for today. Please bring the patients back to their rooms and get back to work or you can go home with no pay. Thank you." Everyone scattered like mice and disappeared. That was the only way Cyndi could think of to quiet down the place and it worked.

When everyone went back to work, Cyndi hid in her office, locking her door and pulling the shade down. Finally alone, she began pacing around like a hamster on a turn-wheel. She opened her window to get some fresh air. Cyndi took a deep breath and sighed. She ran her hands through her hair. The recent turn of events had made Cyndi a nervous wreck and who could blame her? To top it off, she had to make another phone call to Sam Grover. She only had his cell phone number. "Let me get this over with." Cyndi picked up the office phone and put it against her left ear and began dialing it with her right index finger. She also had a note pad and pen on her desk just in case she needed to take down information. Cyndi let the phone ring five times and there was no answer. When Cyndi heard a voice on the other line, she said: "Hello Mr. Grover," and then realized it was only a recording.

The recording said: 'Hello. You have reached the voicemail of Sam Grover. I'm sorry I cannot make it to the phone. Please leave a message and I'll call you back.'

– 190 –

"Mr. Grover, this is Cyndi Gillian from Rigg's Nursing Home. As soon as you get this message, call me back. Your father may be in deep trouble with the police and it involves murder." Cyndi hung up and felt somewhat relieved for a moment just to get that off her chest.

Meanwhile, the Grovers were too busy having a great time at Universal Studios to think about the people at home, especially Sam. Besides, they were grateful to have gone through with their agreement of not bringing any electronic devices with them on their trip. They pretty much went on all of the rides and saw all of the attractions. The three of them were beat and ready to go back to the hotel.

They were just about to leave the park, but Sam saw a sign posted.

Tonight, 7:00PM
Performing Live and for FREE:
Men At Work

After having such a great day, Jude and Todd felt they were about to have a horrible night. They held their heads down in shame. Sam was jumping around and acting like a fourteen year old girl excited to see a boy band. Only a surgeon would be able to remove the smile attached to his face. He screamed, "YES! YES! YES! Isn't this the greatest getaway ever?"

—— THE NURSING HOME ——

Without any enthusiasm, his wife said, "Yeah, Sam. Great."

"Yeah. Great, Dad," Todd said with even less excitement in his voice than his mother. Jude and Todd weren't just unenthusiastic, but embarrassed by Sam's ranting. People were staring and probably thinking: 'What a loser...' and 'What an idiot...'

A man passing by wearing shorts, a Hawaiian shirt, and sandals looked at the sign and said, "1982 is over, man."

Sam wouldn't let the comment bother him. He suggested to his family, "Let's get some grub, 'cause we're gonna have a good time tonight." Sam went to order dinner for the family.

Todd and Jude were starving. They talked amongst themselves. "It could be worse, Todd. You could be in school, right?" his mother said, trying to stay positive.

"Or we could be sitting at the Marlins game, getting rained on again."

"How do you remember that?"

"Grandpa always made fun of us for it."

"Hopefully he's doing alright," Jude said.

"Hey you two," Sam said cheerfully, coming towards them with dinner trays in his hands. He handed his son a tray. "Here you go, Todd. Your baby back ribs and soda."

"Come on, Dad. You're in a good mood... No beer?"

"Don't push it, Todd. I'm letting you drive, aren't I?"

Todd couldn't complain about that. "Like I said, Dad... It looks good." His father laughed.

"A chicken salad for you, my queen," Sam said happily.

"Give it a rest, Sam. We're seeing your little concert tonight," Jude said giddily.

JAMES J. MURPHY III

"Little concert?! Can you believe she said 'little concert,' Todd?" Todd was too busy polishing off the ribs and wearing barbeque sauce on his face to pay any attention to what his father was saying. "Jude, Men At Work only sang one of the greatest songs in rock history! It's the one that got us together and they'll play it tonight."

"I know, Sam." Sam began humming the song as the family enjoyed their dinner. There was nothing that Jude could do but smile at her husband.

After they finished eating, the Grovers headed back to where they originally saw the Men At Work sign. Fans began lining up for the free show. "Sam, are you sure you read the sign carefully?"

"Yeah, Jude. What is there not to get? Men At Work FREE tonight."

"I guess you didn't, Sam..."

"What's she talking about, Todd?"

"It's just a tribute band covering their music," Jude informed her husband.

Sam looked even closer at the sign and felt let down. His family could tell. The expression on Sam's face looked as if he'd lost tickets to the World Series. "Oh, well," he said. "Let's stay, anyway. We'll listen to the cover band. Close enough, right?" All Todd and Jude did was nod their heads in agreement.

After waiting half an hour, an announcer came onto the stage and said that the tribute band was running late. A lot of the crowd left; not Sam and his family. "Can we go, Sam?"

"Yeah, Dad. Let's leave."

–193–

── THE NURSING HOME ──

"You two can leave. I'm staying." The family stuck by him, as if they had a choice. They had no way of getting back to the hotel because Sam had the car keys.

The band arrived an hour late and apologized. The remaining crowd stayed and got rained upon only for the band to play five songs and call it a night.

After the show ended, once again, just like the baseball game years ago, the family was drenched. "Are you happy now, Sam? You got to see your stupid show. Could we go back to the hotel? I'm fucking soaked and tired," Jude complained.

Sam thought that he must be in deep trouble because Jude never cursed, especially in front of Todd. Sam knew it was stupid to stay, but he originally thought it was going to be a really great show and not just a stupid cover band. Since it was free, Sam enjoyed himself. In his own defense, Sam said, "Come on, Jude! It wasn't so bad. So you got a little wet... Boo hoo. You act like you've never gotten wet before. I know you shower. What is it when you shower? 'Happy water?' Just think of it as taking a shower with clothes on. Right, Todd?" Sam desperately tried having someone agree with him. Todd just laughed, thinking: *My parents have the dumbest arguments.* They left the theme park and for the whole ride back to the hotel, there was silence.

Back at the hotel, everyone was in talking-mode again. Maybe it was because they showered and were out of sticky, wet clothing. When Jude was in a better mood, Sam told them: "I don't want this vacation to end. I don't say it a lot, but I enjoy doing this stuff with you guys."

−194−

— JAMES J. MURPHY III —

"Same here," responded Jude. Todd nodded, not showing much emotion. Besides, kids Todd's age probably didn't know what that was. They just had thousands of thoughts running through their heads. Mostly sexual ones.

Back at the nursing home, after Cyndi made the phone call to Sam Grover and the officers spoke with their captain, they met back in her office. "Is everything taken care of, Cyndi?" asked Officer Conway.

"Yes," she replied back.

"Good," said Officer O'Conner. "Can we leave now? Captain's going to kill us with all this overtime we're taking."

"O'Conner, we've earned it and we're not abusing it. It's not like we're spending time at the coffee shop, which I know you want to do soon," Conway said to his partner.

"You're damn right, Conway. I'm fucking starving!"

"Why didn't you say anything, Officer?" asked Cyndi. "There was food in the breakroom. We all had something to eat."

O'Conner felt like a horse's ass because he hadn't thought about the vending machines or nursing home food that the patients ate. He could have had a free meal simply because he was one of Florida's finest. "With all of today's excitement, it must have slipped my mind."

"My ass," whispered Conway to O'Conner. "Cyndi, I know you have top notch security, but obviously, they aren't getting the job done," Conway told her. "So I've hired some guys we've worked with before to put cameras

— THE NURSING HOME —

into some of the rooms of the nursing home to see if anything fishy is going on. You know... the hallways, the breakroom, lounge room, movie room, entrance, and the parking lot."

"You really are a piece of work. You know that, Conway?"

"We're getting to the bottom of this whether you like it or not, O'Conner."

"Cyndi, I had no idea that my partner was up to this hair-brain scheme."

"Stop kissing her ass, O'Conner."

"Officer Conway, personally, I think it's a brilliant idea," said Cyndi. "Finally, we're going to know who the S.O.B. is who's doing this."

"You're both nuts!" O'Conner said, raising his voice.

"What's your problem, man?" questioned Conway.

"Man?! Did you call me 'man?' I think you've been hanging out with those teenage kids way too long, Conway. The only reason you want surveillance cameras is to put cuffs on that innocent old man."

"Mr. Grover may be an old man, but he's far from innocent. If it's him, fine. If not, fine. We'll catch someone in the act sooner or later. Cyndi, all I ask of you is that you treat your staff the way you usually do. Don't let on about anything and don't mention cameras."

"My lips are sealed," Cyndi agreed.

"Rookie, why I've stood by you this long, I have no idea. Just do me a favor... Don't mention this to the Captain. He'll have our badges for this."

"Too late, O'Conner. I already told him that we're going to have surveillance cameras built into the nursing

−196−

home, which we can watch from a van. He thinks we should move on, but I told him that this way we'll definitely catch the culprit. He agreed to it. So guess who's going to patrol at Rigg's?"

O'Conner's blood pressure was rising as Conway was explaining it to him. "Great, just when we thought things couldn't get any worse. Hopefully Jackson and O'Leary don't hear about this. We'll be laughed out of the squad."

"By the way, O'Conner... You didn't hear the best thing about this."

"What's that?" asked O'Conner, with his arms folded.

"I told the Captain it was *your* idea."

After Conway's comment, O'Conner's blood pressure rose to boiling point. "Please excuse us, Cyndi," the officer insisted. Cyndi left the room. O'Conner was heated. "Conway, I know you're a rookie and want to catch these sons-of-bitches, but come on! At least go over it with me first when you're going to make a stupid decision, especially to the Captain."

"Okay," said Conway. "By the way, I took full blame about the surveillance cameras. I'll be the one boiling in hot water, not you."

"That's good to hear," said O'Conner. "Damnit! You know I try looking out for you, kid, so it looks like you better keep that water boiling because I'm going to join you, even though I think this is a waste of time."

"Let's get out of here, O'Conner, and clock out. The Captain's gonna kill us." The two officers found Cyndi and told her that they'd be in touch. Before heading over to the police station and their respective homes, Conway bought O'Conner coffee and doughnuts.

— THE NURSING HOME —

Throughout the rest of the day, the staff stuck to what Cyndi instructed and continued working. A few hours after the cops had left, four technicians showed up and met with Cyndi. She told them exactly what to do and where to install the surveillance cameras. "If anybody asks what you are doing, just say you're testing grounds for leaks. I want to keep this a secret from my staff. I don't want the patients finding out, either. Got it?" They all motioned with a nod in agreement. "Call me if you need help with anything. I'll be in my office."

The gentlemen did what they were supposed to do. Several patients and employees complained about loud noises and questioned her about the technicians. Cyndi told them a bold, straight-out lie right to their faces. "They are just checking out the building for any leaks," she told them. "Nothing to be concerned about. Let's just concentrate on work."

Chapter 24

The following day at Rigg's Nursing Home, the patients and staff felt like shit because of the interrogation with the officers from the day prior. "I can't believe we're back at this dump, man," said Jay, rubbing his eyes.

"Same here. With yesterday's questioning, sitting in the damn cafeteria, and drinking all that beer... I'm totally burnt out. I'm shocked that I can even stand or see straight," said Jeff.

"Yeah, man. And you can't forget about the smoking! We gotta get full time at Kirk's and ditch this place for good."

"I know, but at least we're getting some dough, right?"

"Act cool. Cyndi's coming." Jay noticed her coming from down the hall.

"Fuck," said Jeff.

"Good morning, guys," greeted Cyndi as she approached them. "Isn't today a beautiful day?"

"Why, yes it is," answered Jeff, sounding overly enthusiastic. Somehow he was able to hide his hangover.

— THE NURSING HOME —

"Good to hear, Jeff. Here are the keys to the maintenance room. Get crackin'."

"Will do," promised Jeff.

"If you guys need me, I'll be in my office."

"You got it, Cyndi," smiled Jay. Cyndi started walking away. "What the fuck is 'Will do?'" asked Jay when Cyndi disappeared.

"I don't know. A saying?"

"How the fuck did you sober up so fast?"

"I don't know. Luck?"

"Let's just get to work, man," said Jay. "Will do..." he repeated to himself, laughing.

Over the last few months of working at Rigg's and Kirk's, the boys had worked quite well together, and rather quick and efficiently. Of course, being best friends since high school probably helped. They knew each other so well, it could be frightening.

Around eight o'clock, the boys served the senior citizens their breakfast. They were assigned to the second floor. They worked from opposite sides of the hall, like they always did on the first floor, and met in the middle. Jay started with the lower room numbers, while Jeff started with the higher ones.

Jeff opened the door to room number 243 silently. The lights were off, but there was light in the room due to the sun shining from outside through the blinds. The television was on at normal volume. When being served breakfast, Jeff had to remember that the patients were either sleeping; grouchy; awake, but incoherent; or just plain stubborn, complaining about what the breakfast was. This isn't a five-star restaurant where you get fancy

–200–

meals, Jeff thought. This is a nursing home. Besides, the patients may complain and bitch about the meal, but at the same time, they did it to themselves. Every day they got a menu with a checklist to select from for the following day. It could be worse; if they didn't check-mark it, it was possible that nothing would get served to them.

Jeff walked into Morris's room with tray in hand. It looked like Morris was sleeping. He was going to leave the tray on Morris's lap and leave, but when he placed the tray down, Morris's eyes opened.

"Hey! What's going on?!" asked Morris, all shook up.

Jeff also got startled and spilled the food on Morris's lap. "Fuck! Holy shit! I thought you were sleeping, Mr. Grover."

"It's Morris. And no, I'm not sleeping anymore."

"Cyndi told us to serve breakfast to the patients."

"Doesn't anybody leave trays on the nightstand anymore?"

"I don't know," answered Jeff.

"You've been here, what? Four months, kid?"

"Hard to remember with all the shit that's been going on around here."

"Shit?" repeated Morris. "Is that all you youngsters do? Curse? At least wait until you're my age, kid. Then you can bitch all ya want," kidded Morris.

Jeff laughed. "Sorry, Mr. Grover."

"At least you've got some manners. Once again, call me Morris."

"You got it, Morris. I better serve the rest of the meals."

"Well, at least help clean this food off of me, wouldcha? Thank God it was nothing messy," said Morris.

— THE NURSING HOME —

"Right," said Jeff, beginning to clean the little bits of tapioca pudding that had spilled. Then he picked up the cold eggs, unopened apple juice, and a piece of toast that actually didn't look toasted at all. He held his breath the whole time, thinking, *Could this guy have shit himself in his sleep?* Jeff just couldn't bear the smell of old people. He had been at Rigg's for about four months and still couldn't get used to the smell. "Talk to you later." Jeff was about to close the door on his way out when he heard the old man's voice.

"Jeff, is it?"

Jeff turned around. "Yes, sir."

"I heard a rumor that you and your buddy work at a video store."

"That's right."

"My roommate, Felix, passed away last October. I was left this VCR, but no tapes to play. I hate waiting to watch the Wednesday night movie. Could you pick up some movies if I write the titles down for you?"

"Sure." Jeff gave him a pen and paper. "Shoot."

Morris jotted down the names of three movies. "No rush."

"You got it," assured Jeff. He made his exit and continued with his breakfast stops, while Morris went back to sleep.

The boys met in between. "Yo, man. I just had a conversation with that old dude, Morris Grover."

"You mean that loon who was yelling and screaming at Nurse Helen?" questioned Jay.

"Yeah, man. I did," Jeff told his friend. "By accident, I spilled food on him..."

— 202 —

"Oh, you're fucked, man. Nice knowing ya."

"Oh, would you shut up for a minute, Jay? He only yelled at me for a minute, then he was cool about it. He inquired about us working at a video store, so I told him that we do. He was telling me how tired he is of the Wednesday night movie and asked if we could rent him some VHS tapes, so I said that we can."

"Dude, I know you're completely fried, especially after last night, but do you realize what you just did?"

"No, man. Tell me."

"Since you agreed to get this old bag videos to watch, he's always going to bug you now."

"Oh, would you give it a rest?"

"Don't you get it, Jeff? Now you're going to be his video-bitch. 'Oh, Jeff, rent me this, rent me that.' First, he'll give you money to rent the movie, then slowly, but surely, he's going to pull the 'I don't have the money today' routine. You'll let him slide because you feel bad, then BAM!!! He's got you hook, line, and sinker!" joked Jay.

"Where do you get your facts, man?"

"Horror movies. Besides, you can't trust old people. They're evil."

"I know they smell like shit and it makes me want to gag, but *evil?*"

"Yes, evil."

"How so?"

"My grandfather... nicest person in the world... gave us kids everything and took the family out to dinner a few times a year. He also told us never to steal, do drugs, or abuse alcohol. Well, I've followed maybe a third of what the old bastard told me. Then, one day, out of the blue,

─── THE NURSING HOME ───

we're all food shopping together... the family, that is... and my father's about to pay for the groceries... and I see my grandfather stuffing a pack of gum into his pocket. I asked what he was doing. He said, 'Keep quiet and mind your own business.' Then it progressed to candy, bread, coffee, and who knows what else. Finally, the old fuck died. One time, the check-out lady even caught him doing it. Of course, he said he didn't realize it, so the stupid bimbo let him go. She fell for the old-person-sympathy-act."

"I don't think Mr. Grover would do that."

"Speaking of Grover, Beth wants us to go to the park tonight for a meeting concerning your new friend."

"He's not my friend, dude. Let's continue working. We'll eat lunch together."

"Meet ya in a little bit, man." They went off; task at hand.

Noontime approached and the boys were on their lunch break as Beth and Ron were coming in to work. While they were clocking in, Beth told Ron to meet her at the park later that night. "It's very important."

Ron agreed like a nervous twit, "Oh-oh-okay."

"Damnit, Ron! I've known you almost half a year now. Stop stuttering! I'm not going to scold ya."

"Oh-oh-okay," he said again.

"Park! Tonight! Be there!"

Instead of stuttering, he responded, "You got it, Beth."

Before Beth started with her duties, she rushed to the breakroom and dropped her snack off in her locker. She also put her chicken dumpling soup into the refrigerator.

– 204 –

— JAMES J. MURPHY III —

"Boy, somebody's in a hurry," teased Jay.

"I don't need this right now, guys," she answered quickly. Then she added, "Park! Tonight! Be there!"

"Did you tell Ron?" asked Jeff.

"Yeah, I did."

"Can't wait to heckle him later," Jay told her.

"About what?"

"He gets to work with Rita today," stated Jay.

"How the hell do you guys know about that?"

"Don't you ever see how he acts around her?" asked Jeff. "Whatever she needs, he gets right away. He's glued to her ass," he kidded, "which isn't a bad place to be, if you know what I mean."

"Ohh!" yelled Jay with enthusiasm.

"You guys are too much," laughed Beth.

"Just hope the poor kid gets laid for all his efforts," said Jeff.

"Isn't he saving himself for the girl in *Star Trek II?*" snickered Jay.

"I got to get to work... Later, guys," Beth said.

"Later," they both said simultaneously. They both headed back to work and clocked out at the end of their shift.

Morris was inside his same old boring room, channel-surfing to see what was on TV. *Look at me,* he said to himself. *I'm eighty-four years old, channel-surfing in this pale-white-wall room that looks like a Goddamn insane asylum for the insane. After yesterday's performance, that's what people might think of me. Besides that, the same dead plant has been sitting*

–205–

— THE NURSING HOME —

in this room since I've arrived. Hell, it might have even been here before Felix arrived. God bless his soul. How can I show my face in the lounge room again? Everyone's going to hate me.

There was a knock at the door. Morris did not respond. A hand took grasp of the doorknob and turned it slightly to the right. The person applied body weight and opened the door completely. "Good afternoon, Mr. Grover," a cheerful voice said. Morris was just staring at the television, paying no mind to the lovely voice. It was Nurse Rochelle, a sub-in nurse from another hospital affiliated with Rigg's. She was filling in for one of the nurses at Rigg's who took time off for personal issues. "How are you today, Mr. Grover?" No response. "Do you need anything right now, Mr. Grover?" Still no response. "Do you like me, Mr. Grover?" she asked, with her dark brown eyes staring at him.

"Like you? I don't even know ya, lady."

"Is it because I'm black and yo' nuttin' but a whacked-out white boy?" She began getting racy and started going ghetto on the old man, moving her large body around, waving her hand in the air and putting her finger in his face. She was about five foot six and wearing a lot of gold jewelry.

What was Morris going to do? Fight her? He was eighty-four years old and needed assistance just to go to the bathroom. Instead, Morris said, "You want to bring race into this, I definitely could... but I'm a gentleman, and I'm not racist. What the fuck is 'whack?' The only whack I know is when I misbehaved as a youngster, I got whacked... or a mob member squealing and getting whacked."

– 206 –

JAMES J. MURPHY III

The nurse was absolutely oblivious to the terminology Morris was throwing at her. She was getting frustrated at the old man and was about to knock his dentures out. Good thing for Morris, Cyndi had walked by and witnessed everything from the nurse threatening Morris to her racist comments, and ordered security up right away.

As security escorted the sub out, she yelled: "I kick yo' ass, old man! Yo' dead! Hear me?!" Morris paid no mind to her. Rochelle looked in Cyndi's direction, irate. "Same goes for you, bitch! Bitch! Yo' dead! Bitch! Yo' dead!"

Cyndi was fed up with everyone. "Don't worry, Rochelle. Your supervisor's gonna love me when I send you back. You'll be their problem again, not mine. Before going back, why don't you go back to school? Maybe you could learn to come up with more than two words." As security dragged Rochelle away, everyone could still hear her echoing down the hall.

Cyndi asked Morris if he was okay. All Morris could say was, "Cyndi, where do you find these people?"

"I really don't know, Morris. I'm going to call the hospital where this one came from and report her. I'll have Nurse Helen take you to the lounge room." Morris figured that it couldn't get any worse.

Cyndi contacted Conrad's Hospital to report Nurse Rochelle. The receptionist must have been out to lunch. Cyndi left a message on the answering machine, saying: "This is Cyndi Gillian from Rigg's Nursing Home. I just had the nurse you sent me escorted out by security. Nurse Rochelle threatened a patient of ours with assault because he was not responding quick enough. I don't know how

—— THE NURSING HOME ——

you people do business, but we don't operate like this at Rigg's. You're lucky I didn't press any charges, although I should have." The message time ran out. Cyndi called back again to continue her message: "Don't bother calling back. I won't respond." She purposely slammed the phone hard so that the other end could hear it on the recording. Cyndi felt great afterwards.

Meanwhile, Nurse Helen got Morris into his wheelchair and wheeled him to the lounge room. When he entered, there was a lot of commotion. *Oh, no*, Morris thought to himself. *Hopefully this isn't about yesterday.* Morris felt embarrassed. The patients that still had all their marbles were clapping and whistling, just like at a party when cheering somebody after their fifth beer. The incoherent patients sat there clueless, staring into space.

Nurse Helen said, "I see you have a fan base. I'll leave you alone with your friends." Then she walked away.

A voice from half the distance shouted: "Hey, Mori, old boy! How the fuck are ya?"

Morris wheeled himself over to his buddies. "What's going on here, fellas? By the way, Pauly, my name is Morris."

"We know, Mori," assured Pauly. "You've only told us a thousand times."

"By the second or third time, I'd figured you'd get it right."

"It don't matter how many times you tell good old Pauly. He'll say it the way he wants to say it," stated Ralph.

"He'll always be a ball-buster," added Frank.

– 208 –

JAMES J. MURPHY III

"You're damn right, I am, gentlemen. When I was a wee toddler... young fella, if I may... I had the nickname Nervy Pauly. It's because family and friends said that I can get on anybody's nerves. Since this is the twenty-first century, I think Ball-Busting Pauly serves justice. Don't you?" he asked. They all agreed. "Enough about me. What the hell happened to you yesterday, Mori, old boy?"

"I don't exactly know, fellas. I was called to report to Cyndi's office for questioning, just like everybody else. In the office was Cyndi; that overweight, middle-aged cop, who you could tell has never missed a meal; and the young, wise-ass, Goddamn know-it-all cop in his twenties. Before I knew it, the young punk's questioning everything. 'Where were you this day? That day?' Blah, blah, blah. Let's see, I'm eighty-four years old, in a wheelchair, and in a nursing home; where the fuck do you think I was?" Morris tried not to use foul language, but just thinking about that cop steamed him up. He usually left that type of talk to Pauly. "Maybe he wasn't crazy about my answers. The next thing I know is that this young kid's reading me my rights and placing me under arrest for murder."

"Are you kidding us, Morris?" questioned Ralph.

"I kid you not. Hell, I've never even had a traffic violation."

"Are you going to sue the police force for excessive use of man power?" asked Frank.

"You know, I should sue these bastards, Frank. That was one of the most embarrassing and painful experiences of my life. Did any of you ever have metal bracelets applied so tightly around your wrists, putting so much pressure on your bones, that you are in pain?" Everyone shook their

THE NURSING HOME

heads for 'No.' Morris continued, "If I was younger, would I sue? Damn right; better believe it. Today, I'm not. I even told Cyndi why I won't. By the time I get the lawyers, the paperwork, and a trial, it'll probably be too late. I could see myself winning the case, dividing the shares with my lawyer, and then by the time I receive the money, I'll probably be dead, so that means that I can't enjoy it."

"So, Mori's got this all figured out. Dontcha, old boy?"

"As a matter of fact, yes, I do, Pauly."

"I gotta admit, I have a lot of respect for you after all you've been through, Mori, old boy." Pauly didn't say that to a lot of people, but he meant every word of it when he told it to Morris Grover.

"Thanks. That means a lot, Pauly."

"So, this only means one thing," interrupted Wade.

"What would that be?" asked Morris.

"If you're not the killer, then who is?" They all looked at each other, puzzled.

"That's an interesting question, Wade," replied Morris. "All I can tell you is that it's not me." Morris tried to change the conversation. "That was yesterday, gentlemen. Wait 'til I tell ya what just happened to me a little while ago."

"What was that, Morris?" asked Wade.

"Maybe if ya shut up for a moment, Wade... Mori, here, could tell us," Pauly said.

"Well, gentlemen... I was lying in bed, watching television, feeling ashamed of myself because of what transpired yesterday and thinking of how I am going to explain this. I was walloping in my own misery and this large, colored woman, weighing two hundred pounds

– 210 –

plus, comes into my room, trying to butter me up. I pay no mind to her."

"I don't recall if I've seen her or not," said Ralph.

"Trust me, Ralphie boy, you can't miss her. Her ass is the size of a movie theater screen. How do you think they came up with the idea of widescreen for movies?" kidded Pauly. The gang laughed out loud.

"You've got a million jokes, Pauly, dontcha?" said Frank.

"Yes, I do, Frank. Continue with the story, Mori."

"Where was I, now?" Morris thought for a second. "Oh, yes... so the large, colored woman entered my room. I guess she wasn't happy that I didn't respond, so she started throwing all these racial slurs at me, like she was from the street or something."

"So, what did you do?" Ralph was curious.

"I didn't want to sink to her level, but I did stick up for myself without using any racial slurs."

"That's good to hear," said Frank.

"Then she started moving her arms around and she was pointing her finger close to my face. I never saw so many rings on a hand in my life. If she wasn't working in a nursing home, my guess would have been her working in a jewelry store. Holy crap!" Everyone snickered.

"Continue, Mori," insisted Pauly.

"I think her name was Rochelle; I don't remember. She started with more threats, like: 'I'll knock your teeth down your throat,' you know what I mean? It just so happens that Cyndi heard and witnessed the whole thing. She took action and had security escort her out of the building."

— THE NURSING HOME —

"Cyndi seems to be in right place at the right time," said Ralph.

"I always knew Cyndi was on our side." Frank smiled.

"She's been here for us a lot more lately... I gotta admit," agreed Pauly. "This is only because one of her employees kicked the bucket. I still don't trust her," Pauly stated with confidence. There was no way that anybody could convince Pauly of anything once he had his mind set on it.

"The one thing that definitely caught my eye with this heavy-set, colored woman were the dyed-green streaks in her hair. Or lime, whatever the hell you call it. I never saw anything like it in my life," Morris went on.

"You didn't get out that much, did you, Mori, old boy? That's nothing. Go to New York City," said Pauly.

"No thanks," replied Morris. The gang continued talking amongst themselves for the remainder of the afternoon.

Officers O'Conner and Conway were on their way to the nursing home. "I can't believe you talked the Captain into having us hide outside the nursing home. Also, I can't believe he bought into your stupid idea," O'Conner said.

"When we catch the fucker, who's going to look stupid then?" shot back Conway, all peppered up.

"We'll see, rookie. Just keep driving."

"Let's see what's on the radio," insisted Conway, trying to change the subject. He reached over to adjust the controls.

— JAMES J. MURPHY III —

"Keep your damn eyes on the road, Conway!"

"God, O'Conner, you sound like my old man when I was growing up. 'Eyes on the road!' 'Don't do this, don't do that.'"

"Maybe your old man should have given you a whippin' or disciplined you."

"Don't worry... His mouth did all the disciplining. When he opened it up, that was punishment enough," Conway carried on.

"Man, you poor youngsters have it so tough," teased O'Conner. "'My Daddy raised his voice to me.' Boy, you know nothing about punishment. Growing up, my father took off his belt and gave me a whippin' if I misbehaved. You probably got an allowance for aiming straight into the toilet bowl whenever you took a piss. I also bet you got money from the Tooth Fairy after losing a tooth. I got none of that. Hell, once my old man knocked out one of my teeth because he had a bad day."

"Alright, I get the point, O'Conner."

"You young kids wouldn't know a day of punishment if it hit you in the ass!" O'Conner said, outraged, his hands clenched and spit flying as he spoke.

Conway finally tried to get a word in. "The only difference between you and my father is that he's an asshole. You, O'Conner, are just overweight."

"Real funny."

"Just put something on the radio, would ya?"

"Fine." O'Conner's station-surfing was slower than an old lady with a walker. He had to hear the beat to every song before deciding.

"Get out of the way," Conway snapped impatiently.

—— THE NURSING HOME ——

He turned the radio knob to a pop station. "Now that's what I'm talking about! Listen to that dance beat, man."

"You call that music, kid? Listen to this..." insisted O'Conner, putting on a country station. "Yee-Haw! Now that's what *I'm* talking about."

"Is this where you get your southern hospitality, O'Conner? Listening to the fucking country station?!"

"I was born with good manners." O'Conner smiled.

"Next, you're gonna be wearing a cowboy hat with matching boots and doing a fucking hoe-down." O'Conner turned the music off in disgust. "I'm just kidding, O'Conner," Conway told him. "Play your precious country music."

"No, it's okay. I just wanted a reaction out of you, rookie."

"Well, you got one."

"Truth is, I'm a huge Iron Butterfly fan." O'Conner began singing while playing air guitar.

"Who's Iron Butterfly?"

"I forgot... You only know what's on the top of the charts for today." Then, changing the subject, O'Conner asked, "Don't you think it's going to be obvious? Us sitting outside the nursing home in the same van every night?"

"We'll try not to make it that obvious," answered Conway.

"All I'm saying is that even though the people working at Rigg's may not be the sharpest tools in the shed, I'd still think they'd notice a two thousand pound gray van sitting outside the building."

"Well, it could be abandoned," Conway replied.

"You have all of the answers tonight, dontcha, kid?"

"O'Conner, how stupid do you think I am?"

"Pretty stupid, considering you put me in this situation with you."

"Listen, you big ox, we'll park in back of the building. We will be out of sight. Nobody will suspect anything. All of the employees enter the main entrance of the building and that's where security stands guard. Even if security stood guard in the back, do you really think they would approach us?"

"I just hope you're right, Conway."

"O'Conner, I know security, especially at Rigg's. They don't approach anybody unless they are being approached. All they wanna do is stand, do nothing, maybe take a trip to the vending machine, go home, and get paid."

"I don't want to look like an asshole, or as you would say, a big, dumb ox."

"I never said 'dumb,' but if you want to add it, that's fine with me. O'Conner, we had the best technicians installing the cameras into the nursing home and setting it up so we can watch it from this van right here."

"Conway, not 'we.' *You* had the best technicians installing the cameras into the nursing home. Me, I'm just here for the ride and to keep an eye on you."

"Whatever you say, O'Conner. We are going to see some peculiar action occurring, if any at all. For instance, what's going on in the breakroom, where all of this crap seems to be happening. Plus, I offered the technicians a little extra to plant a camera into Morris Grover's room."

"So, what you're saying is that you bribed the technicians just so you can catch whoever's doing this. Conway, what you are doing is called 'invasion of privacy.'"

—— THE NURSING HOME ——

"If it is Morris Grover... or any other patient, which I doubt... we have the right to know. If that means stooping as low as planting a hidden camera into his room, so be it. Plus, what you call a bribe... let's just call it a tip. We will be the first to see it on video and rush to the rescue."

"I said it once and I'll say it again: I just hope you're right."

"We're here," said Conway as they pulled into the back lot of the nursing home. "All we have to do is turn on the monitors and sit all night."

"Alright," said O'Conner.

"Hell, O'Conner, if you want to sleep half the shift, fine... as long as you let me sleep the second half."

A huge grin came upon O'Conner's face. Getting paid to sleep? he thought to himself. "You know, I apologize. I underestimated you, rookie."

"You may think I'm dumb at times, O'Conner, but I'm definitely not stupid. When we can make some dough without really exerting ourselves, why not? Right?"

"Like I said, Conway, thanks for volunteering us."

Conway shook his head with a smile. "Here, check this out, O'Conner. We can zoom in and out."

"Let's zoom in to the breakroom," insisted O'Conner.

Conway zoomed in. "Nobody there. Let's check out reception." A staff member was answering phones and filing her nails. "I've got an even better idea," insisted Conway. "Let's zoom in on room 243."

"Come on, Conway. Besides, haven't you done enough damage to this old man?"

"I'm not accusing him of anything right now. I did

— 216 —

all of that yesterday." The camera zoomed in to Morris's room. "What's he doing?"

"Looks like he's eating dinner and watching a television series."

"Ha, ha, ha," Conway laughed. "What stupid show is he watching?"

"How would I know?"

"Should I get a close-up?"

"Leave the guy alone," barked O'Conner. "The guy can't even eat in peace. At least he doesn't know we're watching him." O'Conner got up to stretch. A big laugh came from Conway's mouth. "What's so funny now?" O'Conner looked over and began laughing hysterically. Morris Grover had been innocently eating dinner... then, out of nowhere... his hand went down south and he was scratching his ass. O'Conner and Conway were in tears from laughing their asses off. "Holy shit!" yelled O'Conner happily. "I sure as fuck needed a good laugh. I just felt like I was fourteen again."

"Picture if we got to do this every day," Conway told the older cop.

"Yeah, we'd be having the time of our lives. God, I miss being young. Enjoy it while you can, kid. Don't end up like me."

"You're too hard on yourself, Dad," kidded Conway.

"I'll give you 'Dad,'" he shot back. "This old man still has a few good years in him." The two looked at the screen and bursted out laughing again.

"Could you picture putting this on You Tube, O'Conner?"

"What is 'You Tube?'"

—— THE NURSING HOME ——

"You gotta get around more, my friend. With You Tube, you can record yourself or somebody else, post it online, and anybody or everybody could watch it."

"Really?" asked O'Conner, interested.

"Yeah, all you have to do is come up with a title for the video. For instance, it would be awesome if we could post what Morris Grover did. We'd title that one: 'Old Man Scratching His Ass.'" The two had a great time. All O'Conner and Conway did was laugh at the patients and staff and made sure nothing fishy was happening.

They were assigned to work at night because that was when all of the incidents were occurring. Until something happened, O'Conner and Conway would be paid to sit in a van, eat doughnuts, drink coffee, and laugh their asses off.

Jeff left his house, driving a used 1998 sedan that he purchased eight months ago for about fifteen hundred dollars. Actually, his father bought him the car so Jeff didn't have to bother him or Mrs. Randle for their keys every five minutes. Mr. Randle figured that maybe Jeff would become more responsible if he had a car. He hadn't changed and probably wouldn't anytime in the near future. Jeff still drank, smoked, and acted like a slob, except with a car, he could take his actions anywhere he wanted to instead of just under his parents' roof.

Even though the car was not in the best of shape, it did not bother Jeff. To him, it was an escape from his parents and it gave him independence. The car had the loudest engine. It could wake up somebody who was in a coma. The back doors had been smashed in and there

– 218 –

were dents and rust spots all over. It was a black car fading to dark gray, but it was Jeff's baby.

Before Jeff even pulled into Jay's driveway, Mr. Kent called to his son: "Jay, your annoying friend is here."

"How do you know?"

"You can hear that engine a mile away. What are you? Stoned or something?"

"That's a good one, Dad," Jay said, considering he did get stoned a lot with Jeff. "See ya, Dad." His father said nothing. Jay closed the door behind him.

Jeff was sitting in his car with the engine running and music playing. "Hop in, man!"

Jay opened the door on the passenger's side and got in. Him and Jeff give each other a high five. "Yo, what's up, bro?"

"Nothing, man," Jeff responded.

"Do you know what's so important that Beth needs us to meet for?"

"Not sure, dude."

"Hopefully she goes over it quickly because I'm filling in for someone tonight at Kirk's," informed Jay.

"Lucky bastard," said Jeff. "Can't believe you were asked to work without me."

"I know, dude. That never happens. Why don't you just come with me, anyway? You can keep me company."

"What's the point, Jay? I'm not getting paid to be there."

"You can look at the horror section and help me out."

"I'll pass. Besides, I think I'll fall asleep watching *Dracula* tonight."

— THE NURSING HOME —

"Dude, I'm putting away the imports tonight. Hopefully I rent out a few. What do you say?" Jay said cunningly.

"Sorry, dude. Got the movie in the DVD player already."

"Whatever, man. I offer you great horror and you go to sleep to *Dracula*."

"Well, he is The Count, man. Don't mess with the most famous vampire in the world!"

"Alright, man. Just chill, wouldcha?"

"Here we are. Beth and Ron should be here, too. They got out at eight," Jeff informed his friend.

"It's eight already!? Fuck! I was supposed to be at the video store a half hour ago. Let me call Alan," Jay insisted. Jay had his cell phone in hand. He scrolled down to the number for Kirk's and hit the green button.

The phone rang three times and finally a voice on the other end said: "Kirk's Video Store."

"Yo, Alan, man... It's Jay."

"Where the hell are ya, Jay? You were supposed to be here a half hour ago."

"Car trouble," Jay told him.

"You don't have a car."

"Exactly," Jay responded. "Well, I'll get there as fast as I can."

"Don't sweat it, Jay. If you make it, fine. If not, oh well. Hopefully we'll see you tomorrow."

"Thanks, Alan," said Jay. "And Alan..."

"Yes?"

"Please don't start the horror section without me."

"Goodnight," he laughed. Alan knew Jay and Jeff were burnouts, but he also knew that they were good for

— 220 —

the store because of their genuine love of movies. He just wished Jay would stop losing track of time.

"So, how did Alan take it, man?" Jeff asked his friend.

"He understood and was cool about it. But I hate letting him down."

"Wait a minute... Jay actually giving a damn about somebody?"

"Well, I like this video store, dude."

"Hopefully we open our own video store one day, as well."

"Between the two of us, we probably own enough movies to open a video store," Jay kidded. Him and Jeff got videos and DVDs real cheap because they were employees. Having a Kirk's card helped even more because they accumulated points. Prices were lower because videos didn't sell anymore; everybody wanted DVDs and Blu-Rays. Not to mention many people even downloaded their own movies for free. However, Jeff and Jay preferred the original product. "Hopefully Beth gets her ass over here soon, man," complained Jay.

"She will, dude. Just relax," said Jeff. "She's probably getting changed and Ron is probably checking if any dust got on his action figures."

"Women! Why the hell does she have to change?"

"Dude, to be honest, I can't blame her. Do you want to smell like 'old person' when you're meeting people?"

"Well, no, but it's only us. She doesn't seem to mind our smell."

"That's the difference between them and us," Jeff pointed out. "We carry 'young people' smell. Our smell goes away after a shower. With 'old person' smell,

— THE NURSING HOME —

they could wash, shower, and spray. It doesn't make a difference what they do; it doesn't go away."

"Dude, you think too much," kidded Jay.

"No, man. Not enough."

"What is up with Ron and his space DVD collection?"

"He's a nerd; enough said."

Beth and Ron finally arrived at the park. What seemed like a lifetime to Jay was only forty-five minutes. "Where the fuck were you guys?" he asked, waving his hands around in the air.

"What's the matter? Is it past your bedtime?" teased Beth.

"Yeah, past his bedtime..." repeated Ron, mocking him in a shy, little boy voice.

"No, it ain't," Jay snapped back. "Thing is... I have to work at Kirk's tonight."

"Thought you were off," said Beth.

"They wanted to give me extra hours. Plus, I get to put away the horror movies."

"Sounds like fun," said Beth. "Like I was saying... we worked until eight, went to my house to get changed, and then came to see you bone-heads."

"Let's just get down to business," insisted Ron, seeming interested.

"What's the scoop, Beth?" asked Jeff.

"What is this meeting about?" questioned Jay.

"Do you guys remember us talking at Moe's Diner two nights before we all got interrogated at Rigg's?" asked Beth.

"Yeah," answered Jeff. "That was one of my sober nights."

— 222 —

"Okay. Do you guys remember me saying I have every patient's profile on a CD?" They all nodded in unison. "I have everybody's profile from 1893 and up."

"So what?" said Jay.

"All you can say is 'So what?!'" asked Beth.

"Tell us, Beth," encouraged Jeff.

"Well, right after we all got interrogated, I was at work looking up these profiles of past patients on the computer. It listed what I told you: 1893 to the present. Out of nowhere, all of the prior dates were listed. I thought somebody was playing games with me. I was getting nervous. Kind of like someone sending me a death threat."

"Maybe you missed the numbers the first time, Beth. It happens," interrupted Ron.

"Don't you dare accuse me of missing something, you worthless twig! I know what I saw!" Beth's face changed color. She was so enraged about Ron's comment that she wanted to kill him. Ron was so frightened that he nearly wet his pants. He kept thinking that he felt dampness on his boxers, but it had to be his imagination.

"Alright, guys... Let's just calm down," said Jeff, playing referee.

"I thought somebody was holding out on us, but did you notice that now, after Sue died and after the interrogation, somebody wants us to see the first fifty years? I'm telling you guys, this is our clue!"

"I hope you're right," said Jay.

"I know I am," insisted Beth. "You explain to me... Why *now*? Why not before?"

"Maybe it was a computer error," Jay suggested.

—— THE NURSING HOME ——

"Computer error?! Are you kidding me?" Her frustration was growing because her friends weren't seeing things from her point of view.

"Beth, I have no clue. I'm clueless, alright?" said Jay.

"Can't you see that someone obviously wants us to see this information?"

"So what are you saying, Beth?" asked Jeff. "That whoever posted those patients' names may be the killer?"

"Yes!" yelled Beth.

"This is too much for me to handle all at once," Ron said, feeling worried. "I need to sit down."

"Don't sit down yet, Ron," Beth told him. "It's Tuesday night. It's been too quiet at Rigg's lately, so we'll give it a few days."

"Give what a few days, Beth?" asked Ron.

"Until Saturday night, around nine-ish."

"What happens around nine-ish?" asked Jay.

"We break into Rigg's and we find this thing!" Beth told them.

Jeff's response was, "Cool!"

"We don't even know what we are looking for," said Ron.

"Yeah, we do," said Beth. "Whoever posted those names on the screen. I have the CD right here." Beth showed her friends the copy of the CD in her bag. "Saturday night, we break into Rigg's and that's all she wrote."

"How do we get past security?"

"Easy, Ron. Bribe them with doughnuts."

"Be serious, Beth."

"We'll have Jeff and Jay distract security. While security is being distracted, me and you sneak in."

– 224 –

— JAMES J. MURPHY III —

"Oh, dude! Saturday night's gonna be awesome! I can't wait!" yelled Jeff as he and Jay looked at one another and gave a high five.

"You guys may not be able to wait, but I sure as heck can," Ron told them nervously in a low voice.

"Ronny, my boy, you gotta stop acting like a pussy and grow yourself a pair," Jay told him.

"I am not a P-U-S-S-Y." He actually spelled out the word. "Grow a pair of what?"

"No wonder why Rita hasn't fucked ya," Jay teased him. He must have struck a nerve.

"Leave Rita out of this, Jay!"

"Dude, we all know you like her. If you keep acting shy and talking low, how are you gonna get laid?"

"It's possible. Maybe some girls like a low-key man."

"Fine, Ron, but you're still a little boy. Rita talks to you all the time, man. I'm tellin' ya, she wants to jump your bones," Jay said. Ron was all smiles. "All you gotta do is make a move. Besides, Ron, if you don't make a move, how are you going to prepare for the girl in *Star Trek II*?" Jay tried reasoning with him.

"Well, I wanted to save myself for Lieutenant Saavik."

"Rita is here, the space babe is not."

"Oh, now look what you did, Jay," complained Beth. "And I have to drive him home!"

"Did what?" laughed Jay.

"Why don't we call it a night?" announced Jeff.

"Jeff calling it a night so early? That's unusual," said Beth.

"Well, we got no beer or pot. Might as well go home and finish watching *Dracula*."

THE NURSING HOME

"Loser," said Jay.

"Hey, Jay... don't you still have to go to work?" Beth knew how forgetful he was.

"Fuck it. What's the point now?"

Before they all left, Beth reminded everyone to meet at the park Saturday night at approximately 8:50pm.

"Why can't we just meet at Rigg's?" asked Jeff.

"Too risky," she said. "Besides, we're trying to sneak in and your car could wake the dead."

"I like my car," he kidded.

"We're taking my car to the nursing home Saturday night. We're sneaking in, so wear all black or camouflage so nobody sees us. Also, remember your cell phones, so we can contact each other," she said, laying out the rules. Just like soldiers, they all nodded.

After Beth's speech, they gave each other high fives and said goodnight. Beth was going to drive Ron home and Jay was going to bum a ride off Jeff. Before Jeff and Jay left, they had one last cigarette outside of Jeff's car.

"Do you believe we're actually doing this, man?" asked Jay.

"Saturday night's gonna be nuts," Jeff smiled.

"Just hope we know what we're getting ourselves into, man." Jay began to worry a little.

"Dude, don't sweat it. Here... listen to this horror mix I just made." Before Jeff even started playing horror movie theme songs for his anxious friend, they were already at Jay's house.

"Goodnight, dude," said Jay. "Be safe, alright?"

"Same to you, dude. I'll pick you up Saturday. Besides, we're working together this week, anyway." Jeff said one last thing before he backed out. "Jay, just chill." Then they both gave each other knucks with their fists. Jeff went home and Jay was in a better mood.

For the first few minutes of the ride to Ron's house, there was complete silence. Ron was sitting in the passenger's seat with his hand under his chin, thinking, with a sad expression on his face.

"For God's sake! What's wrong?" Beth asked, breaking the silence.

"Nothing," he said, as if he got all F's on his report card and was hiding it from his mother.

"You can tell me, Ron."

"Okay," he started. "I didn't mean to upset you back at the park."

"You're still on that, Ron? I got over that a while ago. I let out some steam; end of story."

"I just don't want our friendship to be affected by this."

"Ron, you know you're always going to be my friend. You are just a nervous twit who needs to relax," she smiled. Ron felt better with Beth's encouraging words. "Also, Jeff and Jay like you, too."

"That's good to hear."

"They just like chopping on you. Especially about the whole Rita thing." Ron began blushing. "By the way, I never told them anything. They figured it out on their own."

"I wonder how..." Ron said.

"They may be burnouts, but they're not stupid."

"You're right, Beth. Maybe I should cover my tracks," he kidded.

– 227 –

— THE NURSING HOME —

They arrived at Ron's house. "This is the end of the road, kid."

"Yeah, I'd better get out. After all of this is over, maybe one day you can come over."

"That would be nice; a trip to the geek museum." Beth could picture all the entertainment memorabilia in his room.

"I'm not just about science fiction shows, you know. I'm also a huge history buff, as well."

"I'll pick you up Saturday night."

"Okay," he responded. "I'll see you then, unless we are working together another time this week."

"You got it, Ron. And remember: Wear black or camouflage!" Beth reminded him, yelling out the window. Ron waved and Beth drove off into the night.

Chapter 25

The Grovers packed their suitcases the night before and had planned to get a good night's sleep. They had only left out their toothbrushes and mouthwash to freshen their breath in the morning. They knew the next day they'd have to check out of the hotel and hand in the keys to reception.

When Wednesday morning came, the Grovers woke up and washed their faces. Sam left the television on so he could hear the score of Tuesday night's Marlins game. Also, he wanted to hear what the temperature was going to be and if it was going to rain.

"We had a great time this past week, didn't we?" asked Jude.

"We sure did, Mom."

"Yeah, Jude. We did have a good time," Sam agreed. "I wish we didn't have to leave."

"Unfortunately, somebody's got work tomorrow," Jude brought to his attention.

"Don't remind me," begged Sam. Sam and Todd

— THE NURSING HOME —

grabbed the packed suitcases and were on their way out. They left the light on for the maid. When Jude closed the hotel door numbered 2217, they heard the click of the lock.

On their way to the car, Jude made a comment to her son. "It looks like you're struggling there a little... aye, Todd?"

"Do you want to carry this suitcase, Mom? Most of your stuff is in here, anyway."

"We'll switch, Todd," requested Sam. "You carry this one and I'll carry that one." Todd quickly agreed, knowing his father's suitcase couldn't be any heavier. Todd took the suitcase Sam had and Sam made an effort to pick up the suitcase Todd had. "Holy shit! Jude, did you pack the hotel? How much crap do you need?"

"It's not that much, Sam. Women always tend to bring more stuff than men. It's natural, you know?" she explained to them.

Sam and Todd looked at one another and laughed while saying simultaneously: "Women."

The Grover family was on line, waiting to return the keys and find out what their total was for the week. The person at the desk, a woman with a southern accent, said: "Next." The family approached the desk and the receptionist asked, "Now, how did y'all enjoy it here?"

"We had a great time. Thank you," responded Sam.

"The bill is $660.00. How would you be paying for this?"

Sam was just about to answer when a thought popped into his head.

"What are you waiting for, Sam?" Jude interrupted.

"Nothing, dear." He looked at the woman's name tag. "Tan-ya, is it?" he said with a salesman-like smile.

"Tanya," she said back.

"How much would it cost if we wanted to stay three more nights?"

"About $330.00, I believe, but we'd have to give you another room."

"Why's that?"

"What are you doing, Sam?" Jude asked curiously.

"Because," Tanya began explaining, "we have another guest who is next to get your room and it wouldn't be fair to him if we broke our promise for him to stay here at The Blue Inn."

"I see," said Sam. "Would we be able to get another room?"

"How about your job, dear?" Jude was getting nervous.

"In a minute, Jude," he told her, as if she was bothering him. Todd didn't know what to make of the situation. If his father wanted to stay, he'd be all for it. For Todd, that would be more fun and bikinis.

Tanya checked availability on the computer and informed him that he wouldn't be able to get a room until later that afternoon.

"That would be fine, Tanya," agreed Sam.

"The only payment due right now would be for the room you've already rented for the past week."

"Here you go," Sam said in a show-off way, handing her his credit card. She swiped his card and handed it back to him with a paper to sign. He signed the piece of paper and returned it to her. Then she handed him his receipt and told him his new room, room 1122, would be available after 4:00pm. Sam thanked her. Then they got

—— THE NURSING HOME ——

into Sam's sedan, which was one of the very few beat-up cars in the parking lot, considering just about everyone else was driving rentals that were up-to-date. Sam looked at Jude and Todd and said, "Let's go to the diner."

"The diner?!"

"What's the problem, Jude?"

"Sam, we've got things to do at home."

"Like what, Jude? You cleaning the house?"

"How about your job? Your father? And I can go on."

"Please don't, Jude. I'll call my boss and say I'm extending my vacation. Hell, Jude, I'm entitled. Besides, Mr. Mills owes me for all the overtime and six-day weeks I've done over the past seven years. As far as Dad goes, that's another story."

"You haven't talked to him in a really long time. You should at least call him."

"Jude, he's fine. What trouble can he get into? He's being taken care of. That's what we're paying for."

"I just hope you're right, Sam."

"Trust me," Sam said. "You want to stay here another three days, aye, Champ?" Todd nodded with excitement. "Case closed, Jude. Three more days of fun." Jude smiled at her husband as he went on rambling. "I don't know about any of you, but I'm craving some French Toast." The family seemed to be on the same page and agreed. They went and ate at a nearby diner and looked forward to enjoying the three extra days of their vacation.

Wednesday night, the cops were heading to Rigg's for another night of nursing-home-spying. Officers Conway

— JAMES J. MURPHY III —

and O'Conner were in an unidentifiable police van listening to some fine tunes. "Here we go again," reminded O'Conner, sounding giddy. "Are you ready for Part II of sitting on our asses in Rigg's parking lot?"

"You bet I am, buddy," responded Conway.

"Hell, I'm ready for Parts III, IV, and V." They both laughed and high-fived each other like immature, adolescent youths. "The only good thing about this stupid stunt you pulled, Conway, is that the Captain said that we don't have to wear our uniforms. It feels great just wearing jeans and a T-shirt."

"I couldn't agree with you more, O'Conner. Don't get me wrong; I like being a cop and all, but wearing the same thing all the time becomes a drag. Wearing these cargos and a T-shirt feels great. I can breathe and move. I was going to wear sandals, but I couldn't find them in my apartment."

"Now you're too relaxed, rookie."

"We still have another hour or so before we have to be at Rigg's. Do you want to get dinner?"

"Oh, boy! Do I?" O'Conner exclaimed, rubbing his large belly. "First, let's stop at the newsstand."

"You and that damn newsstand," teased Conway.

"Well, excuse me," said O'Conner. "Maybe I like to read and find out what's going on in the world."

"Hey! I do, too," Conway defended himself.

"I mean some real news, Conway. Not just going online and finding out what loser celebrities bought with their credit card last week or what loser celebrity is going to appear on so-and-so's show."

"That's not the reason I go online, O'Conner. I go on

— THE NURSING HOME —

to read about nationwide robberies, muggings, shootings, and so on."

"That's what I do, as well," O'Conner agreed. "Maybe it's me, Conway, but I need to hold something in my hands to read. I can't just go online and scroll down at what I'm reading. I'd get a headache. Don't get me wrong; I'm not computer illiterate. I keep records on the computer, considering in the future we may have to file everything electronically because our station is doing away with personnel."

"Do the people in those departments know that they may be unemployed?" questioned Conway.

"Not yet. It's all talk at the moment. Who knows what is true anymore at this station?" O'Conner sighed.

"Hopefully that's not the case."

"I hope not, either," agreed O'Conner. "Hell, I knew some of these people when I was a rookie... and that's going back twenty years."

"Damn, that's a long time." Conway felt sorry about the situation. "If these people get let go, can't they fight it?"

"All they could do is collect off the bastard government until the unemployment checks stop coming. All I can tell ya, partner, is that some of the stations already let go of some hard-working people. Hopefully it doesn't happen to our people," the veteran said.

"Hopefully not. You know, O'Conner, having all this advanced technology is great for some things. Easy access with just a click. Unfortunately, our society also doesn't know how bad modernizing can be for workers. The more advanced technology gets, the sooner laborers get replaced."

— JAMES J. MURPHY III —

"You're not as dumb as you look, Conway."

"Thanks, O'Conner. I think."

"The sad thing is that us humans will eventually get replaced by machines. Look at the way I'm talking," he kidded.

"Yeah, you sound like one of those robot movies."

"You know, you're absolutely right."

"Well, we're here," announced Conway, pulling up to the curb.

The two officers parked the van and went up to the newsstand. O'Conner grabbed the newspaper and studied the cover. The headline read: '**Wrong Place, Wrong Time for Youngster**.' "Isn't that a shame..." O'Conner had a disgusted look on his face.

"I heard about this. Seven year old shot in a deli for no reason."

"Let me buy this."

"Your coffee and doughnuts are on me," offered Conway.

"I'll meet you outside, Conway. Hurry up!"

"Be right there," he responded. Before O'Conner stepped out the door, Conway questioned him. "Isn't that one of the kids from the park?"

"Damnit, Conway! I'm hungry!"

"I won't be long."

"Damnit! I'll be outside." O'Conner stormed off.

With coffee and doughnuts in hand, Conway started walking over nonchalantly towards the kid he recognized. "Hey, I know you."

"I know you do," agreed the girl. "I also know you, Officer Conway. I'm Beth. I work at Rigg's Nursing Home. You questioned us about Sue's death and always talk to us at the park."

—— THE NURSING HOME ——

"Right," said Conway. "The park. You always hang out with Shy Boy and Stoner 1 and Stoner 2."

"You can say that, but they do have names, you know."

"I know. It's just easier remembering people by description."

"That's not very nice, you know," Beth scolded the officer, as if he took a cookie without asking for permission. "They are people, too."

"I know," the officer said. "It's something I have to work on."

"You're a cop. You should know better. I just wonder what you call me when I'm not around."

"Nothing bad. Don't worry. Let's get off the subject, okay?" he suggested.

"Fine with me," said Beth.

"So, what are you doing?"

"Well, it's really none of your business, but since you asked nicely, I'll tell ya. This is a newsstand; thought I'd buy a book and coffee for work."

"You've got work tonight?" questioned Conway.

"Yes, I do."

"Has anything weird been going on at the nursing home since we've interviewed everyone?"

"Not really. Everyone's just quiet. Too quiet, if you ask me."

Conway tried picking the young woman's brain. "How about the patients? How are they acting?"

"Acting like patients, I guess," she said to the officer.

"What do you think of the patient who goes by the name Morris Grover?"

"Oh, Mr. Grover? He's a kind old man and treats me

– 236 –

like his granddaughter, if he had any. Only problem with him is he talks too much. You know old people."

"I certainly do, Beth. Why don't you work with my partner for a few hours?" he kidded. They both laughed. "I was just wondering," the officer told her. "We interviewed Mr. Grover and he seemed *not* so kind. For some reason, I believe he has something to do with the murders."

"Mr. Grover having something to do with those murders? That's ridiculous!" she said, her voice getting louder.

"Lower your voice a little, Beth. We don't want to draw attention."

"I'm sorry." She didn't realize how loud she had gotten.

"I just wish I could put my finger on it."

"Come to think of it, you might be right, Officer."

"Why? What are you getting at?"

"I didn't tell anybody this yet, but I did notice one thing," Beth informed him.

"What was that?"

"After two or three deaths, I came across Mr. Grover's word search book in the breakroom."

"Really?" Conway seemed concerned. "I wonder how my partner and I didn't catch that."

"Beats me," she said. "I just found it very odd how after every death, Grover's word search appeared."

"At the scene of the crime?" Conway tried getting as much information as he could. He couldn't wait to share it with O'Conner.

"Yeah. At first, I thought a staff member, such as Bill at the time, was playing a prank on Mr. Grover. But as the deaths continued, his word search was there, but Grover wasn't."

— THE NURSING HOME —

"I'm still confused. Grover's in his eighties. He can't walk, but he's able to kill? No, it just doesn't seem to make sense," said Conway. "Unless..."

"Unless what?" Beth sounded eager.

"Unless Grover's paying someone to kill off the staff members and having the killer put Grover's word search in the breakroom in order to frame him, so we go after Grover instead of the real killer because Grover's the mastermind behind all of this."

"Officer, I think you've been hanging out with my friends more than I have. I have to get to work." Beth went on her way.

"Inform me if you notice anything strange while your working tonight." Beth kept walking and put her hand up in acknowledgment. Conway didn't blame Beth for walking away when he thought about how stupid he sounded. Even he had no idea what he had said because he knew he couldn't repeat it without sounding like a bigger ass than he just did. Conway paid for the coffee and doughnuts he promised O'Conner. He dreaded going back to the van. Time to face the music, he thought to himself. Conway opened the passenger's door and O'Conner was behind the wheel.

"How fucking long does it take to talk and get coffee?" O'Conner complained.

"Sorry," responded Conway with a shrug.

"Now we're going to be late. There goes dinner. If you want to have cookies and milk with your friend, do it off the clock."

"She's not my friend."

"Oh, I forgot; you have to sleep with 'em first before

– 238 –

you consider her or him to be a friend."

"Fuck you, O'Conner!"

"No thanks. I'll pass." The two cops could go at it for hours. "I'm just messing with you, rookie. What did you and the kid talk about?"

"Mainly Grover."

"You what?! I can't fucking believe this! Don't tell me you blew our cover, you moronic numbskull!"

"O'Conner, chill. I didn't say anything about us being undercover or hiding in a van. Nothing like that."

"Phew," O'Conner mustered out as he wiped his forehead.

"But Beth did provide something informative."

"And what was that?"

"Did you notice a word search, at all, in the breakroom after each death occurred?"

"No, but there was a book there, if I remember."

"And you didn't say anything or bother mentioning it to me?"

"What's the big deal? Book's a book. Maybe someone likes reading. Or it could be a recipe book. For cooking or baking."

"No, it's not!" yelled Conway defensively.

"How do you know this?"

"Beth said that it's a word search book that belongs to Morris Grover."

"If the book belongs to Morris Grover, how the hell did it get in the breakroom?" the older officer asked. Conway gave O'Conner a look like he was about to explain it. "Don't even bother," O'Conner warned him. "We got another night to see if anything fishy happens."

— THE NURSING HOME —

"You're right," agreed Conway. "Let's enjoy our video-watching. We should have some good laughs tonight."

"Don't worry... We will, Conway. But could anything be funnier than Morris Grover lying in bed, scratching his ass?"

"Maybe if he let one loose while one of the nurses were in the room changing him."

"That would be hilarious," said O'Conner.

"Hello, You Tube!" yelled Conway. "Picture it now: 'Old Man Farts on Nurse.' Number one download!" The two cops laughed hysterically. The officers had arrived at the nursing home and were set up with coffee and doughnuts. They were ready for a night of good laughs and relaxation.

Beth arrived to work on time and followed her usual routine of greeting patients, directing guests to their family member's rooms, updating the computer files, and so on. After a few hours, she went on her break. She went into the breakroom to eat dinner and read her new astrology book. When her break was almost over, she decided to send text messages to her friends.

Jay's phone happened to be off, but Jeff felt the vibration in his pants pocket. He reached in and dug for his phone. "Yo, dude. Beth just texted me."

"Oh, man. We're watching a movie."

"Don't worry, dude. There's a 'Pause' button on the remote, so hit it."

"Hit it?"

"Hit it, tap it. Don't act stupid, Jay. You know what I mean," Jeff told him sternly.

"Well, what does the text say?"

"God, I hate texting. I feel like a girl."

"Just read it so we can continue with the movie."

"Beth said she spoke to Officer Conway." Jeff texted Beth back, asking what Officer Conway had told her.

Jeff read Beth's text response aloud: "'**His imagination is worse than yours.**'" Jeff texted Beth back, typing: '**Dude, that's awesome.**'

Beth heard somebody coming. She texted Jeff, and then hid her cell phone because they weren't supposed to be used in the nursing home. It was only Nurse Blanche. They both said 'Hi' to each other. Beth went back to work.

Jeff read the text he received from Beth aloud again. "'**TTYL.**' What does that mean?" Jeff asked Jay. He texted Beth back, asking more questions.

"Don't know," Jay said.

Jeff waited for a response from Beth, but didn't get one. He called Ron.

"Hel-hello Jeff."

"Enough of the stuttering shit, Ron. We've got a problem."

"What is it, Jeff?"

"Beth talked to Officer Conway."

"Really? What did he have to say?"

"Beth was texting me and I think she was going to tell us, but instead, texted 'TTYL.'"

"'TTYL?'" repeated Ron.

"Yeah, man. What does that mean?"

"Talk to you later."

"No, dude. Tell me now."

"Jeff, 'TTYL' stands for 'Talk To You Later.'"

— THE NURSING HOME —

"Oh, okay. Cool. Guess I'll talk to you later, Ron."

"Goodnight, Jeff."

"Well, dude, what did Ronny boy come up with?" Jay asked.

"He said that it stands for 'Talk To You Later.'"

"So we paused the movie for nothing."

"Yeah, man. Told you... texting makes me feel like a girl. Let's just finish the movie, man." The two boys enjoyed the movie, while Beth finished working another night at Rigg's.

— Chapter 26

Beth had set her alarm clock for 4:55am. She had some exciting news to tell her friends. Beth had a hard time sleeping and her news kept her up during most of the night. When her alarm went off, Beth went to grab it. Because of her dreariness, she knocked the alarm clock off of the nightstand. The alarm was still ringing. She finally turned it off, hoping not to have woken anybody in the house. Since she was awake, she stretched her arms above and across, posing like Jesus. She replaced the white T-shirt that she wore to bed with a blue one and put on a pair of blue capris to match.

At 5:02am, she finally began calling her friends. She scrolled down to Jeff's name on her cell phone and hit the green 'call' button. She held the phone against her ear and could hear it ringing. After the fourth ring, Jeff picked up.

Jeff opened his cell phone and started talking on the outside of the cell instead of into it. "Hel-ro," his groggy voice said.

— THE NURSING HOME —

"Jeff, it's Beth. Talk into the phone, please."

"What time is it? What day is it?" he asked, still groggy.

"Thursday, 5:04am," she answered eagerly.

"I'm going back to sleep. Goodnight."

"Don't hang up!" her voice said loudly. "Don't hang up," she repeated in a normal tone, hoping not to wake her family. "It's an emergency, Jeff. Please meet me at the park."

"Damnit! I'll be there in a half hour, alright? Let me throw water on my face and grab a cereal bar."

"Thanks, Jeff. See you soon."

"Yeah." Fucking five in the morning and I'm going to the park. I could have slept an extra hour, Jeff thought. He had to be at Rigg's by seven.

Beth tried calling Jay, but his cell phone was off and he was probably sound asleep, like anybody would be at five in the morning. She then tried calling Ron, but there was no answer. He's either sleeping or watching a science fiction program, Beth thought with a smile. She was dressed and just about ready to go. Before leaving to meet Jeff, she wanted to make some toast and have a cup of milk.

After breakfast, she was about to leave, but she stopped herself. Damnit, she thought. Why do I always have to have clean teeth? It's only Jeff. He probably didn't even shower, she thought.

Jeff actually made it to the park on time. At five-thirty, he was walking back and forth, wondering what was taking Beth so long. It was about seventy-seven degrees outside. At least he wasn't cold in his gray sweatpants and black

T-shirt that read: 'I Am A Demon - Hear My Sound.' He hadn't bothered getting changed. He ran out the door with a change of clothes and ate his breakfast on the way.

Beth arrived ten minutes late. "Thank you for coming. I'm sorry I'm late. I had to brush my teeth."

"So, what's up?" asked Jeff, still wishing he had that extra hour of sleep.

"Unfortunately, Jay and Ron couldn't make it. I wanted to tell you all as a group."

"What would that be?"

"Remember I texted you last night about talking to Officer Conway?"

"Yeah, what was up with that?"

"We were talking about Morris Grover."

"Why talk about that old dude?"

"Conway thinks the murders that have happened are revolved around him."

"No way!"

"Yeah! Conway told me he thinks Grover's paying somebody to do the killing. He thinks Grover wants to get framed because he is the mastermind."

"I doubt it very much," Jeff told her. "Could Grover be under a spell, like in those old horror movies?"

"I don't know who is worse, you or Conway!"

"Hey, at least I don't think Grover's paying someone off. First of all, do you know how much money it costs to live in a nursing home?"

"How much?" questioned Beth.

"Well, like, a lot," explained Jeff. "I doubt very much that he can afford to hire anybody. Look at his clothes and look at the fact that he smells like shit."

— THE NURSING HOME —

"Jeff, you think all old people smell like shit."

"Because they do. Besides, it's hard to believe Grover's capable of something like this."

"All I know, Jeff, is that someone's playing us and we will find out who."

"I sure hope so."

"I didn't tell you this... but besides the files suddenly dating back to the beginning, Grover's word search has been at the murder scenes."

"Did you tell Officer Conway and the other guy?"

"Do you mean Officer O'Conner?"

"Yeah, that's him," Jeff said.

"Just Conway. O'Conner was waiting in the car, as usual. Anyway, I doubt very much he'd believe me."

"Why not?" he asked.

"To him, we are just kids who don't know anything."

"Fuck him, then."

"At least Conway would be on our side... but at the same time, Conway probably just wants to make an arrest to kiss his captain's ass," Beth went on.

"You know those rookies..." Jeff said, shaking his head. "Beth, we'll have all of the answers on Saturday night."

"I know we will," she said confidently. "Well, tell Jay when you get a chance and I'll inform Ron. Right now, I'm going back to sleep."

"Yeah, I gotta head to work. I already have a feeling I'm going to be late."

"Oh, I forgot to tell you. Meet me here tomorrow night."

"Again?" asked Jeff.

"Yes," Beth said sternly. "We have to go over layouts."

– 246 –

"Okay, Beth. I gotta jet." He started heading to his car.

"Tomorrow night!" she yelled as Jeff was walking away.

He waved to signal acknowledgment. Layouts, he thought. What the fuck is she talking about? He revved up his car and blasted his music. His car could already wake the dead, but to top it off, his music was going to wake up the community. Jeff was on his way to work playing the title track "Master of Puppets" by Metallica. Jeff wasn't even alive in 1986 when the album came out.

He pulled into the parking lot at Rigg's, feeling pumped. He was surprised to see that he actually arrived on time with a few minutes to spare. Jeff walked into the nursing home, changed into his work clothes, and then was instructed to do his usual tasks. It was a pretty quiet day at Rigg's for once. Nobody heckled him. He worked until one in the afternoon, and then put in a few hours at Kirk's Video Store later that night.

Ron and Jay were scheduled to work the same shift on Thursday night. Ron had to deal with the regular wise-ass, disrespectful patients and answer the phones. Jay had to do maintenance, as usual. He was flying solo because his best bud, Jeff, was working at the video store.

Ron's first mission after he clocked in was to go to the cafeteria. The cafeteria was on the first floor. Ron felt like an idiot because he was always stationed on the third floor. He was instructed to collect and serve food on the first floor, then serve food on the second floor, and then go back to the first floor to get food to serve to the third floor. What a pain in the ass this is, he complained to

— THE NURSING HOME —

himself. He normally only had to work the one floor, but someone called in, so Rigg's was short-staffed. Ron only had to cover for someone a few times before and he was grateful that he didn't have to bring patients food on all three floors every day because he'd be burnt out.

He went into the elevator and pushed the number '1' button. The '1' turned orange and the door closed slowly. Hopefully Jay is having better luck, he thought. The elevator came to a stop. The orange on the number '1' disappeared and the door opened slower than molasses. Maybe I should have taken the steps, he thought to himself. Now I have to deal with this damn elevator all night.

He finally made it to the cafeteria. "Hel-Hello," he spitted out.

Before Ron could finish, the lunch lady said, "Just save it, kid. Here are the dinners labeled to the rooms."

"Thanks," he said nervously. The lunch lady continued on with her business.

Ron started wheeling the cart with the dinner trays to the rooms. He wanted to be in and out as quickly as possible. He was making great progress until he made it to room 243, Morris Grover's room. Ron was bringing him chicken, cold mashed potatoes, apple sauce, and apple juice.

"What kind of slop are you giving me today?"

"The food you checked off on the menu the night before."

"Listen! I don't like a smart ass," Morris growled back.

"Smart ass? I didn't even want to talk to you," Ron defended himself in a shy voice. "All I wanted to do was give you your food and leave."

– 248 –

JAMES J. MURPHY III

"So leave!" Morris shouted. Ron was startled by the old man's boisterous yell. He started walking away. Then Morris called out, "Hey, kid! Where's Beth tonight?"

"Beth?"

"What are we playing? Copycat? Everything I ask, you repeat."

"No," Ron spoke up. "She's off tonight. What concern is it of yours?"

"Tell her that Morris has some chocolates for her." Morris felt he was in luck that the nursing home had a gift shop, considering his family hadn't been around or even given him a phone call in months.

"Morris Grover?"

"Yes."

"Yeah, I've heard about you."

"Good or bad?"

"Both," Ron said. "Well, I gotta get going before the other patients yell at me even more than you just did."

"You call *that* yelling?" Morris said. I wonder what he thinks screaming is, Morris thought to himself, and then started laughing as Ron went on his way.

Ron completed the three floors as he was assigned. He got cursed at, as usual, and actually had a tray thrown at him.

"What the hell happened to you?" asked Rita as she approached him in the hall.

"A patient threw their tray of turkey gravy at me." His face was blushing with embarrassment. The girl of his dreams seeing him covered in gravy... How humiliating?

"Well, clean it up before it stains," she told him in a motherly way.

— THE NURSING HOME —

He stuttered out, "Oh-oh-okay." The whole situation made him even more nervous. Ron went into the bathroom and cleaned his shirt. "Damn, no-good patients," he said, looking into the mirror. After he cleaned himself, he went to work at the reception desk.

After Jay clocked in, Clevon went to get him the maintenance supplies on the first floor. Jay was used to working with Jeff. They were a cohesive unit, considering back in high school they were the biggest fuck-ups on the planet and their parents still thought that to be the case.

Clevon was talking to himself out loud as he was fiddling with the maintenance keys. "Nows, which one's da key?" There were eight keys on the loop and he tested each one. Jay figured he'd be working with someone more responsible. The guy's only been here since 1996... You figure he'd be a pro by now, Jay thought. "Rappa-tap-tap, Rappa-tap-tap..." Clevon sung to himself. "Now, yous wuz da one," he said, talking to the correct key as he was testing it in the keyhole of the doorknob. The door opened.

All Jay said was, "Cool." He took a close look at Clevon and thought: *Man, I definitely don't wanna end up like this guy. Me and Jeff gotta open our own video store.*

After Clevon got the supplies needed, Jay suggested to the closing maintenance guy, "You want to start at this end and I'll start at the other end?"

"No, dat aright. We's work da same rooms." Jay found it really odd and creepy, but did what he had to do. As Jay tied up the old garbage bag of each patient's room, Clevon was right behind him replacing the full bag with a new

– 250 –

one. Even with Jay next to him in the room, all Clevon kept saying was 'Rappa-tap-tap' because he was so tuned in to his music through his earphones. The maintenance man was getting on Jay's nerves. "Yo, kid... Yous seems ta know wutts yous doin'. If yous want, I's tell Cyndi ta put yous full time wit me."

"No thanks, Clevon. I got another job."

"Wutt yous do?"

"I work at an antique shop," the young kid told him. If Jay told Clevon that he worked at a video store, he'd never hear the end of it. Also, he didn't want to do the dirty old maintenance guy any favors. Jeff was gullible enough to have that old man, Morris, trick him into renting him VHS tapes, which still hadn't happened as of yet.

"Antique shop?! Boy, works here... Greats pay, medical benefits, sick time, vacation..." Clevon tried persuading him.

"Listen, Clevon... I got to go eat dinner. Talk to you later."

"Yous didn't finish yet. I's tell Pearl on yous."

"Go ahead," Jay said. "Work's going to be there later, anyway." Jay left Clevon and the bag of garbage behind and went to the breakroom. Jay snuck out his cell and phoned the third floor reception desk.

"Thank you for calling Rig–."

Before Ron could finish, a voice on the other end said: "Hey, asshole! Come to dinner, man."

Ron laughed. "I'll be there in a minute, Jay. Let me tell Rita."

"Dude, then give it to her."

"See you soon." Ron hung up the phone. He turned towards Rita. "Rita, may I go to eat dinner?"

— THE NURSING HOME —

"Sure, Ron, and save me a piece," she kidded.

God, this woman wants me, the young man thought to himself. Ron left the third floor all happy and went into the breakroom to meet Jay.

"Ronny, my man. What's up?" Jay started laughing as he looked at Ron's stained shirt. "Dude, what the fuck happened to you?"

"One of the damn patients threw their turkey gravy tray at me," he explained as he was feeding the soda machine three quarters once again.

"Hee-hee-hee," Jay laughed. "And I thought *I* was having a bad night with that annoying maintenance guy."

"Who?" asked Ron inquisitively after he selected his beverage.

"Clevon. That dude's a pain in the ass."

"Is he a bigger pain than Morris Grover?" He sipped his cold drink and let out an 'Ahh' afterwards.

"That's a tough call, dude. You know, Grover could croke any day now, but Clevon has no future and will probably be here another forty years."

"You're really cynical, Jay."

"I can't help it. How's it going with your girlfriend?" Jay enjoyed teasing Ron about Rita because he knew it got on his nerves.

"Who? Oh, would you shut up, Jay?! Rita's just fine."

"Dude, just fuck her already."

"She would never go for a guy like me."

"You won't know if you don't ask," Jay told him. Changing the subject, Ron asked Jay if he had talked to Beth. "No, man, but Jeff told me that he met her at the park at five-thirty in the morning."

— 252 —

"What for?" asked Ron. "She called me, too, but didn't leave a message."

"About Saturday night."

"I think I'm having second thoughts."

"If you pussy out, I'll tell Rita right now that you're in love with her!"

What choice did he have? "Alright, alright," Ron agreed in a desperate voice.

"All I know is that Jeff told me that Beth wants to go over some plans with us tomorrow night at the park."

"So we better be there," Ron said hesitantly.

"I will," Jay said. "Personally, I thought me or Jeff would have been the leader of this operation, but Beth knows most about what's going on around here and she seems really gung-ho about it."

"We need women leaders," confirmed Ron.

"Don't push it, man," Jay said. "Oh, fuck! I was supposed to clock in ten minutes ago. See you soon." Ron nodded as he watched Jay rush back to work. Jay hoped that nobody would notice that he was late.

Ron read a page or so of his new science fiction novel before heading back to work. They both worked until their shifts ended and called it a night.

— Chapter 27

Friday, April 4, was bright and sunny. By the afternoon, the temperature had to be in the eighties. There was no humidity and it wasn't breezy, either. Unfortunately, the patients at Rigg's were cooped up in the nursing home. Patients were brought to the lounge room, like they were every day. "Hey gang. Where's Frank today?" asked Morris.

"Yeah." Ralph had also noticed Frank's absence. "I don't remember the last time he's been sick."

"What's your problem, Ralph?" questioned Pauly. "Does he need to get a permission slip from you when he's going to get sick?"

"I was just concerned, that's all," said Ralph, touching up his silver sideburns.

"Next, Ralphie boy's gonna want to know if Frank went to the bathroom today." Pauly, Morris, and some of the patients who could actually understand what was going on laughed their heads off.

"See what you started, Morris?" Ralph shook his head.

– 254 –

— JAMES J. MURPHY III —

"One question leads to this? Damn," said Morris.

"I don't think Frank is sick at all," Pauly stated.

"You don't, Pauly?" asked Ralph.

"No, I don't. According to my source, one of the dumb-ass staff members must have mixed up someone's dinner order last night and the patient threw the tray at him out of frustration."

"Are you sure about this, Pauly?" asked Morris.

"I'm positive on this, Mori, old boy. I'll bet my bottom dollar that that patient was Frank."

"You're out of your mind, Pauly. And it's Morris to you. Frank is one of the nicest, most sincere people in this place."

"He may be, Mori, but you know him as an architect and his love for nature and so on."

"So? What's wrong with that?" asked Ralph.

"Nothing's wrong with that, but don't forget, Frank also fought in the Korean War," Pauly informed them.

"What does that have to do with anything?" asked Morris.

"Since he fought in the war, maybe something triggered in his head or he was having a flashback. Frank told me, at one time, he was able to load a gun in a matter of seconds. Unfortunately, because of his arthritis, he can't really do anything now. He'd be lucky if he could doodle a picture," Pauly told them. A lot of the patients, especially Morris and Ralph, felt bad about their close friend. "His family checked him in here about five years ago because he couldn't move around like he used to."

"Trust me, guys. I know all about having a hard time moving around," kidded Ralph. Ralph began to tell his story. "Originally, I grew up in New York during the 1930s

—— THE NURSING HOME ——

and 40s. Those were peaceful times, my friends. You could go on a street corner and get a slice of pizza for ten cents and not worry about being mugged."

"What happened to those days?" asked Morris.

"Innocent times ended when all of the riffraff took over the turf," reminded Pauly.

"You're absolutely right, Pauly," agreed Ralph. "That was why I moved up to Worcester, Massachusetts."

"That's a long hike, Ralph," said Morris.

"I know, but at the time, I was offered a position in Massachusetts. A friend of mine owned a bus company over there, and he told me I could become a bus driver. I was offered a better salary there than in New York, so I had to go where the money was. Unfortunately, I fell in love with an Italian girl named Maria."

"Unfortunately? Why was that, Ralphie boy?" Pauly was quite curious.

"I'll get to that soon," Ralph continued. "So, I'm in love with this bitch, Maria." Morris and Pauly could see his nostrils flaring. It looked like he was about to breathe fire like a dragon. "We get married and have two children. I'm busting my ass all these years trying to support her and the kids. And what is she doing, do you ask? She's having an affair behind my back with the manager of a tool store down the street. We got separated. Divorce, in those times, was very rare; not like today, where it's an everyday thing." The gang nodded in agreement.

"So what happened to your kids, Ralph?" Wade interrupted the story.

"If you would be quiet, Wade, then Ralph could continue," insisted Pauly.

– 256 –

JAMES J. MURPHY III

"Sorry, Ralph," Wade apologized.

"My kids lived with that rotten bitch while they grew up. I tried keeping contact because they were my kids, too. When they were in their twenties, I was still giving them money. I always cared for and loved those kids... and how do they thank me? By waiting six years to talk to me."

"When did you get your back problems, Ralph?" asked Morris.

"To be honest, I'm not sure. I'm still talking about the pain in my ass," he kidded. The gang laughed. "While the kids were in their twenties, Maria was having heart problems. May I remind you, these spoiled kids don't say a damn word to me for six years... and then all of a sudden when their mother's dying, they give me the news and ask for more money. I told them to fuck off. Maria eventually died, not that I care, and I finally retired from the bus company and moved my ass down to Florida. I've been down here for over twenty years, now, and I love it."

Everyone then noticed Frank getting wheeled into the lounge room by one of the nurses.

"Well, well... Look who it is," mocked Pauly.

"Are you okay, Frank?" asked Ralph, concerned.

"Yeah, I'm doing okay. I was just tired."

"Glad to hear that you are doing good, Frank." Morris felt relieved.

"Why wouldn't I?" Frank asked. "I'm not sick or anything. Are you guys trying to tell me something?"

"Nothing major, Frank," responded Pauly. "All types of rumors are flying around here," he laughed. "I can't say it, guys."

— THE NURSING HOME —

"Plain and simple," said Morris, getting to the point. "Is it true that you threw a tray of food at one of the staff people?"

Frank began laughing. "It's true, I'm the guilty party. I did it."

"But why, Frank?" snuck in Wade.

"Because... first, I was served the wrong meal. More importantly, the dumb-ass hit my left hand. I have arthritis, you know. All I could see were stars and I felt infuriated, so I let him have it." The gang was laughing hysterically because Frank was such a nice, down-to-earth guy, unlike Pauly, who had thrown a couple of trays at staff members during his stay.

"I thought you were having a flashback from Korea or something," Pauly told him.

"Not again with the Korean War, Pauly," Frank responded. "Guys, let me tell you a story. First of all, you guys know how much I love art." The gang all nodded in unison. "Before I made a career in arts and crafts, I grew up in Detroit." He assumed they all knew that was in Michigan. "I had nothing going for me there, so I signed up for the Korean War. I only fought in the war for the last year. I was so grateful I didn't kill anybody or vice-versa."

"How couldn't you have killed anyone?" Pauly sounded a little disappointed.

"I was a horrible aim. I was so bad that I'm shocked that I wasn't discharged."

"You shoulda been," said Pauly.

"I know," agreed Frank, "but I'm grateful that I wasn't or I wouldn't have been able to get my scholarship in the arts and crafts field."

"What did you do for the first three years?" asked Morris.

"Some of the other guys and I were on potato duty."

"Potato duty?" repeated Ralph.

"Yeah, all we did was clean and peel potatoes constantly. Maybe that's why I can't eat potatoes anymore. After seeing, cleaning, peeling, and smelling like potatoes for three years, you grow sick of it." Laughter broke out in the lounge room.

"What's all the commotion?" asked a new nurse who walked over to the group.

"I was just telling a story about potatoes."

"Oh," the nurse said, as if not interested. "If you need me, I'll be over there." She pointed to the corner of the lounge room.

The story continued. "After serving my time, I went back to Michigan to study arts and crafts, met a girl named Betty, got married, and had a daughter named Nicole."

"Is that the one who always visits?" asked Ralph.

"Yes, she's my pride and joy. I'd do anything for her." The gang could tell that Frank was getting emotional by the tone in his voice. "Unfortunately, Betty passed away when Nicole was twelve. Cervix cancer," he told them. The gang felt bad. "After Nicole grew up, we moved down here. It's just so peaceful. Nicole got married and had children... and I got arthritis. They took care of good old Dad for a while. Then it became too much. We talked it out. At first, I wasn't happy about it, but I knew it was right. We still have a great father/daughter relationship to this day."

"That's always good to hear," stated Ralph.

── THE NURSING HOME ──

"Since we're telling stories... you're up, Pauly," Morris pointed to his friend.

"I don't think so, guys. Besides, everyone here knows my story. Wife died, family abandoned me, and I don't trust the staff."

"Yeah, we know that story, but we want to hear and know the *whole* story," insisted Morris.

"Goddamnit! I'll tell you lug-heads. I was born during The Great Depression of 1933. After I was born, I have a feeling my family really was depressed." There were laughs within the room. Pauly always had a sense of humor, even when he was livid. He'd curse someone to death, and then by the next day, he'd be back to his regular self. "I grew up in the bad area of St. Louis. Back then you had to be street smart or you'd end up getting your ass kicked; basically the same as today. As time progresses, you learn, just like I did. One time, I got jumped by these low-class Gavones who thought everybody owed them something. I showed them a lesson or two."

"What lesson would that be, Pauly?" questioned Morris.

"Well, I'll tell ya, Mori, old boy. One of the Gavones was at a drive-in movie seeing *White Heat*, if I remember correctly. You know, one of those mob movies."

"Yeah, I remember that one," said Ralph.

"Yeah," agreed Frank. "A young Jimmy Cagney."

"Go on, Pauly," encouraged Morris.

"The Gavone was about to make out with his dumb harlot and I scared the shit out of this fucker. During the shooting scene in the movie, I go to the driver's side of his car and BAM!!! I smashed his windows with a baseball bat. He threatened me, saying: 'I'll kill ya! Wait 'til I get the boys!' I tell him there's more where that came from. God, I hated those fucking street thugs. You know, they'd have stupid names for their gangs, like: 'The Bats' or 'The Lizards.' But I think these gangs should have called themselves 'The Assholes' because that's exactly what they were. I got them back. He paid. They all paid."

"Were you in the army, Pauly?" asked Morris.

"No army for me. I dropped out of school at the age of fifteen and became a mate."

"What's a 'mate?'" Frank was interested.

"To put it in easy terms, I cleaned boats. When a ship came to shore, I cleaned it. Because the boats were along the Mississippi River, I also got to sail to Wisconsin; Iowa; Illinois; Missouri, which is where I'm from; Kentucky; Arkansas; Tennessee; and of course, Mississippi itself. I loved traveling so much. It was such a fun job. I did that for about ten years. I did some bum jobs for another five years, like moving furniture and traveling from state to state once again. I was enjoying life. Finally, when I was thirty, I settled in Florida and met Mary, the woman of my dreams. We had a daughter named Stephanie." Pauly paused to collect his thoughts. "When Steph was fourteen, we found out her mother had lymphoma cancer and she died nine months later. That was it for me. My daughter was fifteen when this happened. Explaining to her that my wife, her mother, was no longer with us was one of the hardest things a parent could do." Frank nodded his head, remembering going through something similar. "My daughter was the closest person in my life, until maybe ten years ago. I was getting on her and her family's nerves, and vice-versa, because of my bad leg. Years ago,

— THE NURSING HOME —

I tripped down some steps after dark and broke my leg. It still acts up here and there. That's mainly why I'm in a wheelchair. You know me; that can't hold me down. I still try to learn as much as I can. I loved using the Internet. It's great for communication."

"You can't set me up to do that," said Morris.

"Are you scared of new experiences, Mori, old boy?" Pauly said in a mocking tone.

"No!" he shouted back, even though he knew Pauly was right. Morris was old-fashioned.

"Finally, those pieces of shit sent me here. I haven't spoken to them since."

"Why don't you let bygones be bygones, Pauly?" asked Ralph.

"Not a chance, Ralphie boy. That old Battle-Axe up in the sky would have said the same thing to me," he kidded as he pointed up in the air, acknowledging Mary, his true love. "Well, I told you my story, fellas. Now it's time for you, Mori, old boy."

"You guys don't want to hear about little old me. I'm boring," Morris tried convincing the gang.

"We all shared our stories, Morris," Ralph told him. "Your turn."

"Come on!" Frank jumped in.

"Okay, okay. Give this old man some space. And that's Morris to you, Pauly. Well, there's not that much to tell," stated Morris. "Growing up, my father was an asshole and I had a worthless mother who did nothing to help us kids. If I wasn't picked on in school, I'd sure as hell be picked on at home. Basically, I was physically and verbally abused. My father was a coal miner. He worked over fifty hours a

— 262 —

week. All he wanted in life was to eat his dinner, drink his beer, ignore us kids, and give us a whippin' when he was bored. Personally, I liked being ignored."

"We all got whipped, Mori, old boy. That's how it was in those days," Pauly explained.

"I know, Pauly, but my mother could have said something instead of just letting it happen. All she did was knit her precious sweaters or rugs while my brother, Dave, and I got the snot beaten out of us."

"I didn't know you had a brother, Morris."

"I did, Ralph, but after I grew up, we distanced ourselves from one another. It was nothing personal."

"Is he still alive?" asked Frank.

"No, he died in New York City around 1993, I heard. All I know is that a couple of darkies jumped and mugged him for wallet money. Manhattan is a much safer place today than it was in the nineties."

"That's what I hear, also," agreed Ralph, "but it would never be like the 1930s or 1940s."

"Go on, Mori," urged Pauly.

"I also had a sister named Mary. She was a sweetheart, my kid sister. She grew up to be a housewife. Gertie loved her."

"Who's Gertie?" Frank was being inquisitive.

"Don't worry, Frank. I'll get to that. All I know, gentlemen, is that I had dreams and goals, but my father crushed them. For instance, I wanted to be a war pilot; my old man said 'Not in a million years.'"

"Mori, old boy, stop feeling sorry for yourself," Pauly told him. "You can't blame your family for you being a failure."

—— THE NURSING HOME ——

"Well, Mr. Hot Shot, if I can't blame them, who can I blame?"

Pauly stared Morris right in the face from his wheelchair and said: "Yourself." After a brief silence, Pauly continued. "Hell, Mori, all of our parents belittled us back then, but we try to do our best so we don't end up like they did. Ralph's and Frank's parents weren't saints, either, I bet. Hell, probably even Wade's, here, as well." Everyone nodded in agreement and noticed how serious Pauly was about the subject.

"Maybe you're right, Pauly, but I can still hate them."

"Who said you couldn't, Mori, old boy?"

"What happened next?" Wade asked Morris.

"I still blame them for me not being able to follow through on any of my goals, but one goal I did achieve was Gertrude Berkowitz. When I first saw her, I was twenty-four and she was twenty-two. I was a landscaper. She must have been walking home from her job and I just had to meet her. I introduced myself and I was nervous as hell and she could tell, but she was nice to me. The following night, we went to a ten o'clock matinee. After that, it was an easygoing experience."

"Mori, old boy. You sly dog."

"Not like that, Pauly. I mean we got married."

"You went to the movies and got married?" questioned Frank.

"No, Frank. We dated for two years. I was twenty-six and Gertie was twenty-four when we got married. We had a son named Ben when I was twenty-seven. He was a happy-go-lucky kid and loved being the center of attention, especially since I gave all of it to him. My second

— 264 —

son, Sam, was born when I was forty."

"Is he the one with the wife and kid that visits you?" Ralph asked.

"Yeah, that's my no-good, dumb-ass son." There was snickering among the patients in the lounge room. "I forgot to tell you guys... A year before Sam was born, I was landscaping. You know, layering bricks. I lost my balance and fell off the roof, like an asshole, and broke my leg. I landscaped for two more years and then I worked at a bank for fifteen years, then retired."

"Who said you had a boring life, Mori, old boy?" asked Pauly.

"I did!"

"Mori, you're such a ham."

"Go on, Morris," insisted Wade.

"Like I was saying... we loved Sam as much as Ben, but a freak thing happened."

"What was that, Morris?" asked Frank.

"Ben was killed in a car accident. He died instantly. Goddamn drunk driver," he muttered with a lump in his throat.

"We're sorry to hear that, Mori," Pauly said in a serious tone, feeling bad for his friend. The other patients were also sorry for Morris's loss.

"This incident put a black cloud over my perspective of life. Even though Ben was gone, I still had Gertie and Sam, but unfortunately, I may have taken them for granted. This is one reason why Sam and I aren't so close."

"You lost a son, Morris. They have to understand."

"I know, Ralph. No excuses. It took me a long time to get over his death and by the time I tried taking an interest

—— THE NURSING HOME ——

in Sam's life, he was all grown up and didn't need his old man anymore... not like I was there for him, anyway."

"Mori, old boy, don't be so hard on yourself," said Pauly.

"Eventually, Sam married Jude and the rug-rat was born. My knees got worse over the years. I got arthritis. I never wanted to be like a paraplegic. Gertie and I were growing old together and, unfortunately, I was still having flashbacks of Ben here and there. Gertie took care of me for seven years. She died in her sleep and, of course, I had to tell Sam. They took me in and took care of me for a year. I know Sam didn't want to. Jude must have twisted his arm to do so."

"My old Battle-Axe would also twist my arm to do things," interrupted Pauly. "'Pauly, do this,' 'Pauly, do that.'" The gang was laughing like a bunch of kids. Pauly motioned to Morris so he could continue.

"Sam couldn't put up with me anymore, so here I am."

"Morris, you're not boring at all," said Frank.

"Just because you lived in Florida all of your life, don't ever say that you didn't experience anything," Ralph told him.

"Yeah, these lug-heads are right, Mori, old boy." Pauly had a way with words.

As the gang were talking amongst themselves, a couple of staff members interrupted and said, "Time to go back to your rooms, gentlemen."

"Gentlemen? You must be new here, Nurse," said Morris.

"Name's Lucy," she told them.

"Well, I'm Morris."

"That sly dog," joked Pauly to the others.

– 266 –

— JAMES J. MURPHY III —

"You all can continue your get-together tomorrow," Nurse Lucy told them. She and the other staff members wheeled the patients back to their respective rooms.

At around eight at night, Jeff and Jay headed to the park, as planned. They had just clocked out of Kirk's Video Store thirty minutes prior, after working into the evening.

"Oh, dude! What a relaxing day," said Jay.

"Yeah, I know, man," agreed Jeff. "I'm so glad we didn't have to work at Rigg's today. I hate that fucking place." He went on a tirade.

"Dude, we still dealt with some old people today."

"Yeah, I know, man. But at least they didn't drop a torpedo in their pants."

"Pants?!" Jay laughed. "That's a good one."

"Good one? What do you mean by that, dude?"

"Some of those patients don't even wear pants. I hear some have a hole in their bed, under their ass, where a pan is placed underneath. They're like animals in nature, but without the fur. They just go when they have to and leave some poor sap to pull the treasure out from underneath."

Jeff looked like he was about to be sick. "Alright, dude. Change the subject. Talk about a horror movie. Or even the economy. Anything but those old people."

"Well, Beth and Ronny boy should be here momentarily," Jay told him.

"Big word coming from you, Jay."

"Yeah, man. I got it from some movie I saw last night. You know, when they say: '*Help will be here momentarily.*'"

– 267 –

THE NURSING HOME

"Yeah, I think I know that one," agreed Jeff. "Jay, I don't know if I told you..."

"Told me what?"

"Beth is bringing a layout of Rigg's."

"Why am I always the last to know everything?"

"Don't know, bro."

"You said she's bringing a layout?"

"Yeah," Jeff confirmed.

"What the fuck? Are we building a house? We're not carpenters, you know. Do I look like a fucking carpenter, Jeff? Does it look like I'm wearing a tool belt?"

"No," Jeff responded, "but I wouldn't mind a bullet belt. Jay, you worry too much, man. You just gotta chill."

At a quarter after eight, up pulled Beth in her blue car. Beth and Ron got out of the car and began walking towards their friends.

"Do you have my layout, Ron?" Beth reminded him.

"Right..." said Ron. "I'll get it." He went back to the car.

"Glad you could make it!" yelled Jay sarcastically from a distance.

"Glad to be here," Beth said with even more sarcasm when she approached. "Trust me, guys; this isn't fun for me, either. I wish we could go to the movies or go bowling, but we have to go over the plans for tomorrow night if we want to beat this thing." Beth seemed confident.

Ron finally made it over to the group. "Hey guys," he greeted shyly. "Here ya go, Beth." Ron handed her the layout.

Beth extended her hand and grabbed the layout from him. "It looks like it's getting a little dark, guys. Let's go over to the picnic table."

"Why there?" asked Jeff.

"So we can unroll the layout," she told him. Jeff looked at Jay, thinking: *This chick's really serious.* They followed Beth to the picnic table and she took a flashlight out of her bag.

"Did you guys notice that Officer Conway and the other guy haven't been here lately, patrolling and telling us to stay out of trouble and to be good and all that bullshit?" Jeff said, changing the subject.

"I know, man. I miss that dude," Jay said.

"Well, guys... they have lives, too!" Beth told them loudly. "Maybe they are off trying to solve a case, just like we would be now, if only I can get your attention." The boys settled down, like students did when a teacher was getting a class in session. Beth was beginning to lose her patience with the burnout kids, but realized that she had to keep her cool, considering she needed them in order for her plan to work. If they refused to help because of her attitude, then it'd just be her and Ron. More likely, just her, and she couldn't afford that. Plus, they were her friends, she reminded herself.

The flashlight lit up the area where they were standing. Beth unrolled the layout of the nursing home. It took up most of the picnic table.

"No way!" yelled Jay.

"Dude, this is fucking nuts!" said Jeff enthusiastically. "Is this the inside of Rigg's?"

"Beth, did you draw this map yourself?" asked Ron.

"I wish. I did an online search for 'Rigg's Nursing Home' and I actually found a link for it."

"So what did the Rigg's website say?" Ron seemed interested.

—— THE NURSING HOME ——

"There was a bunch of the usual information. For instance: inviting new patients, visiting hours, directions, and contact information."

"Did you find any information about the first fifty years Rigg's was open?" Ron inquired.

"I was hoping to find more information on that, but there was absolutely nothing about it. Just a bunch of garbage trying to convince people what a great nursing home it is. Unfortunately, they didn't have any history of Rigg's, which is kind of unusual," informed Beth.

"As if it's a mystery!" Jay jumped in, seeming a bit intrigued.

"Actually, Jay may have a point here. It is kind of weird that there's no information about the early years of Rigg's. The only mentioning of its past is the fact that Rigg's was established in 1841, but we already knew that because of the engravement on the entrance of the building."

"There were no answers at all on the site?" Ron seemed surprised.

"Nothing," confirmed Beth. "However, what they *did* have was a map of the inside of Rigg's! Everything from the entrance to the boiler room to the breakroom. It's insane!"

"So what? Maybe Cyndi put it there," Jeff pointed out, not seeming phased.

"I doubt Cyndi would display the entire inside of the nursing home on the website – especially with this much detail. Maybe she'd put up some pictures of the rooms, but not a floor plan." Beth didn't think Cyndi was the type to do something like that.

"How could someone have posted a map of the inside of Rigg's online?"

JAMES J. MURPHY III

"Well, Ron, every building does have a blueprint or an outline to use for emergency evacuations, so I guess that somebody got their hands on the one for Rigg's and made it available to the public."

"I guess you can get anything online nowadays. But look at all the detail!"

"Yeah, and somebody familiar with Rigg's must have filled it in. This is pretty accurate. I'm amazed that you can even make out the rooms. It had to be added in by someone who used to work here."

"Yeah, you can even see the vending machines!" Ron sounded thrilled.

"I saved the image to a disc. Then I had a guy at the photo shop enlarge it, like the police do when they solve cases. I'm still impressed with how clear it came out."

"Yo, man... This layout is really colorful for a black and white photo and I didn't even smoke anything yet," said Jay.

"Blueprints and emergency maps use little color to begin with. I had it printed in black and white. You can still see all the detail of the inside of Rigg's. And guess what, Jay? You're not going to smoke anything. Got it?!" Beth commanded.

"Bummer, dude."

"Don't worry, Jay. After tomorrow night, you and Jeff could fry your brains all you want." Jeff and Jay both had happy grins on their faces. "Now let's get down to business!" she instructed them.

"I still can't believe how detailed this is," Ron went on about the map.

"'*I still can't believe how detailed this is*,'" Jay repeated, mimicking him in a feminine voice. "Oh, dude.

–271–

— THE NURSING HOME —

No wonder why Rita won't fuck you," he laughed.

"Why do you always have to bring up Rita's name, Jay?"

"Because I know you won't," Jay told him. Jeff was too busy laughing at the two arguing to intervene.

"Hey! Focus, everyone! This is serious, damnit!" Beth said with enforcement. "Nobody's fucking this up!" Beth was not going to waste any more time. "Jay, just listen tonight and after tomorrow, smoke all you want; I don't care. Ron, if you're going to fuck Rita or any science fiction actresses, do it after tomorrow. Concentrate now! Got it?" The kids were once again put in line. They obviously didn't like being yelled at, but they knew they had to work together as a unit. Outside of all the chopping on one another, they were friends and they didn't want to see each other getting hurt in any way, shape, or form. They all settled down.

"Wow, check out the people on this map." Jeff noticed tiny stick figures drawn on the map in blue ink.

"That's us, Jeff. I drew us on the map the other night. We want to get to this point here." Beth pointed to the reception desk that she worked at. "We can use any means of a computer, but why not use the one you know, right?"

"Why don't we just use Cyndi's office?" Ron asked her.

"Because Cyndi may be in there, working. Also, we don't want to be trapped in there."

"Are we going in together?" asked Jeff.

"No!" Beth told him. "We're being divided into teams. Ron and me are going in."

"Ma-ma-me?" Ron quivered at the news. "Are you sure Jeff or Jay wouldn't be more useful?"

— 272 —

— JAMES J. MURPHY III —

"Yeah, Beth... Sending Ron in with you is like getting thrown off a ship into the ocean with no life preserver. No offense, Ron," stated Jeff.

"None taken." Ron knew Jeff was right.

"Yeah, Beth. It's really risky," added Jay.

"Don't worry, guys. It's under control," Beth reassured them.

"You better be right," said Jay.

"Question, Beth..." interrupted Ron.

"What is it, Ron?" she replied.

"I know I asked this Tuesday night, but you didn't give me a serious answer. How are we getting into Rigg's?"

"Ron, don't you know anything?" said Jay. "You just walk into Rigg's, considering you already work there, and tell them you forgot your book."

"No way, dude! That's way too obvious," jumped in Jeff.

"Do you think Bronski would let us in?" Jay asked his friend.

"He hates us."

"Where did you get that idea?"

"Because he's told us numerous times," Jeff reminded him. "The only solution is to sneak in from the other side of the building. There's never security over there."

"You are one hundred percent right, Jeff," agreed Beth. "Normally, we would do that, but I have this gut feeling that the police are going to be hiding out there."

"Why would the police be hiding there?" asked Ron.

"Maybe they're on the lookout, trying to solve this case," Beth told them. "Like I told you guys... I bumped into Conway at the newsstand on Wednesday night. He was very talkative. I'm shocked he didn't ask me for

THE NURSING HOME

my phone number."

"Damn cops!" yelled Jeff. "They can get away with anything."

"Yeah, man," butted in Jay. "Maybe *they* have something to do with the murders at Rigg's and are trying to frame one of us."

"That's absurd!" exclaimed Beth. "So you're saying that the police have nothing better to do with their time than to frame one of us?"

"That's exactly what I'm saying," expressed Jay.

"It's true," confirmed Jeff. "They only look out for their own."

"Alright, guys. This is how we get in." Beth went forward with explaining the plan. "Since the police may be on the opposite side of the building, we have no choice but to confront security."

"Are you nuts?!" Ron raised his voice.

"Yeah, Beth. Ronny boy is right," Jay told her. "Bronski will fucking kill us with no problem. The dude's, like, six foot two and two hundred and seventy-five pounds of pure fucking muscle."

"He won't go after all of us," she informed him. "Ron and I will stand by the car, while you and Jeff distract him. I'm pretty sure you two could make him angry enough for him to leave his post."

"Trust me, we can," Jeff said, although not feeling so confident.

"You two do that while Ron and I sneak in, rush past the staff, and find an available computer. Hopefully it's the one at the reception desk where I work."

"What are you going to accomplish on the computer,

– 274 –

anyway?" Jay was curious as to what Beth had in mind.

"I have a CD listing every single patient who has passed away at Rigg's. I'll insert the disc into the CD-ROM so all of the names pop up and it's easy pickings from there." She felt strongly about her plan.

"'Easy pickings?!' Put the car in reverse!" Beth, Jeff, and Jay looked at each other, confused as hell, after hearing Ron's comment.

"Dude, if she puts the car in reverse, she'll hit the parking cement block," Jeff warned him.

"Not the actual car, Jeff," Ron explained. "I mean just back up the story for one minute." He looked at Beth. "How do you know if any of the names on the CD have to do with the murders?"

"It's a hunch, Ron," Beth told him. "All I have to do is call out the names, and we'll see what happens."

"I don't know about any of you, but I don't want to risk my life on a hunch. I hate to say it, but the officer you spoke to the other night may be right."

"How so, Ron?" she questioned.

"By pointing the finger at Morris Grover."

"Are you sure you didn't speak to the officer yourself, Ron?" Beth's voice was rising.

"Beth, I met that nasty old man the other night. He's the meanest bastard on this planet," Ron said angrily. "Too bad I wasn't a few pounds heavier and more sure of myself because if I was, that old windbag would be lying right on his keister!"

"'Keister!?'" enthused Jay. "Where the fuck did you come up with that word? Just say 'Knock him on his ass.' No wonder why Rita won't fuck you."

THE NURSING HOME

"Leave her alone, Jay."

"Well, if it is Grover, he has to be getting help. I think the help he's getting is on this disc," Beth declared, feeling positive of her opinion.

"Dude, Mr. Grover doesn't even know how to turn on a computer," informed Jeff.

"We know that, Jeff," voiced Beth again.

"Maybe it's you, Jeff," kidded Jay. "You are his VHS-bitch now, aren't ya?" He couldn't stop laughing.

"Just stop, dude."

"No, guys. It's definitely one of the people listed on the CD who is working with Mr. Grover, or whoever, to do these horrible acts."

"By the way, Beth..." Ron interrupted. "Morris told me to say 'Hi' to you."

"Greeaaat," Beth's voice dragged on unenthusiastically. "Still, for some reason, I can't picture kind, old Mr. Grover doing anything like this."

"He's not kind at all," Ron told her, acting like a high school girl.

"I don't know about the *kind* part," joined in Jeff, "but the old man sure as hell smells like shit."

All Jay could say was, "Don't trust old people. Like I said, Jeff: We're the bait and they're the big fish. We're just waiting to be eaten."

"Guys, I believe we covered all the bases. Correct?" asked Beth. They all nodded. "Just remember: Be at the park tomorrow night at 8:50pm. You know the plan."

"Yeah, Beth. Me and Jeff get Bronski away from his post, where he'll probably murder us before we catch up

– 276 –

to you," summarized Jay.

"Then you and Ron go into Rigg's and find a computer," continued Jeff.

"Beth yells out names from the CD," Ron concluded.

"Glad you all remember." Beth was satisfied.

"What happens if a voice responds?" Ron asked, shaking in his white sneakers.

"Then we respond back. Be prepared!" Beth felt confident.

Jeff and Jay looked at each other. "Awesome!" they said in unison.

"Let's call it a night," Beth decided. "We'll meet here tomorrow night."

"I can't believe we are calling it a night at nine-thirty on a Friday night," Jeff complained, feeling bummed out.

"I hear ya, bro," agreed his buddy.

"Don't worry, guys. Tomorrow night will be a night that we'll never forget," promised Beth. Everyone said goodnight to each other. Jay was leaving with Jeff, while Ron was going to leave with Beth. Beth rolled up the layout of the map and put the flashlight away. On a final word, Beth screamed out, "Don't forget your camo!" as everyone left.

Chapter 28

It was a dark, dreary, gloomy day. Thunderstorms were in the forecast and flood watches were in effect. On every channel, there was print scrolling along the bottom of the screen warning people who did not have work to stay in. Even though it was ten in the morning, it looked like it was ten at night because of how black it was outside. The town lights never turned off from the night before because it was so dark.

In room number 243, Morris was sound asleep. He hadn't bothered eating the breakfast that was served to him earlier in the morning. Morris thought rainy days were great to catch up on sleep. Who would want to get up out of bed by the looks of it outside?

At about a quarter to one in the afternoon, Morris was still at peace. Then, out of nowhere, somebody entered his room. The person began to shake the sleeping senior citizen. "Why are you still asleep, damnit?! Wake the fuck up, Grover!" demanded the intruder. "You old windbag!"

Morris came to. "Help! Help! What's going on here?! What the hell?"

"Shut up, Grover, you old fuck. I was supposed to feed you an hour ago. Cyndi's gonna have my head for this."

"Whoa! Whoa! Take it easy, Pearl."

"Don't you tell me how to do my job, you old fuck. One of the damn newcomers called in sick, so thanks to her, I have to work a fucking sixteen hour shift and I don't need no lip from you. Got it?" Pearl was irate.

"I was in peace until you disturbed my sleep, you dumb harlot."

Pearl became infuriated. It could have been because of what Morris called her or it could have been because Pearl has no idea what the word 'harlot' meant. "Who gives a flying fuck about your sleep? You can sleep whenever you want. It's not like you are going anywhere anytime soon, except maybe to your grave."

"How dare you say this to me, Pearl?! How dare you?!" Morris started boiling up. His wrinkled hands clinched together to make a fist. "What horrible thing did I ever do to you?"

"Besides getting shipped here by your scum-bag family? Let's see: Bill's dead; Sue, my best companion, is dead; Nurse Anne is no longer with us; and Eddie... God only knows where he is."

"I agree with my buddy, Pauly. I'm glad none of 'em are here. Personally, I'd be happy if you disappeared, as well." Morris snorted heavily like a bull, not flinching one bit. He was eyeing her dead-on.

Pearl looked outside to see if any other staff members were around. There was nobody in sight at the moment.

—— THE NURSING HOME ——

Everybody was either at lunch or sitting in the corner of the lounge room, babysitting the patients from a distance. Pearl slowly closed Morris's door. "Guess what, you old fuck? Nobody's in sight. How would you like to repeat what you just said to me?" Morris was fuming. He wanted to spit the words out, but he was so anxious that a lump formed in his throat. "Just like I thought," she mocked him. "Cat got your tongue? You gutless coward." She laughed at him and WHAM!!! An open-hand slap right across his wrinkled face. Morris didn't expect that, especially from a woman. He was stunned. It was followed by a back-hand slap, leaving Morris dizzy.

"Augh!!!" Morris was aching in pain. The back-hand slap busted his lip because Pearl had made sure the sharp ring on her finger connected with his mouth.

With all her power, Pearl yanked Morris out of bed and flung him into his wheelchair, which was placed against the wall. "What's wrong, Morris? Cyndi's not here to save your pathetic ass."

"I don't need Cyndi. I don't need any of you. You are all nothing to me."

"Keep it up, Grover, and I'll make sure this is an everyday occurrence," she threatened him. "I know people, too, so don't fuck with me." She paused after her warning, and then continued. "Like I said, you're late for lunch, so let's get going. If anybody asks about your lip, you say nothing, or it will be open season on not just you, but everyone here." Morris hated to be threatened, but didn't want anything bad to happen to any of the other patients, especially the ones he became close with. In his only defense, he gave Pearl a nod in agreement, knowing that he'd just made a deal with the devil. "Now that we've got this behind us, I'll wheel you to the lounge room so you can spend some time with your pathetic friends."

Morris was silent. He was wondering what made Pearl go ballistic on him. Could the job have finally gotten to her? Could someone in her family have died? Could it be that time of the month? It was a mystery to him. Still, he thought: *If this bitch fucks with me, I'll get her back in more ways than one. You can count on it.* He gave a somewhat distorted smile with his blown-up lip. Pearl was too busy wheeling him to notice or care.

When they entered the lounge room, Pearl just left the old man at the door entrance to wheel himself to his buddies. Going outside to satisfy her nicotine fit was way more important to Pearl than servicing the patients. She walked down the hall, digging in her purse in search of her cigarettes. By the time she got outside, the pack was in her hand. She stood under the roof, staring at the darkened sky. *Can't believe how dark it is today and thanks to that bitch calling in, I'm stuck here*, she thought to herself. She hit the box of cigarettes so that the ashes wouldn't fall on her when she smoked. She learned that old trick from her friend, Sue, who was no longer around.

While Pearl was outside, puffing away on her cigarette and looking above, a voice from behind her said, "Hey dolly. Can I join you?" Pearl turned to see who it was, and then shrugged her shoulders as if she didn't care. The voice continued. "Miserable day, huh?"

"What do you want, Helen?"

"What? I'm not allowed to make conversation?" Nurse Helen asked her.

—— THE NURSING HOME ——

"Not now! I just have things on my mind, okay?"

"What could be on your little bird-brain mind?" joked Helen.

"None of your business," Pearl shot back.

"If you're having personal issues, keep 'em at home. Don't bring it to the work place because nobody cares," retorted Helen. "By the way, I noticed the fat lip on Morris Grover."

"What are you talking about?" She pretended not to know what Helen was referring to.

"I'm not stupid, Pearl. You hit him, didn't you?"

"And if I did, who cares? He's a useless piece of shit, anyway."

"Listen, Pearl... I'm not going to say anything about it. See no evil, hear no evil," Helen said, trying to get on Pearl's level. "But if Cyndi finds out, you're toast."

"Don't you think I know this, Helen? I'm just having a horrible day, and then having to fucking deal with Grover... I'm telling you; I just want to kill somebody and Grover just makes it so easy. I admit, I could have killed him right there, but I restrained myself," she explained, breathing heavily.

"We're all having a bad day, Pearl. Especially since the new girl called in saying that she can't make it. I think her excuse was something about her son. I don't even know her name."

"Me neither," said Pearl. "To top it off, after I got out of work yesterday, I went to my mother's for dinner. She cooked her usual Friday corned beef and cabbage. We enjoyed the meal and talked, as usual. She told me about her Tuesday Bingo, yapped about going shopping,

– 282 –

complained to me that there are too many commercials on television, and went on about how much she misses Bob Barker hosting *The Price Is Right*."

Helen was thinking about how, outside of work, Pearl actually seemed like a caring person and not a bitch twenty-four seven, as she appeared to be. "My mother does all that stuff, too, but she's hooked on all of those morning talk shows. I just hope that I'm not like that when I'm her age."

"I couldn't agree with you more."

"So what happened next? You and your mom enjoying dinner..." Helen repeated.

"Yeah, so I go downstairs to look for the circuit breaker because we lost power. I don't know what happened, but five minutes later, I come back upstairs and I see my mother lying on the floor by the dining room table. She must have tried to grab the table or chair because the chair was on its side, as well."

"Damn."

"I called an ambulance. The E.M.T. came right away and raised her into the ambulance, and away they took her. I followed her to the hospital."

"Which hospital?"

"St. Mary's."

"I heard they're pretty good," Helen said positively.

"Me, too," agreed Pearl. "I'm just worrying about their staff."

"Don't worry. Your mother's in good hands."

"That's what I'm afraid of. When families drop their loved ones off here, we treat them like shit... and don't deny it, Helen." Helen was speechless. "Especially me; I had no excuse for what I did to Grover, that old fuck.

— THE NURSING HOME —

Now, because of my mother's heart attack, she has to stay there for a few days and I keep picturing what's happening to her." Pearl's voice began to get lower as tears started to build in her eyes.

"Take it easy, Pearl. It's gonna be fine. I've got to get back in there before these patients have a fit. The ones who actually know what's going on, that is."

A laugh came out of Pearl's mouth. "See ya soon." Her co-worker made her way back inside the building. "What goes around, comes around. I deserve this," Pearl said to herself out loud. She flicked her butt after finishing her smoke and went inside.

Morris had wheeled himself to his buddies when he had seen Pearl abandon him.

"Hi ya, Morris," greeted Ralph.

"Why are you always coming to lunch so much later than us?" asked Frank.

"I'll tell you why, Frankie, my boy," said Pauly cheerfully. "You see, guys... We're not good enough to be in the same room as Mori, here. He has to have his grand entrance like he's some Hollywood big-shot."

"That's not true, Pauly. And it's Morris to you."

"Well, Mori, today's Saturday. No news on in the morning; only cartoons. Were you watching some cartoons, Mori, old boy?"

"No!" Morris growled loudly. "I'm an old man. Cartoons are for kids." He tried to keep his face down so that nobody would notice the swelling on his lip.

"Come on, Mori. It's nothing to be ashamed of."

— JAMES J. MURPHY III —

"Yeah, Morris. None of us minded watching the Saturday morning cartoons with our kids," Ralph told him.

"Well, I wasn't watching any stupid cartoons. I woke up a little late and didn't even get a chance to eat my bowl of oatmeal. It was probably cold, anyway."

"That's what you get when you oversleep, Mori, old boy," Pauly reminded him.

"What I wouldn't do for a nice stack of hot pancakes smothered with syrup and butter." Frank's mouth was watering.

"Don't forget the whipped cream and the cherry on top," added Ralph. "Personally, I'm a French Toast person myself. I could go for a few golden slices right now with some sausage on the side. Mmmm."

"Look at you two lug-heads! What do you think this is? Some damn buffet?! I wouldn't mind some bacon, eggs, and toast, either, but don't expect any of it from this place. All we are getting is some cold slop. Right, Mori, old boy?"

"I can't believe that we are having this conversation. It's pathetic. First cartoons, now breakfast."

"Holy shit! What happened to your face?" Pauly was the first to get a good look at Morris's face. The rest of the patients took notice, as well.

"No need to worry, guys. I'm fine. I'd rather not discuss it." Morris knew he couldn't avoid eye contact any longer, especially since nothing could get past Pauly.

"Who did that to you, Morris, if you don't mind me asking?" questioned Wade.

"I do mind, Wade. Now leave me alone. It's no big deal, guys. Really." Morris tried to convince them of

— THE NURSING HOME —

that because he cared about his buddies, but he was also waiting for the perfect time to blurt out that Pearl was the perpetrator. Commotion ensued in the lounge room over Morris's fat lip. "Goddamnit, guys! Would you keep it down?!" Morris told them. "I don't want to draw attention to myself."

"Don't worry, Mori. That lip's doing enough without my big mouth," joked Pauly.

"Guys! Before Nurse Helen comes over!" Then Morris shook his head. "Too late," he whispered.

"Hey! Hey!" yelled Nurse Helen as she approached the gang. "Now you guys keep it down, would ya? This isn't a stadium. Got it?!"

"What? Are you gonna make us?" asked Pauly in defiance.

"I'm warning you guys." Helen was getting angry. "You'll get yours one day, Mr. Gardener," she promised Pauly, and then walked away. Pauly began bursting out with laughter.

"That wasn't funny." Morris had a serious look on his face.

"Don't tell me you're losing your sense of humor now, Mori."

"No, I'm not, Pauly. I don't want to be the center of attention, either."

"Don't worry, Morris. Pauly was only kidding," assured Ralph.

"Yeah, Morris. Pauly's never going to put you in harm's way," agreed Frank.

"I know, guys. But..."

"But what?" Pauly asked Morris.

– 286 –

— JAMES J. MURPHY III —

Before Morris could spit out what he was going to say, Pearl entered the lounge room after a long cigarette break. She walked up to Morris's group. The smell of smoke on her was so strong that Frank's eyes got watery. "Hi guys. Does anybody need anything?" she asked politely. Nurse Helen overheard Pearl and wondered if she was trying to be nice because of how she treated Morris or if it was because of how she thought the hospital was going to treat her mother. Pearl was acting like she actually cared about the patients, but deep down, she didn't. She just felt guilty. If somebody else mishandled the patients, she wouldn't give a damn.

The patients gave a shrug in acknowledgment. They might not all be able to help themselves, but the ones who still had their senses were definitely not stupid people. They knew a con when they saw one, especially Pauly. He hadn't trusted the staff since Day One and still didn't. The patients pretended to act interested in the program that was left on the television.

A few moments later, Brian cheerfully entered the room. "What's happening, fellas?"

"Don't we see enough of you during the week, Bri?" kidded Pauly.

"Trust me, I see enough of *you* during the week, as well, Pauly," he shot back with a laugh. "Please call me Brian."

"Whatever, Bri."

"So, what brings you to this neck of the woods today, Brian?" asked Ralph.

"Yeah, what's the deal?" chimed in Frank.

"I forgot my check again."

— THE NURSING HOME —

"They must pay you pretty damn well, aye, Bri?" Pauly egged him on.

"Well, I can't complain, but we all need a little more here and there. Why are you asking?"

"Because usually when pay day comes, people need it that day. They can't wait a day or two later, like in your case, Bri."

"First, can't you ever call me Brian?"

"No," Pauly responded. His buddies laughed.

"Second, yes, I do have expenses. That's why I need my check. I'm already a day late with the rent money. Thank God my landlord is an understanding and cool guy because if he wasn't, my ass would be thrown out on the street."

"Maybe you should look into direct deposit," Pauly suggested to him.

"Maybe I will." Brian hated when Pauly called him 'Bri,' but enjoyed talking to him because he was very up to date for an old man. "I gotta jet, guys." Ralph, Frank, and Wade all said goodbye. "Wait a minute. No goodbye from you, Morris?" Brian got a good look at his face and noticed his fat lip. "What the hell happened to you, Morris?"

"I've tried talking to these guys," Pearl quickly jumped in, "but they didn't respond."

Anger had been building up inside of Morris, and finally, he exploded. "It was Pearl!" he screamed. "She did this to me!"

"Are you feeling okay, Morris? You're getting too loud. Please keep it down." Pearl immediately tried to change the subject.

"FUCK YOU, PEARL!!! This horrible bitch did this to me," he accused her, pointing his finger in her

– 288 –

direction. Pearl was ready to go off like dynamite. If her fuse had been lit any other time, she would have exploded on whoever or whatever, but it was her mother she was thinking about. "I swear, if I wasn't crippled, I'd bash your fucking face in, you bitch!"

"Okay, settle down, Morris," Brian told him. "I didn't witness anything, Pearl, but if I ever see you mistreat these patients in any way, shape, or form, I'll bash your head in myself."

Pearl was turning pinkish-red. She really wanted the old man to have it, but at the same time, she knew she deserved it. But who was to say she couldn't unleash on Brian? "Brian, why don't you just grab your check and get out of here? You're not on the clock, so I suggest you leave."

"I'm warning you, Pearl," threatened Brian.

"I'm also warning *you*, Brian," she retorted back. "Cyndi comes in on Monday. Take it up with her. I'm in charge right now, so get out of here."

Brian didn't want any more of a riot, so he took his check and left.

Pearl stared right into Morris's face. "Never again," she warned him, pointing her finger, and left.

After the noise level got lower, the patients either watched television or talked amongst themselves. Morris explained and apologized to his friends about the incident. He told them he was threatened and didn't want anybody to get into trouble. They all understood and cheered Morris up. The gang enjoyed the rest of the afternoon together, telling old stories about themselves until they had to go back to their rooms for dinner.

—— THE NURSING HOME ——

"Off to the nut house once again, aye, Conway?"

"It's a nursing home, O'Conner, and yes," he verified. "Let's see... a fuckin' rainstorm – and we have to travel in it."

"Hey, this was your idea, rookie. You bargained for this. Don't let a little rain keep you down."

"You're right," agreed Officer Conway. "I just hate when these damn mirrors fog up."

"Use the defogger, kid."

"What?"

"I said, 'Use the defogger.'"

"Don't you mean the defroster?"

"You know what I mean!"

Conway shook his head and decided to talk about something else. "Hopefully something happens soon."

"What? Are you kidding me, Conway? I hope nothing ever happens. This is great; getting paid to watch patients scratch themselves or miss their mouths when they eat!" laughed Officer O'Conner.

"I know, or when a nurse bends over. Too bad there aren't that many attractive ones here."

"Oh, well. That's what happens when the oatmeal dries up."

Conway turned his head towards his partner while his left hand was on the steering wheel and gave him a look that conveyed that he had never heard such a dumb comment in his entire life. O'Conner saw the look and didn't bother responding. He knew it was a stupid comment. There was silence for a moment. "Do you know what this place needs?" asked Conway.

"What's that?"

– 290 –

JAMES J. MURPHY III

"Sound. Watching the staff and patients on film with no sound makes me feel old."

"If I remember correctly, sound was first introduced into motion pictures around the 1920s. All of those Charlie Chaplin movies had no sound, you know," informed O'Conner.

"Charlie who?"

O'Conner forgot that Conway was a young man. He couldn't comprehend anything from 1995 or earlier, like a lot of people his age. "Charlie Sheen." O'Conner gave him a quick response.

"Dude, Charlie Sheen's the man!"

"Yeah, you've been talking to those kids again, I see."

"I haven't spoken to those kids since the day we interrogated them at Rigg's. The only reason I talked to that girl when we were at the newsstand was to get info."

"Are you sure it wasn't to get into her pants, Conway?"

"Fuck you, O'Conner."

"Or fuck her." They both laughed.

"She's not that bad lookin', O'Conner, don't you think?"

"Listen, rookie... I'm in my mid-forties, paying off a house, and married. I'm not blowing any of that away for some young tang. Got it?"

"Yeah, Dad. Just chill, okay?" responded Conway.

"Next light, make a right."

"For what? I thought we were going to the nursing home."

"We are, rookie. But what's wrong with eating dinner first?"

"Nothing's wrong with that." Conway made the turn.

— THE NURSING HOME —

"Make a left on Oak Street," instructed O'Conner.

Conway jerked the wheel, while O'Conner held on to the hand brace above his head. "Are you going to tell me the name of this place or do I have to guess?"

"It's gonna come up on the left, Conway. Don't soil your boxers."

"Ha, ha. Very funny, old man."

"Who are you calling old? Just because I got a good few years on you..."

"Those gray hairs do it for you," Conway kidded him.

"Don't worry, rookie. Your time will come. And your next partner will say the same to you."

"I know, O'Conner. That's why I need to get my jokes out while I'm still young."

"Wait! There it is up ahead," O'Conner told him.

"What?"

"Bob's Steakhouse! Only the best steakhouse in Florida."

"We'll find out," Conway said.

"Bob and I go way back."

"Is he the owner?"

"Yes, he is. Why do you think it's called 'Bob's' Steakhouse?"

"Are our meals going to be free?"

"Of course they are. He favors cops," O'Conner told his younger partner.

"Let's see... You know the guy and the food's free... Of course you're going to kiss his ass and say how great this place is."

"That's not true, Conway. Let's just go in and eat, okay?"

"Fine with me."

— 292 —

—— JAMES J. MURPHY III ——

The police officers got out of the van and into the rain and started walking. When they entered the steakhouse, the hostess greeted them and asked, "How many will there be tonight?"

"Two," replied O'Conner. "Is Bob here tonight? I'm his old buddy, Officer O'Conner, and this is my partner, Officer Conway."

"Hey," greeted Conway.

"Who's Bob?" the hostess asked.

"The owner," O'Conner said with attitude, starting to get pissed off.

"Oh, him," the brunette said, twirling her hair with her finger.

"Yeah, him."

"He, like, died six months ago or something."

"What? Are you kidding me?"

"No, Officer. His son, Tim, runs the place now... but for how long is the question. This place has gone downhill since he's taken over. No offense. He's really a nice guy, but he doesn't know what he's doing."

"Is Tim around?" asked Conway, knowing that his partner was speechless after hearing the bad news.

"Not at the moment. He comes and goes. Party of two, was that?" she asked, trying to change the subject.

"Yes," said Conway.

"Follow me, Officers. Is the booth okay?"

"Just fine-" Conway hesitated. "Sally," he said as he caught the name off her name tag.

"A waiter will be here shortly to serve you. Don't worry, Officers, it's still on the house." She placed two menus down on the table. They both thanked her and nodded with a smile.

— THE NURSING HOME —

"I can't believe my buddy, Bob, died six months ago," O'Conner went on, still fixated on the death of his friend.

"Things happen, O'Conner. People die."

"I know, Conway, but someone could have told me."

"If you weren't informed, maybe you weren't really that close."

"Maybe you're right, partner," the veteran responded. "Let's eat! I'm starving."

"Me, too!" They quickly glanced at the menus.

A few minutes later, a waiter came over with two glasses of water. He was a young man between the ages of eighteen and twenty-one. He had short brown hair that was combed forward and gelled up in the front. It appeared that he'd been trying to go for a trendy hairstyle. "Would you gentlemen like anything to drink?"

Both officers said, "Coffee" simultaneously.

The waiter took out his notepad and jotted it down. "Have you Officers decided on what to order?"

"I'll have the London Broil with mashed potatoes," O'Conner told him.

"How would you like the steak cooked?"

"Medium-well."

"And how about you, sir?" The waiter turned in Conway's direction.

"I'll have the Charcoal Triple Decker Burger with fries."

"Would you also like it medium-well?"

"Yes, please," Conway told him kindly.

"Your food will be here shortly," the waiter told them. He picked up the menus and walked to the back.

"Thanks for suggesting this place, O'Conner."

– 294 –

"No problem, buddy. Conway, could I get serious with you for a moment?"

"What about?"

"Rigg's," he said sternly.

"Let me guess. The murders, right?"

"What else? You know, Conway, the Captain ain't gonna let us patrol Rigg's forever."

"Don't worry, O'Conner, I believe we'll catch somebody very soon. I've been having my roommate, Ryan, go through the tapes to see if he sees anything fishy."

"The Captain's gonna kill you if he finds out."

"O'Conner, the Captain's not going to find out and I know you enjoy getting paid for doing absolutely nothing."

"You're right about that, Conway. Can you trust this Ryan character?"

"He's my roommate, O'Conner, for over a year now. I believe I can trust him. Besides, if he screws me over, I know where he lives." They both laughed. "So let's enjoy it while we can." O'Conner agreed on it. The officers' dinners came. They enjoyed the free meals and then went to Rigg's to stake out.

"Oh, shit! Eight-thirty already?!" Beth's voice echoed.

"Keep it down up there!" a voice yelled from downstairs.

"Sorry, Mom!" Beth was almost done touching up her face in camouflage, being extra careful around the eye area. She wished she had a camera because she couldn't stop looking in the mirror. Beth was not one of those glamour-type girls that always needed a mirror so they

—— THE NURSING HOME ——

could touch up their makeup, but she sure outdid herself with the camouflage. To go with her camouflage face were her black boots, army pants, and tight shirt. Her shirt rose up a little. She hated when that happened because guys got turned on by it. After the shirt would rise and they'd see a belly button, they'd want to see more. There was no need to worry about Jeff and Jay; they were always in their own little fantasy world, anyway. But she had to worry about Ron. It wasn't that he'd make a move or do anything, but she knew he'd probably shoot his load and get her seats sticky from being so nervous. I don't want to be the one to clean up the mess, she laughed to herself. Beth walked down the steps.

"Where are you off to tonight?" her mother asked. "Don't you know there's a damn thunderstorm out there? I wouldn't be shocked if there are floods."

"Going out with friends."

"Why do you have all that paint on your face? You look like an idiot."

"Nice talking to you, too, Mom." Beth left, closing the door behind her, while her mother was still talking. She got into her car and backed out so quickly that she hadn't looked to see if any cars were coming. Thank goodness there weren't any, she thought. She was really pissed off about her mother's comments, but realized that there were more important issues at hand.

When Beth was driving to Ron's house, she pictured him looking like a stick figure in camouflage and began laughing hysterically. Ron was waiting inside his house when she arrived. Beth beeped her horn and Ron came running outside with the rain hitting his skinny body.

–296–

"Ha-ha-hi Beth."

"Stop with the bullshit and hop in," she said, amused. Ron's face was covered in black. He wore black pants; a black T-shirt that looked like it would fit an eight year old boy, which Ron was built like, anyway; and black sneakers because boots hurt his ankles. They went off to the park to meet Jeff and Jay.

"I can't fucking believe this!" Jay bitched to Jeff.

"What, man?" asked Jeff.

"It's 8:50 and it's raining. We could be watching a horror movie. Where the hell are those two?"

"Don't worry, dude. They'll be here. Beth probably had to touch up her camouflage or something."

"Yeah! Heh! Women!" said Jay. Jeff just laughed. Jay was wearing his usual baggy black pants and low-top black sneakers with a black shirt. He had light black Halloween makeup on his face, looking more like a Goth kid than someone who was in disguise.

Jeff went all out for the occasion, as if it was actually Halloween. He camouflaged his face perfectly with the green, brown, tan, and black colors. He even one-upped everybody and did his arms. If Jeff didn't work at Rigg's and Kirk's, he'd make out to be a great makeup artist. To accompany his face and arms, he was wearing camouflage pants; a black T-shirt with no actual writing, pictures, or logos on it; black boots; and he brought an army helmet just for fun. It was up to him to decide if he wanted to wear it. Jeff's favorite holiday was Halloween. He wished he could dress up every day, but he'd rather

— THE NURSING HOME —

dress like a ghoul than a soldier. All he needed was his pumpkin trick-or-treat bag.

Jay was worrying too much about the time. He kept looking at his cell phone and pacing back and forth. "Damnit."

"Jay, give it a rest! You are really pissing me off right now. It's not like we're really getting wet. At least we're under these park umbrellas."

"Oh, wow! Park umbrellas! Well, tell them to get their asses over here!"

"Fine. I'll give them a call." Jeff took his cell phone out of his pocket, and then saw headlights coming towards them from a distance. "Never mind."

Beth parked her car next to Jeff's and shut the lights off. She and Ron got out of her car and walked towards Jeff and Jay. "Sorry we're late," Beth apologized.

"Yeah, let me guess... Touching up your camouflage?" Jay said, being sarcastic.

"Jay, is there anything else you can do besides complain?" asked Beth.

"Lots of things," he shot back.

Jeff was staring at Beth. He was very impressed with how she did her camouflage so neatly and really liked her short shirt, as well.

After Jay and Beth finished with their child's play, Ron spoke up and greeted Jay and Jeff.

"Holy shit, Ron! Did you borrow that T-shirt from your kid brother?" Jay asked, laughing at him.

"For your information, Jay, I do not have a kid brother."

"It must have been your sister."

— JAMES J. MURPHY III —

"Ha, ha... very funny. Let's get this over with." Ron was still nervous about breaking into Rigg's.

"You know, Ronny boy, when you break in, at least you'll get to see Rita."

"Leave her alone, Jay."

"'Oh, Rita! Yes! Oh, yeah!' 'Oh, yeah! Fuck me, Ron! Please! That kid-sized shirt makes me wet,'" Jay teased him, mimicking the voices of both Ron and Rita.

"Shut up, Jay!" Ron demanded. Even Jeff started laughing at how stupid his buddy was acting.

"Alright, guys. Break it up," Beth interrupted, acting as a referee. "Ron, use your anger for when we break in. And Jay..." She paused.

"Yeah, Beth?"

"Are you sure those pants are baggy enough for ya?"

"She's got a point, dude," Jeff jumped in. "You could fit a family in there." How Jay was going to be able to run from the security guard, Bronski, was a mystery to everyone. But Jeff knew better than to underestimate the young rebel. He had run from the best in high school, while Jeff usually got his ass handed to him.

"Don't question the power of the pants," Jay told them with a laugh.

"You guys know the plan?" Beth double-checked with them.

"Yes. For the hundredth time, yes, Beth. Me and Jeff get Bronski's attention. He'll probably eat us for dinner, but at least you and Ronny boy get to go in and see what's up."

"Glad you guys understand. We'll take my car."

The four of them began walking to her car and Jay shouted, "Shotgun!" He sat in the front with Beth, while

– 299 –

— THE NURSING HOME —

Jeff was seated in the back with Ron. "Got any good tunes, Beth?" asked Jay.

"Nothing that you'd be interested in. I have some sounds of wildlife and nature."

"Sounds of wildlife and nature?! Damn! I need something heavy."

"Tough luck," she said. "There was a special on an animal channel and they gave a website where you could go and sample the sounds of the wildlife and nature. Instead, I downloaded it and burned it to a CD. I really enjoy these animal sounds."

"It's cool," Jay told her.

The kids pulled up to the side of the Rigg's building, not too far from where Bronski was patrolling. Beth didn't want the car to be within Bronski's sight. "You guys know what to do, right?"

"Don't worry, Beth. Piece of cake," said Jeff.

"More like *road kill*," commented Jay.

"Just distract him so me and Ron could get in," instructed Beth.

They both said, "Okay."

Bronski was standing in front of Rigg's all chiseled up. He stood six feet, two inches and weighed two hundred and thirty-seven pounds with not a single ounce of fat on his body. He could be the guy of some girls' dreams. He was very tan and had a flat-top hairstyle with the sides shaved.

"I hope you're ready. It's time," Beth told them.

"Nice knowing ya," said Jay.

"Good luck," she wished them. The boys got out of Beth's car and made their short walk to confront Bronski.

– 300 –

On the other side of the building sat Officers Conway and O'Conner.

"Another dull night, aye, buddy?" said O'Conner. "But at least we're getting paid for it."

"Very dull, if you ask me."

"I just did."

"Oh, real funny, O'Conner," Conway said sarcastically. "Hey, O'Conner!"

"What?"

"Did you remember seeing a blue car on the side of the building?"

"I don't know, Conway. Maybe it belongs to one of the employees."

"Well, they're parked in an awful weird spot, wouldn't ya say?" he asked with curiosity.

"Maybe they got lost driving around the building in the rain," suggested O'Conner.

"Oh, you're full of answers tonight, buddy." Conway went to grab a can of soda from the back of the van. He opened his cola and took a gulp. "Oh! That hits the spot." Conway was in his glory.

"Holy shit!" yelled O'Conner from the front of the van.

"What is it, O'Conner?!"

"You better get your ass up here and take a look at this." Conway rushed back up. "What's going on?"

"Look at the screen. Aren't those the two burnout kids from the park you always talk to? It's hard to tell... Is that face paint they're wearing?"

"Shit!" yelled Conway. The officers were watching the screen to see what the kids could possibly be up to.

"Do these kids have a death wish? Look at how big the security guard is compared to them," O'Conner went on.

— THE NURSING HOME —

"Let's break it up."

"Give it a minute."

"A minute may be too late. That security guard will bury them into the ground." Conway was worried.

"I know," said O'Conner, "but nothing seems to be happening."

"If even one thing begins to happen, we rush our asses over there - *pronto*," Conway warned him. The officers continued watching the screen.

"Hey Bronski. I forgot my pen. Be right out," said Jay, overdoing his attempt to be casual.

"After hours, if you're not scheduled… leave," Bronski told them, grabbing Jay by the shirt and shoving him away.

"What the fuck's your problem, Bronski?" asked Jeff.

"You two string beans," said Bronski, mocking them. "Just get out of here. I don't want to have to hurt either of you or smear your makeup."

"Hurt us? You couldn't even hurt your virgin girlfriend, if you know what I mean," teased Jay.

"Ohh! That's a good one, bro," cheered Jeff. Bronski's brown eyes filled up with rage. "That was a low blow because his girlfriend won't give him any. She's saving herself for a real man, who actually knows what he is doing." He kept egging the huge security guard on.

"Get out of here - NOW!!! I better call the cops because there will be two more deaths if you guys don't knock it off."

"I'd like to see you try, you jacked-up Frankenstein!" Jeff yelled to him. "We know Bronski can't fight his own

– 302 –

battles. Right, Jay?"

"No, man... He can't," answered Jay. Bronski was fuming so hard that he looked like he was about to chase a matador like a bull. "You know what they say about juice-heads?"

"What's that, Jay?"

"They can't do anything by themselves!" Jay shouted. "Ohh!" The kids gave each other a high five, as if they scored a touch-down against the giant.

"I will kill you both if you two don't leave!"

"Just try it!" Jeff spat right in Bronski's face. The blob of white gooey phlegm that hung on Bronski's face began to drip. When they saw Bronski look up with the spit on his face, they knew it was time to run like hell.

"Damnit!" shouted O'Conner, who witnessed the entire incident from inside the van. "You were right, Conway. Step on it! Now!" The officers headed to the entrance way because they believed a fight was going to break out.

"Augh!" bellowed Bronski.

"Run!" yelled Jeff. The kids started running like there was no tomorrow. If Bronski caught them, they'd be dead.

"I'm going to fucking kill you two little turds!!! You're fucking dead!!!" Bronski yelled at the top of his lungs. The bull went on the attack. Jeff and Jay succeeded in luring Bronski away from the fort to help their friends go in.

—— THE NURSING HOME ——

"That's our cue!" announced Beth. She and Ron exited her car and ran to the building.

The officers arrived at the entrance of the building, but Bronski and the boys were nowhere in sight. They got out of the van and began searching the premises. "Damnit! Where are they?!" Conway wanted answers.

"Look! Two more sneaking in!" O'Conner said, pointing from a distance. "Let's get 'em!" The officers then focused on Ron and Beth.

"Run faster, Ron!" Beth screamed. "They're gaining on us!"

"I am! I am!" Ron shouted back. "I need new shoelaces!"

"Not now! Keep running!" Beth demanded. The officers were hot on their trail. "We're almost there. Just a few more feet, Ron," she told him as she was running out of breath. Finally, Beth made it inside, while Ron scurried in behind her and locked the door. "They could open it easily," Beth warned him.

"I locked it," Ron told her.

"I know, but cops could break a lock just like *that*," Beth explained with a snap of her fingers. "We gotta get to the second floor."

"Let's go," encouraged Ron. "It wouldn't be shocking if Bronski chased Jeff and Jay out of the state."

— 304 —

"Damnit! The door won't budge," complained Conway as he pushed the door with all his muscle.

"Stand aside, kid! Let a man show you how it's done." O'Conner cracked his knuckles.

"Man? My ass!"

O'Conner took over. "You're right, rookie. It won't budge."

"Told ya!"

"What could be holding it closed?" O'Conner had a puzzled expression on his face. The officers continued their attempt to open the door, but had no luck. The two of them never met a lock that they couldn't break.

Beth and Ron ran to the elevator, passing staff members on the way. They heard voices of fellow co-workers. Comments filled the air, such as: *'Hi Beth. Little late, isn't it?'* and *'Where are you going in such a rush, Ron?'* and even *'What's with the get-up, you two?'* referring to their attire. Beth paid no mind to the staff and Ron followed behind her. Their goal was to get to the second floor. The kids got in the elevator and Beth pressed the number '2' button. The doors closed and the number '2' lit up in the color orange. *'Ding!'* was the sound of the bell as the elevator stopped on the second floor. The kids got out and ran past more staff members.

"I gotta go, Ilene," Pearl said into the phone as she caught sight of Beth and Ron. "Unwanted visitors just zoomed by me." Pearl hung up the phone and turned around to see where the kids were heading. "Hey!" Pearl called out to them. "You two aren't on the clock. Get out of here!"

— THE NURSING HOME —

They didn't say anything to her as they made it to the free computer at the reception desk. The computer was on, but running slow. "Put the CD in, Beth! Pearl looks furious," Ron warned her, noticing Pearl was on the march.

"Not my problem."

"What exactly are you going to do, again, when the names pop up, Beth?"

"When the list comes up, I'll call out the names of each patient."

"Isn't that evil or something?" Ron was having second thoughts.

"No! Do you see me at a campfire with a fucking Ouija board?"

Pearl was getting closer. "I told you that you're not allowed here! Get the fuck out of here or I'll call security!"

"Do it!" Beth dared Pearl, knowing that Bronski was off chasing Jeff and Jay to God-knows-where. "And I'll call the police for harassment! Now get out of my fucking sight!" The names popped up on the screen. Beth didn't waste any time. "Arnold Green! Lee Casey! Debbie Cooler!" She was yelling out the names like there was no tomorrow.

Pearl thought that Beth was crazy. "What the fuck are doing, girl? Have you gone nuts, like our patients?"

"Not even close!" Beth shouted, not bothering to look in Pearl's direction. Many names had appeared on the screen, starting with the most recent death on the top. Beth had been calling the names out in no particular order and finally decided to scroll down and yell the last name on the list, which was the first death ever to happen at Rigg's. "GLORIA MIGUEL!"

– 306 –

— JAMES J. MURPHY III —

"Beth, you won't believe this..." Ron didn't know what to think.

"What? I'm busy!" Beth looked up to see down the hall. Patients were walking out of their rooms very slowly. "Holy shit!"

Pearl looked down the hall, as well. "No way! But how?" Pearl picked up the phone to make an announcement on the intercom. "Helen, page reception - NOW!"

Helen paged her back. "Yes, Pearl?"

"Look! Fucking patients *walking*! Without wheelchairs! Am I seeing things?"

"I see it, but I don't believe it. Pearl, I'll be right- AUGH!"

"Helen! What's going on?"

"Pau- Augh!" She couldn't even finish saying Pauly Gardener's name. He was suffocating her with a plastic bag. Other patients who were passing Pauly's room saw Helen struggling. The mob went into Pauly's room and started attacking Helen. A pair of scissors were sitting on the nightstand in Pauly's room. It caught the eye of one of the patients. The patient dragged his wrinkled, old body to the nightstand, grabbed the scissors, and made his way towards Helen. As Helen was fighting for her life against the mob of patients, the patient with the scissors in his hands made his way to her and stabbed her repeatedly in the back until she fell to the ground.

Dr. Owens, Rita, and some of the other Rigg's employees ran to the reception area. "I don't believe it," expressed Dr. Owens, completely amazed.

"Can't be..." said Rita with her eyes wide open in shock.

— THE NURSING HOME —

"It is," Beth responded. After Beth had called Gloria Miguel's name, a cloud of smoke appeared as a ghostly figure. "Gloria Miguel? Is that you? And why are you doing this?" Beth asked the figure. She didn't exactly know what to expect, but she was hoping to get some answers.

A voice came from the cloud of smoke. "**I am not Gloria Miguel. She is dead, thanks to this incompetent nursing home. Refer to me as Rathul!**"

"Well, Glor-, I mean Rathul..." Ron corrected himself in a shy manner. "Why are you doing this? Why?!" he repeated, growing angry.

"Yeah," Beth said, demanding to know. "We never harmed you in any way."

"**Oh, no!?!**" he bellowed. "**How about today? A patient in room 243 got beaten earlier this afternoon... by that one.**" The ghostly figure pointed to Pearl.

"Sorry," Pearl said, putting her hands in the air.

"**How about the other patients who have died here in the past, thanks to you? But I got some revenge. One of my best victories was when I had that arrogant asshole die. I believe his name was Bill,**" Rathul revealed to them with a boisterous laugh. "**Now it's time for me to get my major victory, and that would be to put an end to all of you,**" he told them with an energetic, evil smile.

"Look down the hall," instructed Dr. Owens.

"They's gettin' closer," Clevon said, still wearing his earphones.

"Do you believe this?" Pearl asked in astonishment. "They're dragging their worthless bodies like a couple of-"

"Zombies." Beth finished Pearl's sentence.

"Never thought I'd see this in a million years," said Rita.

– 308 –

— JAMES J. MURPHY III —

"You already killed Helen, I'm presuming," Beth said to Rathul.

"You presume right. And you're next."

"But you never answered our question. Why are you doing this?" Beth asked him again.

"You want to know why?"

Everyone replied with: "Yes."

"Well, let me begin..." Rathul said, prepared to explain himself. **"The story goes like this: I was born on May 3, 1800 in Tampa Bay, Florida... Growing up, my family was really poor... At one time, Florida was an all-Spanish state, but I noticed the colony was changing... It started becoming all-American... This would mean that us Spaniards would be wiped out... My family and my people were being driven out of our own homes..."**

"There was a great special on a history channel about the 1800s Spanish American Revolutions," Ron interrupted. "I'm going to be–"

Before Ron could finish his sentence, Rathul looked right at his geeky face and said, **"Shut your mouth, you useless sack of shit. Just because you watched a television special or studied the subject in school, it doesn't make you an expert. Guess what, you waste of life? I didn't watch it or study it; I lived it and suffered through it."**

Ron's face turned red and filled up with guilt. "I'm sorry. I didn't mean any harm." He tried explaining himself to the evil ghost.

"Let me continue," Rathul warned them. **"I wanted to seek revenge on the Americans for what they had done to me and my people... This hatred built up inside me for a very long time."**

—— THE NURSING HOME ——

"So, wutts yous do?" asked Clevon.

"**About thirty years later, my wife and I were wandering in Tampa Bay... seeing how the state of Florida has changed... We went back to the house where I grew up in, or got kicked out of, however you want to put it... just to find out that my home was no longer in existence.**"

"So, what did you do?" asked Dr. Owens, seeming very interested.

The patients dragged their bodies past room 240. "They're getting closer," Rita notified the group.

"**Shut up! What was once my home was now a field for slaves.**" Explaining how his people were slaves still put tears in his eyes just like it did nearly two hundred years ago. "**I ran away and out onto the dirt road like a gutless coward, just to take a deep breath.**"

As Rathul was telling his story to the staff on the second floor, patients had already taken the lives of three staff members on the first floor and four on the third floor. Rathul was very pleased with the results.

Patients were dragging their bodies past room 237. The staff members were so preoccupied with the patients making their way down from room 250 that they had no idea that the rest of the patients from the other side of the hall were creeping up as well.

Rathul went on with his story. "**A horse was charging, pulling a wagon... It was about to hit me, but my wife, Gloria, pushed me out of the way...**"

"At least you weren't hurt," interrupted Beth.

"**Trust me, I was. When Gloria pushed me out of the way, she got hit by the wagon instead... It should have**

JAMES J. MURPHY III

been me, damnit!" Rathul screamed, remembering the painful time.

"It shou-shou-should have been no one," Ron stuttered.

"Quiet!" Rathul yelled, pointing his ghostly finger at Ron. "I don't want your sympathy... Nothing happened to me... The gentleman who was riding the horse looked concerned... He offered assistance. This person and I helped Gloria up and we went to the newly built Rigg's Nursing Home... At the time, Rigg's was the closest thing this town had to a hospital, so we took her..."

"Was Gloria okay?" asked Beth, making sure she didn't upset Rathul any more than he already was.

"Why don't I show you all a picture of what happened?" The staff members were nervous about what they would see and the patients seemed to be making their way closer. Suddenly, another figure of smoke got conjured up. "See that woman lying in bed?" What the group saw was a lady lying helplessly in a hospital bed. "That's my wife, Gloria... And now... do you see this prick?" Another ghost figure appeared next to Gloria. Instead of paying concern to Gloria, the ghostly figure was reading a newspaper and laughing. "He's the doctor." The vision continued. "A few hours later, Gloria woke up... '*Where am I.*' she wondered to herself... A doctor came in and clarified to her that I, her husband, had said that she got hit by a wagon... '*It looks like you'll remain here for a really long time,*' the doctor told her." Rathul paused with a sad look on his face. "Unfortunately, there was nothing that I could do," he said in sheer disappointment. "Now, if you thought that was bad, listen to this..." he told them. "Watch!" The staff obeyed the ghostly cloud.

– 311 –

—— THE NURSING HOME ——

"'*I need to get out of here*!' my wife screamed. That's when she realized that she was condemned to a wheelchair. She stayed at Rigg's Nursing Home for two years and I tried visiting her every chance I got. During those last two years of her life, it was a living hell... The staff was American... You know how they felt towards Spanish people back then... The staff ridiculed her and her people... They made fun of her because she was in a wheelchair... They beat her, and even more degrading, they raped her. She was fed every few days... Basically, the Rigg's staff had fun seeing how long she could suffer." Rathul took a moment to pause. "I hope you all enjoyed the history of this miserable nursing home. I sure as hell haven't." The staff members felt guilty and were speechless. "So, to answer your question of why I am doing this is quite simple. From what you have witnessed, can you blame me?"

"So, you're the one who carved '1843' into Bill's body," Pearl stated.

"Did you mean the year 1843?" questioned Beth.

"Be-eth," whined Ron. He was growing more nervous as he saw the patients slowly getting closer. Beth didn't pay any mind to Ron. She was too busy listening to Rathul's story, like the others.

"In 1843, the staff working at this place thought it would be fun to see how long my wife could go without eating or drinking. She died only after a few weeks and, coincidentally, it just happened to be on my birthday. Over the years, I have come back, through the minds of the patients, to seek revenge on abusive staff members. But never before have I seen so many helpless patients die due to lack of responsibility as I've seen in this past year.

So now, I have come, once and for all, as their only defense. I can't watch them go through what my wife went through." He paused, and then added, "I love you, Gloria."

"But we never did anything to you," argued Beth.

"Yeah. We weren't alive at the time," said Ron.

"Why are you making such a big thing over this?" asked Pearl nonchalantly. Everyone looked at Pearl, as if to tell her to shut up. "It was a long time ago."

The patients were only a few rooms away on each side. The staff was being surrounded.

All Rathul said to them was: "**Prepare to die.**"

"Now look what you've done, Pearl," said Dr. Owens in frustration.

"I's don't wants ta die," said Clevon, scared shitless.

Rita was speechless.

"They're coming, Beth. What do we do?" asked Ron, hoping she had an answer.

"If it's a fight Rathul wants, it's a fight Rathul gets," Beth said, determined. The group of staff members was trapped. "It's time to fight. ATTACK!"

The staff knew they were in for a war against the possessed patients. They searched for what they could use as weapons. Clevon took the chain off of his wallet, ready for battle, with the earphones still in his ears. Dr. Owens got a club from under the reception desk. Pearl yanked the keyboard from the computer and intended to be hostile. Rita reached for pepper-spray from her purse. Ron had nothing, so he grabbed a ruler. Beth had a hunting knife that she stole from her father earlier in the evening to be prepared.

"Oh, shit!" screamed Rita. They all turned around, realizing that they were being trapped from both sides.

— THE NURSING HOME —

"Fuck!" shouted Beth.

"What do we do, Beth? We're dead," said Ron.

"Yeah, with that attitude, we are. Hopefully we get some help." Dr. Owens tried to stay positive.

"Immediately," added Pearl. "I'll call the police." She picked up the phone and dialed 911.

"I's don't wants ta die," repeated Clevon.

A patient who had gotten their hands on a butter knife from the breakroom was about to stab Rita from behind. Ron attempted to play super hero. He pushed Rita out of the way and got stabbed in the arm with the butter knife. He fell to the ground, like a sack of potatoes, holding his arm. Ron began to whimper like a girl. His skin was punctured, but he was not bleeding profusely as if he'd been shot.

Pearl listened on the phone as the operator asked her about her emergency. Holding the phone away from her mouth, Pearl told Beth: "By the time the police come, we'll all be dead."

"Keep trying!" encouraged Beth.

As Pearl was beginning to inform the operator of the situation, she got disconnected. "Hello? Hello!?!" Pearl yelled. A patient had ripped the cord out of the phone socket. Pearl then joined the fight. She hit Mildred from room 233 over the head with the telephone. Beth was trying not to hurt the patients because she knew they were under Rathul's power.

Three staff members came from the third floor down to the second floor. It looked like they were entering a new fight after just escaping the possessed patients from the third floor. "Watch out, Carlos!" a staff member warned

– 314 –

— JAMES J. MURPHY III —

his co-worker. Carlos didn't have enough time to answer. He got stabbed in the back of the neck with a pen. He fell to his knees while being attacked by the mob.

"Help him, David!" yelled Dr. Owens.

"Get your ass over here, Jackie!" yelled Pearl to another co-worker. "Hopefully we get more help; we need it."

"Tell me about it," said Jackie. "We were lucky enough to get off the third floor in one piece. What the hell is going on here?!" Pearl's attention was so focused on defending herself that she couldn't respond.

Clevon began swinging his chain. He was hitting some of the patients with it, making them stagger. "I's goin' ta kick yo' ass." He was full of energy until he got stabbed in the gut by a patient. Clevon fell to the ground, holding his stomach while the blood was pouring out. He continuously got mauled by the mob of patients.

"Take that, fuckers!" shouted Dr. Owens, who hardly ever swore. He was clubbing the patients. The doctor was doing great, but he was strongly outnumbered. Two patients got Dr. Owens from behind. He tried to swing, but there were too many of them. He got stabbed on the side of his stomach with a screwdriver, which made him fall to the floor. He had to fight for dear life. There are just too many damn patients, Dr. Owens thought, feeling defenseless. They did a number on him as he continuously got stabbed with the screwdriver. He was scared about the amount of blood he was losing.

"Do something, Beth!" Ron yelled, still on the floor, holding his arm.

"I'm trying!" she yelled back.

"Ha, ha, ha, ha! How does it feel now?"

– 315 –

THE NURSING HOME

David, from floor three, went after the patients with a heavy-duty flashlight. There weren't that many possible weapons available around the reception desk to choose from. Pearl ripped the computer from the outlet and used the wire to choke out a patient. The war continued inside of the nursing home.

From outside of Rigg's, the officers called for back up. Officers Jackson, O'Leary, and a few others arrived right away. "I hope this is good, O'Conner," laughed O'Leary.

"We can't get the fucking door opened," O'Conner told him.

"You wasted our time on *this?*" complained Jackson.

"Watch your mouth, Action Jackson!" Conway told him off. "Help us open this fucker, wouldcha?" The officers who arrived at the scene gave it a shot. Still, the door wouldn't budge.

"What's holding this damn door shut?" asked Jackson.

"What's the matter, Jackson? Didn't you do your workout this morning?" Conway teased him.

"Real funny," said Jackson.

"We've been at it for nearly twenty minutes," explained O'Conner.

"On one door?!" argued Jackson.

"No, we also tried the other entrance and the windows while we were waiting for you guys to get here," stated Conway.

"Why don't we split up?" asked Jackson.

"Between all of us, we'll get this thing open," insisted O'Leary. "Let's just stick together." The officers did as he

– 316 –

suggested and worked as a unit.

Meanwhile, Jeff and Jay were racing back towards the nursing home.

"Just keep running," insisted Jeff.

The boys took a breather as they hid inside a Dumpster for a while. They were desperate. Bronski figured out where he could find the two pieces of trash. "How the fuck did Bronski find us?" asked Jay. Before Bronski could catch them, Jeff and Jay jumped out of the Dumpster and ran past the officers, yelling and screaming. Bronski was in hot pursuit.

"Hey!" yelled O'Conner. "Those three are the ones who got us in this mess to begin with. After them!" The police started chasing Bronski around the building, as Bronski was chasing Jeff and Jay.

"Please, God! Let the door on the other side be unlocked," prayed Jeff as his camouflage makeup was getting smeared all over due to the rain.

Rathul had been so enticed in watching the second floor staff get decimated that he lost focus on having the back door locked. Jeff and Jay swung the door open and ran for cover. Bronski and the police followed.

Jeff and Jay saw the unbelievable. Disabled patients *walking*. They knew that their friends had to be in trouble and figured the elevator would take too long so they made a dash for the stairs. They made it onto the second floor. "No way!" exclaimed Jeff.

"Far out!" shouted Jay, witnessing the battle.

"Jeff! Jay! Over here!" yelled Beth. "Help!"

—— THE NURSING HOME ——

"We're coming!" Jeff screamed back.

"You ain't going anywhere!" Bronski grabbed Jeff with his muscular arm.

"Let him go, man!" yelled Jay as he struck Bronski. His punches were like rain on a vinyl tablecloth.

The police had been following and arrived, as well. "Holy shit!" O'Conner came to a halt.

"What the fuck?!" questioned Jackson.

"Is this for real?" asked O'Leary, not believing what he saw.

"Nobody listens to the rookie," said Conway. The officers stared in awe.

Bronski was about to make a dent into Jeff's face, but just before his fist met Jeff's mouth, something stopped him. Bronski got stabbed with a knife in the shoulder blade. It was Morris Grover. He and all the other patients attacked Bronski like piranhas.

Rathul was clapping. He was happy to witness what was in front of him. There were plenty of deaths already: Dr. Owens was lying in a ring of his own blood; Clevon was left for dead, earphones and all; the four staff members on the third floor, plus Carlos; the three staff members on the first floor; and two more followed.

Pearl was grabbing everything possible to fight the patients off, but there were way too many of them. She was being strangled with a computer cable; her own idea used against her. Pearl kicked and screamed, but it was no use. Gasping for air, she began fading. The staff tried helping her, but it was just too late. Ironically, Pearl beat her mother to the great blue sky, without getting the chance to say goodbye.

— 318 —

David was swinging like he was an All-Star baseball player with the flashlight that he had come down with from the third floor.

The officers had their nightsticks and began clubbing away. O'Conner gave a right hook to a patient from room 217. "That felt great," he said with confidence.

"How many of these fuckers are there?" asked Conway.

"A lot," replied Beth.

"Dude, this is like a real-life zombie movie," said Jay.

"Yeah, man! *Night of the Living Dead!*" yelled back Jeff.

"Who's doing this?" asked O'Conner.

"**Look ahead, flat foot,**" a deep voice demanded.

O'Conner looked up. "Am I seeing things correctly or did that cloud of smoke just talk to me?"

"That's not just a cloud of smoke; that's Rathul," informed Beth. "He's behind all of this... The staff murders." Some of the officers were seriously injured, but none were dead yet.

"**I'm not going to stop until you all suffer and die.**" Rathul gave a hearty, devilish laugh. Just then, another cloud of smoke seemed to appear, but in a form of a woman.

"*Juan!*" a female voice yelled. "***What is the meaning of this?***"

"**Gloria! I'm so glad you are here!**" Rathul responded to his given name.

"***Juan, you have to stop this right now! Those kids didn't do anything wrong.***"

"**Maybe not the kids, but the other staff members did. If I don't do anything, the patients are going to get**

THE NURSING HOME

abused on a daily basis, just like they are now."

"*Juan, I know that you are trying to make things right, but you are acting just as bad, or even worse, than these staff members.*"

"I love you, Gloria. I should have been there for you. I really tried everything in my power, but I failed. Because of me, you were abused at this Godforsaken place."

"*Juan, it was over one hundred and fifty years ago. I never held you accountable for anything. There was nothing you could do. I want you to call off these patients right now.*"

"They must pay, Gloria."

"*I believe they've paid enough. Please call them off, Juan. Please?*"

Juan/Rathul got out of the patients' minds. They were no longer under his power. He still wanted to see the staff members suffer. The only reason he called the patients off was for Gloria. He'd do anything for her. "I only wanted to get revenge on the people who did this to you, Gloria."

"*I know, my love. Every minute that I was being tormented here at Rigg's, the only thing I could think of was seeing you again and right now my dream has come true. Grab my hand, Juan. Please join me in the afterlife?*"

Juan/Rathul grabbed Gloria's hand and the two spirits followed the bright light to the sky as they were reunited together for eternity.

Due to all the carnage that had taken place in Rigg's, there were dead staff members on three floors. After Rathul had left the patients' minds, there were injured patients agonizing in pain on the cold floors and some dead, as well.

The staff members and officers were all in shock. A loud voice echoed through the building. "We did it!" yelled Beth.

"We did it!" repeated Jay.

"More like that chick ghost did it," Jeff pointed out.

"Her name is Gloria Miguel," Beth told them. "And we should be very grateful to her."

"If it wasn't for her, God knows what would have happened," said Ron, lying on the floor, still holding his arm.

"Ron, is your arm really that bad? It looks like a paper cut," said Beth.

"Get up, you pansy," kidded Jay.

"Stop teasing him," said Rita as she helped Ron up. She put his arm around her shoulder. Ron had never been so close to a woman before. Not just a woman; a *mature* woman.

"Way to go, Ronny boy," encouraged Jay.

Ron responded by giving a thumbs up with the arm that was resting over Rita's shoulder.

"You okay, Jackie?" asked David, a fellow employee.

"Just a little bruised, but I'll live," Jackie answered.

"Nobody believes the rookie..." repeated Conway.

"How the fuck do we explain this to the Captain?" asked O'Conner.

"We don't," responded Conway firmly. The rest of the officers agreed.

"Who's gonna clean up this mess?" asked Jackson.

"Looks like we're gonna have to help these two numbskulls," complained O'Leary to his partner.

— THE NURSING HOME —

"Watch your mouth, O'Leary," warned O'Conner.

"Let's get to work," said Conway. "For the injured and dead patients and the dead staff members, we'll get an ambulance. You kids and your co-workers, help us bring the remaining patients back to their rooms. Got it?"

"Hey, rookie... what will we tell Cyndi? She has the right to know," said O'Conner.

"We tell her the truth," Conway told him. "She won't believe us, anyway."

"How could she not believe us?" asked Ron.

"Denial, dude," Jeff told him. "Grown-ups don't want to know the truth."

"Yeah, man. Don't trust anyone over forty," said Jay.

"Watch it, kid," O'Conner replied. "I'm still in shock."

"Sorry, Officer," Jay responded.

"Let's just do our jobs," said Conway. "Tomorrow's a brand new day, but tonight will live on forever."

Everyone went on to do what they were instructed. The kids and the other employees helped the patients up, brought them to their rooms, and tucked them in. The staff realized that the patients were obviously unaware of what had just taken place.

Officer O'Conner called for an ambulance to get all the injured patients to the nearest hospital. He also made arrangements for all the dead staff members and dead patients to be ushered off, as well. Then the officer gave Cyndi a call, telling her to come to Rigg's immediately. She told him that she'd get there as fast as she could.

When Cyndi arrived, she was startled. *Why isn't Bronski standing at the post?* she thought to herself. She entered very slowly. The officers, staff, and the kids,

— 322 —

who were supposed to be off duty, were there to greet her. "What is going on here?" asked Cyndi. "Where's Bronski? What are you kids doing here off-hours? David, Jackie... why aren't you on the third floor? Rita... why aren't you on the second floor? Where's Pearl, Dr. Owens, and everyone else who is scheduled? What are you Officers doing here, anyway? Why are there more than two of you? Could someone please give me some answers?!" she asked with great concern, not giving anyone a chance to talk.

"Cyndi, I think you need to sit down for this one," suggested O'Conner.

"Cyndi, what you are about to hear is going to shock you," added Conway.

"Where is everyone? Are the patients okay?" she asked, worried and defensive.

"Unfortunately, some more patients and staff members died, and some patients were seriously injured, but are going to be fine," said O'Conner.

"What do you mean *'died or got injured?'*" She was getting aggravated.

"Do you remember all of the mysterious deaths that were going on around here?" asked Beth.

"I'll take over from here, kid," interrupted Conway. "Well, Cyndi, we figured out who was committing all of the murders."

"Who?!" asked Cyndi impatiently.

"Rathul. Or shall I say Juan Miguel..." Beth couldn't help herself.

"Did you arrest him, Officers?" Cyndi asked.

"We couldn't," said O'Conner.

– 323 –

—— THE NURSING HOME ——

"So you call me to come down here in the middle of the night to tell me that you know who the killer is and that you let him get away? Just great!"

"It's not that simple. Now you could tell her, kid," Conway told Beth.

"Cyndi, Juan Miguel is a ghost. His wife is Gloria Miguel. She was the first patient to ever die in this nursing home. She was abused mercilessly by the staff in Rigg's from 1841 to 1843. Juan, her husband, tried to avenge her death by possessing the patients and having them try to kill us. We had to defend ourselves against them. Gloria stopped her husband and saved us all."

Cyndi looked around the room in disbelief. Everybody nodded to confirm that Beth was telling the truth. "Everybody knows that I don't stand for patient abuse. I'm totally against it." Cyndi made herself clear. "My problem now is that I have to call the families of everyone who has died and tell them *what*? Say a ghost went around possessing patients and killing staff members? I will be sent to the mental institution for sure."

O'Conner suggested, "For the patients that didn't make it, say they died in their sleep. Also announce it to the staff and patients who are still alive, as well."

"So you want me to lie?" she asked the officer. "I'm opposed to lying, but what choice do we have? What about the families of the employees?"

"We'll figure something out at the station. Tomorrow's a brand new day," O'Conner told her.

"Act like it never happened," said Conway.

"At least none of the patients will remember a single thing," added Beth.

– 324 –

"It looks like we all have work to do," said Cyndi.

Cyndi made the phone calls about the deaths of the patients, leaving the responsibilities of the staff members' deaths for the police. The officers had already arranged to have the dead staff members and the injured and dead patients brought to the hospital earlier. The other patients were already in their rooms. For the remainder of the stormy night, everyone cleaned the nursing home and by seven in the morning, it looked like a million dollars. Everyone went to their respective homes, except for Cyndi. She planned to work another ten hours.

— Chapter 29

Returning home on a rainy, gloomy Saturday night, the Grover family was stuck in traffic. "There must be an accident up ahead," commented Jude.

"I see the damn ambulance lights now," pointed out Sam.

"Wow! It's like a three-car pile-up," Todd told them.

"Oh, great!" exclaimed Sam. "Hey, at least we can sleep late... aye, gang?"

"Thank God." Todd wiped his forehead, feeling relieved.

"Yeah, my feet are killing me." Jude took off her shoes and stretched her feet.

"Unfortunately, back to everyday normal life. Me working mostly six-day weeks."

"No need to complain, Sam. It was great that we got away for a little bit, but one thing is good: We get to sleep in our own beds when we get home."

"I guess you're right, Jude. I could sure use some home cooking. How about you, Champ?" Sam asked his son.

— 326 —

JAMES J. MURPHY III

"You bet, Dad. I can't wait to watch my own TV," Todd told them. "Hey, Dad... do you think we could get a big fifty inch flat-screen TV and mount it up on the living room wall?"

"Our television's just fine for now. It's lasted this long."

"It looks like we'll be stuck here for a little bit. Let's try to make the best of it," insisted Jude.

The Grovers sat in traffic for an hour. They reminisced about their vacation and all of the fun they had. They talked about everything from Sam making his family get soaked at the concert to Todd seeing cartoon characters at the theme parks to Jude screaming on the upside-down roller coasters. The family had a wonderful time with each other. A lesson should be learned from going on vacation, Sam thought to himself: Enjoy it while you can because it doesn't happen all the time.

Finally, traffic began moving. Sam cheered loudly, "We're moving, gang!"

"Good," said Jude. "I can't wait to check my voicemails. I can't remember the last time I went this long without my cell phone."

"How about the nineties..." Sam commented under his breath.

"Yeah," agreed Todd. "I have to check my emails and my MySpace page."

"What space?" questioned Sam. "You only have a bedroom."

"No, Dad. It's my profile online."

"Oh," said Sam. "Did you know about this, Jude?"

"Yes. I did, dear. You know how it is, Sam. Today, one thing; tomorrow, the next."

– 327 –

THE NURSING HOME

"I guess, Jude."

"We were young once, too, Sam."

"You're right, Jude. Hell, when I get home, I'm going straight to bed. I'll look at my messages tomorrow."

After the accident had cleared up, traffic flowed smoothly, and the Grovers ended up getting home at 1:23am. Pulling into the driveway, Sam announced: "We're home!" Todd and Jude had fallen asleep for the remainder of the ride. They woke up groggy. Jude got out and opened the front door and put the outside light on for Sam and Todd. Before the men went into the house, Sam pulled Todd aside. "Son, I know you're not a little kid anymore and that you think you're too old to be seen with your parents, but I did try for us all to have a good time."

"I had my doubts about this vacation, too, Dad, but I really had a great time. Now let's get inside before we get sick," Todd kidded.

"Right behind ya, son." The two of them brought the luggage inside. Sam thought to himself, *God, my boy is growing up so fast*. When Sam got inside, he saw Jude had been waiting for him in bed, sound asleep. He gave her a peck on the forehead and went under the covers after he got out of his damp clothes. The Grovers had a great night's sleep.

Jude prepared bacon, eggs, toast, and pancakes for her family for breakfast. Todd was the first of the two to go downstairs and start stuffing his face. "Home cooking!"

"Save some for your father," Jude told her son.

– 328 –

—— JAMES J. MURPHY III ——

Sam also joined them. "Smells great, dear. I'm starving."

"I told my mother that we've just come back from Orlando."

"How is the old lady?"

"Oh, Sam!" Jude expressed, waving her hands. "She wants to know when we can visit."

"I don't know, Jude."

"She's making her famous lasagna, Sam." Jude knew he was a sucker for his mother-in-law's fine cuisine.

That put a smile on Sam's face. "Maybe next week. I just want to put my feet up and watch the game today."

"Why don't you give your father a call today?"

"What did I do now?" asked Sam with a smile.

"Irene also said 'Hi.'"

"I say 'Hi' to her, too." Sam was just being nice because he knew Irene was one of Jude's friends. He wouldn't remember her if he saw her.

"Did you check your voicemails, Sam?"

"I will now." While Sam was indulging in his breakfast, he took out his cell phone and began listening to his voicemails. He put it on speakerphone. "Just my boss from two weeks ago," he said after the first message played.

The next message played. "Mr. Grover, this is Cyndi Gillian from Rigg's Nursing Home. As soon as you get this message, call me back. Your father may be in deep trouble with the police and it involves murder."

After hearing that, Sam began choking on his bacon. "MURDER!?!" he yelled, still coughing on the bacon.

"Take it easy, Sam. Drink some orange juice." Jude handed him his glass and he washed down his bacon.

— THE NURSING HOME —

Sam, getting his voice back, said: "What the fuck is the meaning of this?"

"It has to be a misunderstanding," said Jude, trying to calm down her husband.

There were six other messages from Cyndi. "I knew we should not have come home, Jude." Sam had been on cloud nine all week. After hearing the disturbing message, his cloud burst and he had nothing to land on except solid ground.

"We'll get it straightened out, Sam. Don't worry."

"You're damn right, we will. We're leaving! Now!"

"That old buzzard couldn't hurt a fly," said Todd.

"That's no way to talk about your grandfather, Todd," Jude scolded him.

"He's absolutely right, Jude. Let's go!" Sam shouted, leaving the food on the table.

"Can't I wash the dishes first? Or at least put the food away?" Jude hated leaving the kitchen untidy.

"No time! Let's go!" Sam was serious and his family could tell, so they did as he said. The family closed the door behind them, not even checking to see if the doors were locked.

Sam backed out of the driveway and booked it. He'd never moved so fast in his life; not even when him and Jude were dating. He was swerving in and out of lanes at high speed, as if he was in a race.

"Would you please slow down, Sam?" Jude begged him.

"It's under control, Jude," he told her. Todd hated when his father was stressed, but loved it when he drove like a maniac. They came to a stop. "Damnit!" yelled Sam, slamming his hands on the steering wheel with anger.

– 330 –

"Sunday traffic, dear."

"Traffic! And aren't they ever going to finish this fucking highway?"

"Hopefully by 2011, Sam."

While the family was stuck in traffic, Sam continued to rant. "No wonder why we're stuck here! Another Sunday accident! What else is new?!" Todd laughed to himself because he knew his father was right. "Almost every day, construction. Almost every Sunday, accident. How hard is it to drive on this fucking highway?" Sam complained. "Look at where our taxes are going! A fucking highway that takes about five years to complete. What a fucking joke!"

"Don't worry, Sam. We'll get to the nursing home and everything will be resolved."

"It better be. Once again, thanks to my incompetent father, I'm missing the Marlins game."

"Maybe there's a rerun tonight." Jude tried cheering him up.

"There's no rerun, Jude." Todd was about to open his mouth, but Sam cut him off. "Don't even mention the VCR, Todd."

"I wasn't," Todd spoke up. "Why don't you use the DVR, Dad?"

"Stop being a wise-ass."

"Todd is right, you know," Jude told him.

"What?"

"Come on, Sam. It's 2008; all televisions are going to be required to be digital next year. Everyone has a DVD player by now, and even TiVo or DVR. Why don't you let Todd teach you how to work ours, so we don't have to hear you complain about missing a television show?"

—— THE NURSING HOME ——

"Yeah, Dad, and the best thing is that you can save it as long as you want."

Sam was beginning to have second thoughts. "Really?"

"Yeah," his son assured him.

"How about sometime this week we sit down as a family and you teach us, Todd?" suggested Sam.

"I already know how to do this stuff," said Jude.

"Okay, then sit down with me, Todd. Maybe it's about time I get caught up to the twenty-first century." Sam laughed at himself. During the few minutes of talking about current technology, he had forgotten about Cyndi's message. But when traffic began moving, Sam, once again, became a raging lunatic. The hold-up wasn't too bad; they were stuck in traffic for twenty-five minutes. In the past, it had been much longer. That was why Sam avoided going out on Sundays.

They finally made it to Exit 4, getting off the Tigress Highway and heading towards Tera Lane. The nursing home was five minutes away. "Damn! I forgot how many twists and turns were on this road," Sam said as he had control of the steering wheel.

"There it is, dear!" Jude pointed out.

"I haven't been here in so long that I forgot how big this place was," said Sam. "Hopefully Dad wasn't moved from his room."

"Yeah, into the insane asylum," commented Todd.

"I am warning you, Todd. Watch it! You're on thin ice, Mister!" Jude raised her pointer finger towards her son.

Sam laughed at her remark. "It looks crowded. Are those the same nurses smoking as usual? They need to get a life."

– 332 –

—— JAMES J. MURPHY III ——

"I don't think they're the same ones," Jude told her husband.

"A nurse is a nurse. They are all the same," said Sam. "Let's just get Dad out of here."

Jude sometimes wondered if Sam ever thought before he opened his mouth. There was no talking or reasoning with him, especially when he was in that state of mind. She loved her husband very much, but wished he wouldn't judge people.

They walked into the entrance of Rigg's and headed for the elevator. "Can I help you?" the receptionist asked. Sam stormed right by her, while Jude and Todd followed. "Sir! You need to sign in."

"Sam, I think the receptionist is mad," Jude informed him.

"I don't give a fuck!"

The receptionist called Cyndi. She wasn't sure what to do. She told Cyndi that a man, woman, and teenager stormed in and refused to listen to her. "Thank you, Katherine," Cyndi said over the phone. "I have a pretty good idea about who it is."

"Should I call security or the police, Ms. Gillian?"

"No need for the police yet. I think I can handle it for right now with just security."

Morris slept until just before noon. When he woke up, he sat in his room, doing a word search and letting the sun shine in.

There was no knock on the door. The Grovers barged in. Morris looked up with his pencil in his hand. "Sam! Jude! Todd! What is this?!"

−333−

— THE NURSING HOME —

"Shut up, Dad! We're getting you the fuck out of here!"

"Have you gone nuts, Sam? What the fuck is going on?"

"I'll tell you later." Sam firmly took the pencil and word search out of his father's hands and put it aside.

"Hey! That's my word search. I'm using that," Morris defended himself.

"I'll buy you a new one. Now shut up!" Sam went behind the wheelchair and gripped the handles tightly. He exited room 243 with his father and family. "We're bringing you home, Dad!"

"I am home, you fucking idiot! Help! Help!" screamed Morris.

"Shut up, Dad! You're causing a scene."

"You're damn right, I am."

Cyndi approached the Grovers with security behind her as backup. "Mr. Grover, what is the meaning of this?" she asked innocently, knowing exactly what the matter was about.

"What is the meaning?" Sam repeated. "You lunatic bitch! You tell me." Sam was irate. He wanted to tear her head off and use it as a basketball. "I get about seven fucking phone calls from you saying my father may be involved in a murder and you're asking me what this is about?"

"What?" asked Morris, confused.

"Oh, that," said Cyndi. "It was a false accusation. We apologized to you about that, Morris, and we are sorry to have inconvenienced you, as well, Mr. Grover. Didn't someone call you? Anyway, you can visit your father if you want to, Mr. Grover. Otherwise, I'll have to ask you to leave."

"Yeah... We'll leave, alright," Sam told her, "but not without my father."

— 334 —

"Morris Grover is going nowhere. This is his home."

"Over my dead body, it is."

"Mr. Grover, it's really not up to you; it's up to Morris."

"I'll get Power of Attorney!"

"That would be Morris's choice. He's perfectly capable of making his own decisions." Cyndi still kept her voice relatively low and calm.

"Well, it won't take much to prove he's incompetent. He can't remember a damn thing."

"Mr. Grover, the only disability your father has is his physical handicap. You can't prove a thing. Besides, Morris was fully aware and content in his decision to remain here. He agreed for us to bill his account from now on."

"You bitch!" Sam expressed his feelings towards her, and then he addressed his father. "Dad! You what?"

"Yes. It's true, Sam. I figured I'd never come to your house again. Hell, I'm going to be here until I die. At least now you, your naive wife, and that bastard brat won't have to fight over who gets what when I'm dead because there won't be anything left for you."

"How could you, Dad?" Sam still could not believe how stupid his father was to have made billing changes with the nursing home without running it by him first.

"Morris!" Jude couldn't believe it, either.

"I told you he was a stupid old man," Todd said straight out.

"Todd!" shouted Jude.

Morris wasn't listening to Jude and Todd argue. He wanted to get stuff off his chest with Sam. "It's simple, son. When you sent me here, I knew it was for my own

— THE NURSING HOME —

good; I understood that. Hell, I even respected that. But when I told you everything that was going on here, you didn't believe a single word I said. That's why I signed everything over to this place. I'd rather have complete strangers get the money than my own family. At least they are honest about not caring about me. Most of the time, that is," Morris concluded.

"Jude, I can't believe this is happening."

"I don't believe it, either, Sam."

"We can contest this, you know! Old people lose their minds all the time."

"Sam, it's not worth it. If this is what your father wants, maybe it is for the best."

As Sam continued his conversation with Jude, Cyndi was feeling guilty, but she had to go with the flow of her own made-up story. She couldn't exactly say that Morris and a bunch of other patients had been possessed by a spirit or ghost named Rathul. Even she had a hard time believing it, considering she didn't witness anything. She didn't know what else to do.

"What have we done?" asked Sam, feeling ashamed.

"You did nothing wrong, dear. There is nothing we can do now. What's done is done. Let's just go home, Sam." Jude turned towards Cyndi. "We're sorry, Ms. Gillian. We'll leave. We don't want to get anyone else involved."

"No need to apologize." Cyndi just wished the whole thing never happened.

Jude grabbed her husband's hand as security was starting to escort them out. Todd joined them.

"Trust me, it was great seeing you, Sam," Morris called out sarcastically. "Stop by anytime."

JAMES J. MURPHY III

Sam refused to acknowledge his father. "Your father's talking to you, Sam," said Jude.

"I told you; he is nothing but an asshole."

"If he was such an asshole, you wouldn't have had us make this long trip just to rescue him."

"Whatever happens to Dad is the nursing home's problem now, not ours."

"Oh, Sam..." Jude sighed.

Sam turned towards his son. "Do you want to get a bite to eat, Champ? There's a restaurant on the way home."

"Yeah!" Todd said with joy. Jude didn't know what else to do but agree.

"You got it!" said Sam. "It's on me, gang." The Grovers left and moved on with their lives from there, without Morris.

Deep down, Morris cared about his family, but he refused to let anybody walk all over him, family or not.

After all of the commotion was over, Cyndi asked: "Do you want to go to the lounge room, Morris? All of your friends are there."

"Sure, why not? I apologize about my family, Cyndi. They mean no harm."

"They're just looking out for you. No hard feelings," Cyndi said, feeling guilty as sin. There was one thing that Cyndi hated and that was lying.

Whoever was left of Saturday night's staff still remained working at Rigg's Nursing Home. Beth went

—— THE NURSING HOME ——

back to school, attending a local college to study science, while working part time at the nursing home. Ron added another science fiction DVD to his collection and also took college courses locally. He still wanted to be a history teacher. He was also seeing Rita here and there. Jay and Jeff worked at the nursing home one night a week. They thought the Saturday night with Rathul was the coolest thing they'd ever witnessed in their entire lives. The rest of the time, they worked at Kirk's Video Store.

Officers O'Conner and Conway still bickered at one another and the other officers still joked with each other.

At Rigg's Nursing Home and at the precinct, Saturday night's incident would never be mentioned again. One reason for that was that everyone was blocking it out of their minds. Another reason was that nobody would believe them, anyway. The patients had no memory of it, so the police and staff stuck to their stories and agreed to keep what happened a secret. When the kids hung out, they sometimes brought it up to each other. Saturday night might be gone, but what happened would live on forever.

After Cyndi had brought Morris to the lounge room that Sunday, she left him with his friends. "Hey there, Mori, old boy!" yelled Pauly with exuberance. Frank and Ralph said 'Hi,' as well.

"Hey gang. Like I said, Pauly... the name's Morris."

"Is it just me, or is it a little quieter than usual?" asked Ralph.

"It's you," said Pauly.

"Well, it wasn't quiet before," stated Morris.

— JAMES J. MURPHY III —

"Yeah, I heard yer yellin', Mori, old boy. Did somebody steal your word search again?" teased Pauly. Frank and Ralph laughed at the joke.

"No, not this time. Thanks for helping me, Pauly," Morris joked.

"Yeah, a seventy-five year old fat man who can't walk is going to come to your rescue?" kidded Pauly.

"Crawl if you have to." The guys were having a ball. "So, back to what I was saying..." said Morris. "My own Goddamn family tried kidnapping me."

"What?!" asked Pauly.

"That's exactly what I said!" Morris told him. "I'm doing my word search and they come in like vultures."

"I thought you and your son weren't talking to each other," commented Ralph.

"My son's an idiot. I don't know how to put it any other way," Morris explained. "So, Cyndi and security had to escort my family out of the building."

"Did they explain why they were taking you?" Frank inquired.

"Sam told me to shut up. Then him and Cyndi had words. Remember that day the cop thought that I was involved in murder?" They all nodded 'Yes.' "Well, that must have been what this was about, but of course, in the end, justice prevailed," Morris said with confidence.

"What justice?" asked Pauly. "You're still stuck in this dump."

"I'd rather be stuck here with friends than go home to family," Morris told them.

"You know, like I've said in the past: You're alright, Mori, old boy. That goes for all of you lug-heads," said Pauly.

— THE NURSING HOME —

"I don't know about you guys, but I had one of the best night's sleep in ages. You know... not having to move, not waking up to adjust myself." The gang agreed with Morris to also having a good night's sleep. For the rest of the day, the guys joked and laughed with each other.

As for the future, Morris; Pauly; Ralph; Frank; Wade, the so-called 'fifth guy;' and some of the others would always be in the lounge room talking and having a good time. Pauly still complained about not trusting the staff. Frank still enjoyed talking about arts and crafts. Ralph remained to be the go-along guy. After all was said and done, Morris still continued to remind Pauly: "It's Morris!" From time to time, he whistled one of his son's favorite songs when he was having a good time with the gang.

— About the Author

James J. Murphy III lives in New York with his wife, Lisa. He loves watching movies, listening to tunes, reading, and chilling. He believes the story he wrote was original and hopes to write many more. More information can be found at LandJPublishing.com.